Bearwalker Alibi

Jake Doherty

ISBN: 978-1-927114-81-0
Print Edition 2014

Cover Design by Holger Majorahn

Author's Note

Although *Bearwalker Alibi* was inspired by true events, and a courageous grandmother, all the characters and narrative are the products of the author's imagination.

For Denise, Francoise, Conall and Liam.

"Let us plunge ourselves into the roar of time...It's only action that can make a man."

"Faust Part One"
By Goethe, as translated by Randall Jarrell

Chapter 1

Mid-winter, 1996

Fergus Fitzgerald suddenly found himself stranded beside a small, frozen lake near Sudbury in Northern Ontario.

Without warning, his big Ford Escape had died silently, no herky-jerky death rattle this time. He still had a lot of gas in his tank, and no warning lights were flashing on the dashboard. This had been a short trip to visit an old newspaper buddy who was house-bound and recovering from knee surgery.

Looking around for help, he saw no traffic on either side of the road, just endless rows of tall trees and rocky outcrops, and the overwhelming ache that he had been here before, a flashback – a shaman would say a curse – that overrode every other memory.

It had started many years earlier, with the sight of a ferociously large black bear rearing up on its hind legs and staring back at him with almost luminous eyes. Fergus had been driving north to escape Toronto after his young wife had died of cancer, and had stopped to ski along an isolated lake. The only sound came from the whistling winds of a snow-squall out of the northwest that blurred his vision.

There was a brief moment, however, when he could make out the torn carcass of a young deer a hundred meters or so ahead, ribs with bits of skin still attached sticking out of the hard-frozen ice, and blood splattered over the cold white surface like an urban crime scene.

As the winds eased for a moment, Fergus's perception seemed to shift, and he saw the bear as almost human – most certainly a different shape now, with a smaller head and an arm that pointed to his kill, and then raised an angry fist at him. The transformation startled Fergus, not knowing or accepting what really had happened: was it a quick flurry of blowing snow like a looming, northern mirage, or was it perhaps something more primordial, left behind from an earlier time in the ancient forests? The image, or images, took root in him as the bear walked off the ice onto the green-grey granite shoreline and disappeared into the woods.

Instinctively, Fergus sided then with the deer, angry at the bearwalker but equally angry at himself for taking pleasure at the savage beauty of the scene. He told himself, this is nature; this is the natural order of life, so just ski away and don't look back.

That, of course, was several years ago. Alone again now, Fergus gulped a belt of scotch from a flask, savored its warmth, and turned the ignition key. The engine quickly restarted. With a last look at the lake, he drove away. Strange, he thought, if those images were real then, where is the bearwalker now?

Chapter 2

Early September, 2001

With five minutes left in their flight across Germany from Canada, Fergus looked at his seat mate, and wondered whether she would simply vanish someday. He and Mary Fraser had been together six months as live-in lovers, but he still found her other-worldly. She's aboriginal, he knew, Ojibwa really. Bright and feisty, more than most. But there were times when she wouldn't go out after dark, as if there were something waiting for her.

What's out there, he fretted, wherever 'there' is? Or does she sense something I can't, reaching in and taking over her life? Real or myth? he wondered, as he brought his seat upright. For good or evil?

Then again, Fergus worried about most things in life.

Minutes later

Lufthansa Flight 211 banked sharply into its final approach to the Dresden airport, a medium-sized city with an incendiary past, tucked away in what formerly had been East Germany. For most of the usual squeeze of business passengers from Munich and a few tourists from Germany and North America, this was situation normal. Not Fergus, always a world class white-knuckler.

And why in bloody hell, he asked himself, am I still with her? Just to meet some fastidious Germans who want to play Indian in Canada, in my backyard, for God's sake, on Manitoulin Island, with beads and bangles and whatever turns them on?

You made your choice, man, for now anyway, he told himself. Even if she thinks I'm a black Irishman with a chip on my shoulder. Condescending bitch, oh yeah, but dammit, she's right. Mary, Dr. Always Right Mary, art historian and general know-it-all.

In Dresden, he finally relaxed, feeling the jet's wheels drop into place. He even stole a look at her as she reviewed her files for their dinner meeting with Max Adler, her new employer. Every section of her expensive binder was color tabbed with schedules, presentations, and even the last minute details of her leave of absence from the University of Toronto where she was a tenured professor.

Fergus pulled himself from the window and faced her. "It's your decision, woman, but does old Max know what could happen if his pretend Indians don't play well with the real natives back home? Could be messy for you."

No reply. Once inside the cavernous Dresden Airport, Fergus said a quiet "Amen" as they approached the carousel for their bags, two large ones for Mary and only an overnighter for him. He was left lugging the bags into the main arrival area, while she strode ahead into the sparse noon-hour crowd looking for Max. She had met him once before to negotiate her contract, and twice on Manitoulin. Now she suddenly plunked her hands on her hips and tapped her elegantly shod foot with an imperious tattoo. No Max in sight.

"Fraulien Doktor? Dr. Mary Fraser?" said a much younger man. "Ich bin Franz Dietrich." He continued in rapid German that Fergus could not understand.

Mary translated quickly, "Max can't get away so he sent his nephew."

"Your German is very good, Fraulein Doktor."

"No, but good enough to get by. May I call you Franz?"

"If I may call you Mary. Yes? Now we must move on. Tell your man to bring your bags to the front entrance."

Fergus grimaced at his sudden demotion, and promptly moved forward, touching Mary lightly on her shoulder, resting his hand there until Franz moved back.

"Ah yes, Fergus Fitzgerald," said Franz, barely glancing at him. "The writer, I am told. Hurry, please, my car is in the VIP zone, but then again, everyone knows my uncle's Mercedes. No silly police will bother us here. So nice, don't you agree?"

Fergus remained mute, but noticed Franz wasn't the crisp businessman he had expected. God, look at him: dark glasses, leather jacket, damn expensive shoes but no socks. And all that jewelry, much too flashy for Manitoulin. So, what's he really peddling?

For the moment, Fergus saw that Mary was overwhelmed, jet lag no doubt. So he demurely did as he was told, and followed Franz outside. With Mary settled into the front passenger seat, Fergus began loading their bags into the trunk, but stopped, perplexed by what he saw. Just an ordinary sports bag, off to one side. Dangling from its lock was a small metallic emblem of a skull with a horn protruding from its forehead, and a large bird wing behind it. An old German cult? Or perhaps, a biker emblem? Curious, Franz didn't look the type.

Fergus was still wondering about Franz during the twenty minute drive into suburban Radebuel. The Steinberger Hotel was chic, tucked into its own lush gardens.

It was a micro-climate, Franz explained, almost Mediterranean, very balmy. He roared past a string of school children.

Weird, thought Fergus, when Franz ushered them into the hotel with a grand sweep of his hand. And when Franz took off his glasses, Fergus saw none of the braggadocio that had been evident at the airport. The German even bowed slightly.

Moments later, when they were alone at the elevator heading to their room, Mary made it clear she wanted a nap.

Fergus was more confused than ever by Franz's quick-change personality.

"Yeah, he can be efficient and gracious," he told Mary, sitting on her bed, "but he's still a presumptuous, arrogant little prick and. . ."

"Enough!" she snapped. "Take a shower, go for a walk. I work for these people."

Fergus knew when to get out of her way. Talk to somebody else. So he skipped the mini bar and opened his laptop computer. Email Matt in Manitoulin, he told himself. Even police sergeants have friends.

To: **Matt Peltier<mattpeltier@sympatico.ca**
From: **Fergus Fitzgerald<Brendan@BMTS.com**
Subject: **Fishing**

I need your help, so stay with me. Am pissed off at an arrogant little prick I've just met. Nephew of Uncle Max, and the money man behind Mary and Max's plan to build a playground for German wannabe *Indians.* Franz Dietrich is his name.

Could be a biker. Real piece of work.

Okay, no shouting. Here's my take: Franz is joining the hotel management team. Rude, dismissive one minute, and then gracious, butter wouldn't melt in his mouth the next. Did I say sleazy, snake-oil type? And I'm sure he's on something. My old newspaper instincts tell me there is a story here, and it ain't no bedtime tale. I can't see why Max is bringing him, or why he agreed to come. Can you run an informal check on this guy, Interpol perhaps? If I'm wrong, coffee on me for a month.

Thanks.F.

Matt had helped Fergus with a few freelance stories for the *Manitoulin Expositor,* and they planned to go hunting in the fall. Fergus grinned at that, because he had never held a gun, draft-dodger from Boston that he was.

Feeling better, he decided to explore nearby Radebuel. No dilapidated factories here, left over from the Communist era, just tony vineyards and up-market homes.

Mary was rising as he entered, and went to his computer again.

"Another note to Conall, your Irish friend or whatever?" she asked in mid-yawn.

"Yep," replied Fergus. "I told him we couldn't stop by on our way home."

"Don't let me sleep past six. Remember dinner with Max at seven. Sharp!"

Fergus decided not to tell her about his end-run to Matt. "Ah shit," he muttered, and deleted the email. "Too much guilt for one day." He turned off the computer, and took a nap himself.

Chapter 3

They slept longer than they had planned – and barely made dinner on time. Max and Franz were waiting for them in a private dining room off the main lobby, reflecting Max's concern that Mary be well-rested, and capable of convincing his financial advisors the next morning that the Manitoulin hotel was a solid investment. Few even knew that Manitoulin was a large island in Lake Huron, one of the Great Lakes north of Toronto and straddling the Canadian and American border.

The dinner went well, and the surprise was that Max and Fergus were open with each other, which, in hindsight, was fortuitous because Mary and Franz had little to say, particularly to each other.

Growing weary, though, after his long day, Fergus began to edge his chair back, only to be stopped by Max.

"Nein, I am not quite ready to leave and, hopefully, nor are my guests here. Fergus, I sense something dark that bothers you, perhaps something much older than this hotel."

"It's too late, Max, to unravel what—"

"No Fergus. Nein. You owe me this much."

"Owe?"

"Share, then, with a fellow traveler, as you obviously have a new role. My English fails me at times, but I think a devil's advocate has joined our little group. I salute you—"

"Just this, Max: Manitoulin is more than an island, more than rocks and trees. Its depths and spirits are restless, dark spirits that can reach into your soul and squeeze it until there is nothing left."

"So?"

"Tell it to your parents, Max. You do talk to them."

"You Irish…your spirits travel with you. Is that it?"

"Just me da along, reminding me that 'travelers are never alone, because we can't leave home without our stories.'"

"So, my fellow time traveler, what do I tell them?"

"Nicely put. I like that. Tell them…tell them there are animals with human spirits, great bears that walk in the night to protect Manitoulin's stories. Just that, Max: don't take away our stories."

Franz, suddenly alert, sat upright, and quietly repeated to himself: "Great bears that walk in the night." No one seemed to notice Franz. They left the dining room without much comment.

Mary, though, was lost again in her own world. Once back in their room, she hurriedly retreated to the bathroom, slamming the door. All Fergus heard was water running, and the soft moan that he had heard so often in their Manitoulin home. Once, several months earlier, he had found her just before dawn, facing the corner of the shower stall, letting the water trickle down her spine, and rubbing herself fiercely. He recalled how she had reached back and scrubbed the pock-like marks on her left buttock, souvenirs from some childhood incident. He never asked where they came from, and she never spoke about them.

Chapter 4

The next morning, Fergus felt Mary enter his bed, and it was the other Mary who began to caress the inside of one leg, and it was his turn to moan, a loud and long moan. Then her hand floated over his groin and down his other leg.

This, too, had happened before, not often, when she would break out of her pupa like a wondrous butterfly, hands and hair fluttering over him. She would give him a glancing, gossamer touch and then run away to begin her day.

And their merry-go-round went round and round again. As if she were on another schedule to get on with the day, she became coolly efficient, no time for a sweaty afterglow.

"Fergus, get dressed quickly. Move it," she told him sharply. "Our trays will be here in minutes, and then we meet Max and Franz in the lobby. Can't you understand why we're here?"

"Whatever," said Fergus, taking cover by turning on his computer and entering his own other world. There was one short note from Matt in Manitoulin. "Bingo!"

> *"Good instincts, man. Call me as soon as you get back. I'll buy the coffee. Safe journey. Matt."*

Buoyed by this news, Fergus complimented Mary on her hair when she stopped by the mirror for a last check. He recognized her job would be on the line today at Max's make-or-break financial meeting. He had also been with Mary long enough to know that her self-image came down to her hair, always aboriginal black in color, but regularly permed into tight curls, and cut short around her neck – the essence of the with-it white world.

"Oh, the hell with it, let it grow one more time," she said softly to herself. "Uncurl who I am, Dr. Mary Fraser, Ph.D. and world…No, No! The sweet little native girl running in the spring, and her long black hair blowing in the wind. Where, where did I lose her? What's gone wrong? What am I missing?"

Once into the meeting, Mary put aside her doubts when the German bankers probed how the proposed hotel could deal with modern Germans coming to Canada to play at being natives.

"Of course, Herr Reschat. I appreciate the opportunity to share my thoughts about my people.

"First, let's begin with the word 'Manitoulin'. It means 'Spirit Island', and the migration stories of the Ojibwa and related tribes all say it is home of the 'Great Spirit', or in their language 'G'ichi Manitou. When they arrived is a matter of debate, but my people do believe that the entire island was once cleansed by fire. The Ojibwa will share their culture with you, but it remains theirs."

"Can you give me an example, Fraulein Doktor?"

"Of course. Let me give you an extreme example. The Ojibwa, like most tribal societies, have a dark side. And, if I may say so, not unlike the conflicts of your own wonderful culture, as we see in Dresden, and, ah, your own military history. To return to the Ojibwa, tribal societies created mythologies that appealed to people intrigued by sinister underworlds and the paranormal. The most controversial element, probably, would be the bearwalker."

"I appreciate your sensitivity, but what is this bearwalker, now that you have mentioned it?"

"For some it's a myth carried over from the time when survival was precarious, particularly in dark winter nights, when predators moved just beyond the campfires. Every tribal society had a bogeyman who lived in the shadows, and his presence grew with primitive imaginations."

"Just a big brown bear, that's it?"

"No, Herr Reschat. Some people believe the bearwalker can change its shape, and take on human forms and lay curses on people. Simply put, the bearwalker theme is best left to the Ojibwa. That's all I can say."

Chapter 5

Lunch went well as Max had intended, with fine foods and wine and lively conversation.

There was one last probing query from Herr Reschat. "So, Herr Adler, the question remains: Can you succeed, or will your bearwalker savage our balance sheets?"

"We have faced many risks, Hans, and, if you will allow me, we – you and I – have more than survived. We are here today because we triumphed together. And now we must go to Canada together. A little challenge on the way, but what is life without risks?"

After several rounds of toasts, Max insisted that Franz spend the afternoon with Mary, while he and his backers prepared agreements and budgets. He suggested the nearby Karl May Museum, which was snug behind the hotel. Even as she agreed, Mary felt a persistent tick in her left eye that she could not rub away or easily explain. She had been advised that it was more psychological than medical in origin. Avoid stress, she had been told. *With Franz leading me? I'm anxious and I feel vulnerable, and Fergus, wherever you are, dammit, you may be right about him.*

She tried to relax, as she knew that Karl May's home was where Germany's great love affair with North American Indians had begun. May himself never made it to North America, but his fictional hero, Old Shatterhand, had become that masterful German superhero who teamed with Winnitou, an Apache warrior, to tame the wicked west. "Romantic nonsense, or was it?" she asked herself. Even Hitler had insisted that his generals read the books.

Her speculation ended abruptly, as Franz took her elbow and led her through throngs of children to the log cabin where native artifacts were on display. He pulled again at her elbow, more of a yank this time, and too forcibly for comfort.

"It's just old stuff Mary. But there are ways to enjoy this."

Mary picked up on a different edge in his voice. His rapid personality changes bothered her.

"Enjoy? That's not what your uncle—"

"Forget Max! People like you and me can make things happen."

"Forget Max?" she repeated to herself, and began to wonder why Franz was taking such chances, what strange compulsion was taking over.

"Really, Franz? Just like that, eh?" She turned to get into his face.

"Ja! Anything you want!"

"Anything?" Mary tried not to laugh at him. "No way. You're too much, way out there. All charm one minute, and then another Franz pops up."

"Ah, delighted you noticed."

"No, I need to understand the May legend. Your uncle—"

"Max?" Franz sneered. "An old man like your Fergus. Charming boors. You need…"

Before Mary could interrupt, Franz slid a hand over her hip.

She stiffened. "I need *what?*"

"Get a life, stupid woman. I can supply whatever you need. Anything!"

His touch, more than his words, blew away her self-control.

Old and darkly painful images battled in her mind. A large predator came first, hovering, holding her, and hurting her until her synapses snapped back, and she became defiantly furious.

"Enough," she screamed. "GET YOUR HAND OFF MY BUTT!"

"Feels good! Very tight, no sagging for a woman of your age."

Mary stepped away, just far enough to jab her index into his chest.

"Leave me alone, you presumptuous little bastard, and stop messing with my head. I need to get out of here."

Fergus found Mary unusually quiet when they met later in their room. She insisted on a long shower before they left for Semper Opera House on Dresden's central plaza along the Elbe River. Most of the buildings had been damaged during World War Two, particularly throughout three successive days of fire-bombing by the Allies late in the war.

Finally settled into their balcony seats, Fergus was soon absorbed by the throbbing fury of *Tannhouser* and the thunderous applause from the gilded tiers of opera lovers. As the third act was about to start, Fergus hummed the major theme again and turned to Mary. "Did you know the East Germans restored this place?"

She continued to stare ahead.

"Some people even miss the Communists," he continued.

"Oh?"

"Yeah, the opera house here, the Zwinger galleries, the old churches."

"Anything for the tourist dollars," she said.

"Partly. But think of the irony. The Allies bomb the hell of this place, and the big, brutal commies put it back together."

"You're the anthropologist. You figure out the politics."

"It's not politics Mary."

"Perhaps not. I'm just...What about the old church you wanted to see?"

"The cathedral?" he asked.

"Yes."

"So many tourists and buses, it was hard at first to capture the spirit of the place."

"But?" Mary asked.

"It was just a small chapel, really, off to the side, easy to miss."

"Your point Fergus. The intermission's ending."

The house lights flickered, and they stood to let two couples pass by.

"You were saying?"

"There was a white porcelain altar made in Meissen," he said, "a rough-shaped Pieta, not at all baroque. Quite stark really, but that was the point. Simple inscriptions on either side."

"And?"

"A couple from Holland translated for me."

"Translated what, Fergus?"

"Two dates with inscriptions. One said simply that 'Our sadness began 1933', when the Nazis came to power, and the other, of course, marks the firebombing in 1945."

Mary turned to face him. "Did you feel the sadness?"

"In part, yes. I went out to the light, and sensed evils pushed aside, as the restorations flourished in the sunlight. The Elbe, its waters felt like they were cleansing me. But I got the point."

"And?"

"Something's bothering you," he said. "Hold my hand, squeeze it!"

She turned as a hush from a nearby patron made her blush.

"Dresden, Radebuel," Fergus went on, "the wineries, they're a resurrection in progress, it's…Don't you feel it?"

The *Tannhauser* motif began again, so Fergus quickly whispered, "Nothing? No resurrection, no awe?"

"Nothing…he just touched me."

She moved his hand to her inner thigh.

"Franz again? I'll deal with the bastard."

"No, let it be. Too much depends on this."

"You're sure?"

"No." She pulled away and burrowed deeper into her plush seat, head down, eyes clinched. "Not sure of anything anymore." Tears leaked out as her hands shook. "Get me out of here….Please, just take me home."

Chapter 6

There was no cuddling when they returned from the opera. Neither mentioned Franz, just said terse "g'nights" followed by lights out.

The next morning Mary, woke slowly and irritably. Night sweats had again left her cold and clammy, shivering under a thin nightgown as she pushed back the duvet.

Then she recalled how, just before waking, she had been startled by brief flashes of another place, a much smaller place where she was unable to move. It had left her with an overwhelming and lingering sense of powerlessness. She had been there before, but this morning the sensation was more intense, a solitary explosion in her head. As always, she saw no faces and heard no voices.

The memory faded, and she managed a little grin as she looked at Fergus snoring. She touched him, aware of his scent, and then traced an eagle totem on his back.

A short knock on the door, followed by breakfast trays, pulled them into their day, the 'going home to Canada' day. They had packed the night before.

Now they had different agendas. Mary had to get Fergus moving quickly in time join Max and Franz at the airport. Fergus knew, as he showered, that getting Mary home was not going to solve her problems.

He'd try to keep Franz at bay until he could talk to Matt Peltier at the OPP. Yeah, high-level spook stuff. Get real, he thought ruefully. Curious process, though. Matt had found something, but didn't want to risk an email going astray, let alone a long distance call.

The first incident occurred during their layover in the old, soon-to-be-replaced Munich airport. He saw Franz touch Mary's shoulder and speak to her. She brusquely swatted his hand, away as her body went rigid. She glared at him for several seconds before stalking into a bookstore.

Fergus followed; Franz, prudently, did not.

Nor did the return flight to Canada go smoothly. Heavy turbulence kicked in near Montreal, with several wing-snapping chops that sent Franz's drink dribbling down the front of his shirt. He didn't notice the dampness until the ice cubes came to rest in his crotch.

Pearson Airport, Toronto

The long walk into the immigration hall at Terminal One also did not go well. Terminal One was an old building, its low ceilings, garish brightness, and unfiltered noise all unwelcoming to tired travelers. Max had his Canadian work permit ready, and expected a few questions about the Manitoulin project. Fergus was just Fergus playing Fergus, worrying, as always, whether some official would still question his reasons for immigrating to Canada from Boston in the early seventies. He'd taken out Canadian citizenship in 1979, just before his marriage to Maureen.

Mary, on the other hand, plunged ahead, trying to avoid any more contact with Franz, who followed along behind her. Once in the immigration hall, she was relieved to direct Franz and Max to the primary inspection line for non-residents, while she and Fergus slipped into the adjoining queue for residents.

She stiffened when Franz reached across the space between the two lines, speaking loudly enough for Fergus to pick up a few words about an offer, and a deal that "still stands." She recoiled, shuddering almost spastically as Franz touched her shoulder again. Fergus quickly put his arm around her, but Mary pushed him away, dropped her briefcase, and abruptly turned to challenge Franz. "Enough, dammit, you're in my country now."

"Hey, woman of the world," countered Franz, his words slurring and his hands dangling lazily by his side. "Lighten up a little. Time to snort, time to play, so who's to know?"

Mary's rage exploded, even as Fergus tried to pull her away. Max yanked Franz back. She broke free first, grabbing Franz by his lapels before anyone could stop her. Quickly, the physical feel of his hands on her body and the fear of powerlessness threatened to overwhelm her.

Fergus was stunned by a rage he had never before witnessed.

"I made a deal with your uncle, kid, that's it. Stay the bloody hell away from me."

"Or?"

"Or? You, you drug-dealing-scumbag. Come at me again and I'll put you—"

"So what can you do? Tell Fergus? Get real, woman! He ran once and he'll run again."

No more repression. "You rotten piece of *shit*, Franz." She was in his face now with all emotional guns blazing. "He's got more guts than you ever had. No, dammit, this is *my* fight. Come at me, and you'll regret it for the rest of your life, if you still have one."

Fergus and Max stepped back to allow a nearby immigration official to intervene, like a hockey referee trying to break up a fight before someone really got hurt.

"What's going on here? Your passports, please." Pete Clarke, a long- time inspector for the CCRA, the Canadian

Customs and Revenue Agency, took charge of the situation. Only his standard-issue black police shoes conveyed his official status. He was one of the roving staff constantly checking the lines for suspicious behavior.

He flipped open a wallet with his badge and ID. Already he suspected drugs, because Germany was a major source of Ecstasy for young Canadians on the make. Though the German sounded nasty, Clarke knew he could be a decoy for the others with him. Perhaps the woman was the real carrier. She's moving too easily, bending too comfortably moving her bags to be carrying a body pack around her waist, but a vaginal pack, well, that wouldn't show. Obviously, she knew something. And Interpol, the international criminal information system of which Canada was a member, had already advised that more E shipments were expected.

Max, sensing the impending danger first, stepped forward and drew himself to his full height. "Nothing, my good sir. My nephew here has had a little too much to drink, too easy, much too easy to do in first class. Just a little family argument."

"Not quite that simple, sir," countered Clarke. "I overheard some of the conversation. We need to clarify a few things. You're German, I assume," and turning to Mary, "and you're Canadian. Are you two related?"

Max tried to respond first, "They both work for—"

Franz jumped in, jabbing a finger in the official's face, almost grazing his nose. "Related to that Indian bitch? Get real, like she's—"

Before Franz could finish, Clarke pushed the finger away from his face, firmly taking Franz's wrist and snapping it down.

Clarke picked up Mary's hesitancy. "You, too, ma'am. Your passport, please."

"I'm Canadian, and this land is—"

"Ma'am, I've heard that song before, and you're not Anne of Green Gables."

Clarke then pointed sharply at Fergus and Max. "Both of you stay where you are. Just show me your passports."

As he spoke, Clarke waved for backup from two nearby CCRA agents and a uniformed officer from the Peel Regional Police Force that had responsibility for domestic incidents, drunk and disorderly charges, and common theft at the airport.

Then hitching up his pants, he looked Franz hard in the eye. "Let me give you a warning, sir. Take a hard look at my ID. You're on Canadian soil now, and you're close to being charged with threatening to assault an immigration officer. One more move like this, and the local police will be delighted to hold you for a bail hearing, and that could take weeks before they ship you home. That's the way we do it here. Got it?"

Franz didn't get it, and turned to walk away. He took only a few steps before a CCRA dog handler joined the group.

"Jackboots in Canada!" Franz said. "Now dogs! Not the glorious welcome we anticipated, Uncle."

"Be quiet, for God's sake, or your mother's. There is too much at stake! Millions."

The dog, tugging on its lead, first sniffed Fergus and Max. Finding nothing, it looked around, nose in the air, and then headed straight for Franz, vigorously sniffing at his hands.

Franz kicked at the dog, now sitting quietly but alert at his feet. "Get that attack—"

The handler cut him off. "It's not an attack dog, sir. Passively trained to point to drugs. That's all."

Franz tried to move away again, but the dog followed, and again sat at his feet, ears alert.

"Cuff him and take him back," said Clarke. "You're being held for threatening a peace officer, and will be searched."

Max whispered something quickly in German to Franz who then quietly nodded to the officer.

Fergus could only hang on tightly to Mary, arm around her shoulders. She now seemed small in his arms, almost terrifyingly so. Even through several layers of clothes, he could feel her heart racing. Emotionally spent and embarrassed by her outburst, Mary was breathing deeply to regain control of herself.

Clarke spoke softly to one of the other officials. "That's enough. Two hits. Escort them back for interrogation and prepare for a strip search."

"Two hits? What else?"

"The woman, a Dr. Fraser from Toronto it seems, said the younger German's been dealing in something. Time to separate the men from the boys."

Clarke turned to Fergus. "Please let go of your companion, sir. Just follow the escalator to your right. The sooner we clarify what's happening here, the sooner you folks can—"

"When do we see a lawyer?" Fergus squeaked, his voice climbing. "This is pretty heavy stuff, even for a loudmouth drunk like—"

"We hope that's all it is, sir. Mr…Mr. Dietrich will have access to a duty counsel, and, if any charges are laid against you and your two other companions, then you also have a right to counsel."

"But?"

"But, until then, we're entitled to follow our routine investigation."

"Routine?" said Fergus. "We come home from a business trip in Dresden with some bankers and wannabe Indians, and we're surrounded by a bunch of guys with guns, a bloody big dog, no rights…and you call this routine? So this is Canada?"

"It is today, sir. You have two choices, and two seconds to decide. Come with us quietly, or the officers here will cuff all of you."

Fergus and Max knew when to cut their losses, and fell in line.

They were processed quickly. Clarke, however, needed time to check Franz' record with Interpol. Just a loud-mouth drunk, or something else, he wondered, and why had he pissed off the Fraser woman?

"Your papers seem in order, Mr. Fitzgerald: a naturalized Canadian citizen, couple of speeding tickets up north in Bruce County. You're living with Dr. Fraser on Manitoulin. The OPP tell us you're working for a local weekly, drink a little beer, but no known drugs. Your bags were clean. That's about it."

"May I go now?"

"A couple more questions should do it. What can you tell us about the younger German with your group, Franz Dietrich?"

Fergus paused, vigorously chewing on his bottom lip. "I think, ah, I think, yeah, this would go faster if you could call the OPP on Manitoulin first, ask for Sergeant Matt Peltier."

"I've already spoken with him. Thanks for the heads-up. Have you heard from Peltier yourself?"

"Really? That fast? I just emailed him a couple of days ago and—"

"So, have you heard from Peltier?"

"No, he said it could wait."

"He's being cautious with a civilian source. Let me give you the summary that was expedited to us. According to Interpol, Dietrich has no record of convictions, or even charges, although he is known to associate with German drug groups, particularly bikers in Berlin and Munich. Aside from the ruckus just now, he's clean as far as we're concerned, but there are allegations you should know about."

"Oh? More drugs on Manitoulin?"

"Peltier and I, we agree that's a real possibility. But drug sources in Munich say our Mr. Dietrich could be caught up in a gang slaying. The investigation there has just started, but there's a rumble that he may know who's involved, or at least can provide some damning evidence. If so, it's not a stretch to expect an attempt here to take him out."

Perplexed, Fergus pursed his lips and shrugged his shoulders. But the inspector probed again.

"Look, either way, he's a nasty piece of business, and there's a good chance someone is going to get hurt. Unfortunately, we can't hold him at this point, even in protective custody. So do us all a favour, including yourself, and tell us what you know."

"Do I know him? Not really. We just met a couple of days ago."

Time froze while Fergus worked his way through the inferences. He was sorely tempted to deep-six the little bastard because of what he had seen and heard in Radebuel and Dresden: little comments and actions that hinted Franz's darker side was well beyond the pale.

However, Fergus knew old Max had taken the kid as an act of mercy for his sister, Franz's mother. Northern liberals his age – leftovers from the sixties and seventies – didn't like final judgments, especially about black-and-white questions with no wiggle room. Be kind, be nice, be humane, and let everyone work out the consequences of their own lives. No sin, no need for redemption or absolution.

Part of Fergus thought everyone would be better off if Immigration put the kid on the next plane back to Germany. On the other hand, Franz might be worth the risks involved if he stayed. As the seconds ticked by, Fergus decided that since Canada had given *him* another chance when he had fled the Vietnam draft, why not give this young punk a fresh start?

Oh, what the bloody hell, Fergus concluded. Take a risk.

"Nah, not much. He's a little free with his hands when Mary's around. Nothing serious, just some growing pains. Nothing she and I can't handle. Besides, Max needs him for the German side of the hotel promotion."

"Sure of that?"

`"Who's sure of anything? But, yeah, what's to fear?"

"I hope you're right, Mr. Fitzgerald," said the officer. "From the little I know so far, I think you're taking a chance. You can wait outside now."

Down the hall in another room, two other officers were taking no chances. Franz was bent over in a corner, naked with his anus exposed and genitals hanging down. All his clothing had been removed and searched. One officer conducted the search while the other took notes. Franz was trembling as the clothing search found a crumbled old toke.

The officers, however, were more interested in the brief intelligence report they'd received from the German police through Interpol, who indicated Franz was known to run with a biker group that peddled Ecstasy, sometimes in large amounts, to the international market. Much of it was trans-shipped from Montreal and Toronto into the U.S. Slick enough to stay in the shadows as a minor player, Franz had never been charged. By far, his biggest contribution had been the arrangements for inventory financing to comfort nervous suppliers. His uncle's bankers seldom asked questions.

"You can put your clothes on, sir."

"That's all? Got your kicks for the day? Look up a good German arse and sausage, a rare treat. You Canadians, you think—"

"I would go easy on that, sir. The senior officials will be here shortly to decide what happens to you. Answer me this, though. What's the tattoo for, the one on your shoulder blade? Not very visible."

"It's an Iron Cross, you dolt!"

"You can still earn those, can ya now?"

"My grandfather did. Normandy."

"Nice and safe was he, tucked back a bit? Survive it all?"

"No, one of your planes got him."

Clarke returned as Franz was buttoning his shirt.

"So, what's it to be with you, Dietrich? You're crude, brash, stupid, no real skills, other than bumming from your uncle, who seems decent enough."

"You left out charming, Inspector, well-dressed and good-looking, a great addition for your boring bloodlines. Yes, I could help people like you."

"Not with my daughters, you don't. Enough of this bullshit, and back to the options at hand: We can turn you over to the Mounties on the possession charge, send you back now, or let you stay. And from what we've gathered so far, you probably have some associates who may not want you back."

Franz was suddenly sober, wary enough to know that he had pushed the official too far.

"On the other hand, sir, I have no record, and I do have a job here. My work permit from your consulate in Dresden allows me to stay here for a year, after which it must be renewed if I choose to live in this country."

The inspector leaned against a wall, calming himself before stepping forward again into Franz's face. "We do the choosing, young man, and right now you're frigging borderline. Your BKA has—"

Franz's head jerked up.

"The Bundeskriminalant. Old men who—"

"Don't push me, Dietrich. Let me repeat: The BKA has informed our national police force that you could be involved in a murder. No charges or warrants yet, but that could change quickly."

Arching his eyebrows, Franz started to reply, meekly lowered his head, and shut up.

Clarke also paused, caught off guard by the sudden shift in the German's demeanour.

"I'm letting you in but…"

"But?"

"Your work permit is being reduced to six months. A caution notice of this complete file, including our interrogation notes, will be forwarded to the RCMP and then the local regional police here. Ultimately, this file will land on a desk at the nearest OPP office, presumably Little Current in your case. And I expect it will also go to the tribal police on Manitoulin as well. Get out of line once, and you're gone."

Across the hall, in another sterile room with bright lights, Mary Fraser had just finished dressing. She had tried to focus away from the strip search, to the sounds and the feelings, and even the smell of a room full of chattering students at university, to the taste of a quiet glass of cold Chardonnay in a rooftop bar overlooking Toronto's evening lights, to her first dinner with Fergus in the Spirit Rock restaurant near Wiarton. The images helped only briefly, as memory quickly slipped further back to another naked moment, as a child.

The two officials, both women, told her they had found nothing.

"This is difficult for you, Dr. Fraser, and we apologize for the inconvenience," said the older one, full of hip and bosom, grey-haired with crinkly eyes.

Mary's shame abruptly gave way to anger.

"INCONVENIENCE! You call a strip search an inconvenience? What do I do now? Say a rosary, let you fondle me like some terrified kid on a reserve?"

"Easy now, Dr. Fraser. It's over."

"No! No! No! It's *never* over! It doesn't wash away that easily."

"Well, it is for me, ma'am. The file says you're a bright woman, well educated, and you damn well know my job is border security, not the resolution of all Aboriginal hardships. That you can do on your time."

"My time? My fault?" Mary fired back.

"Don't go there, please," pleaded the official. "It's not that I don't care, but it's not my job."

"You're…you're right, of course."

"No apologies needed, ma'am. I might say the same if I were in your shoes. May I ask you, if you don't mind, about the marks on your left buttock? They look like nasty burn scars. They're old, but did he, Franz or whoever he is, did he do that to you?"

"No. They're too old for that, from my childhood, really. Who? Why? That's the hell of it, the living damnable hell of it. I can't see them anymore."

"Not at all?"

Mary began to sink to her knees, head down, and fingers burrowing into her ears.

"No more, not now. Please, please. Just, just let me go."

"Take your time. Let me get your coat."

Chapter 7

Little Current, Three days later

Fergus looked like any other middle-aged slug, sitting at the end of the dock, chomping into an ice cream cone, and watching life drift along the North Channel between Manitoulin and the mainland.

The pretence almost worked.

All Matt Peltier had told him so far was that there was little the OPP could do to keep Mary out of any crossfire between Franz and some nasty German bikers. Matt was now was twenty minutes late.

"We'll let you know when we have anything solid," Matt had told him yesterday "We have no reason to pick up Franz, no request from the German BKD to extradite him back to Munich. Hell, Ferg, this is Manitoulin, and I don't think the Krauts even know where Manitoulin is."

Fergus tossed the last of his cone into a trashcan, and felt like jumping in himself. He headed back to the Jeep, but his mind was churning as he drove away. Anyone with rudimentary Googling skills knew that the German bike gangs had close ties with gangs all over the world, including Canada. Moreover, the Hells Angels and Bandidos were known for leaving a lot of blood on the ground in their turf fights. "So where does that leave me?" he asked himself. "No badge, no gun, and only God knows what Mary will do next." Already Mary had bumped into Franz at a local food store and their exchange had quickly become damned heated and threatening.

She's different now, he thought. Something happened in Dresden that has made her far more volatile, less disciplined, perhaps even in danger of hurting herself or others. Little Miss Time Bomb she is. And just keep her out of the crossfire, according to Matt. Oh, that's nice. Do I use ropes or duct tape or just hide her in the barn? Then again, I kept myself out of the crossfire with 'Nam.

South Baymouth, Same day

No one particularly noticed two leather-clad men roaring off the Chi-Cheemaun ferry onto the receiving dock. There was the usual clatter, as their Hawgs hit the metal ramp and then the eastern end of Manitoulin Island, sixty kilometers south of Little Current. Cyclists, both motor and pedal, were always first on and first off for the trip across Georgian Bay from Tobermory on the mainland. No police checks, no security clearance or baggage checks. Cars, trucks, and vans would follow.

The goal of the bikers would soon be clear: to prove that German-funded terrorists could strike at will into the Canadian heartland.

Within minutes, they pulled into a gas station with a payphone booth. Like most bikers, they were dressed entirely in black, even their helmets and wrap-around sunglasses. One had a beard, but neither sported any club insignia. They carried no credit cards, and their ID and licences claimed they were Francois Sullivan from Stoney Creek and Eric Gunderson from Hagersville in Southern Ontario. Their documents, however, had been stolen for them by other bikers.

The shorter of the two pulled out a prepaid long distance card, and punched in the access code and then a 905 number.

The call was short.

"Okay, okay, we're here. No fucking sweat."

"Any curious citizens?"

"No. Any shit-ass changes your end?"

"No. Meat okay?"

"Yeah, lots for breakfast. Still frozen."

"Fucking A then. Time to move out."

Call completed, the black knights roared off. At the Manitowaning Road, they signalled a right-hand turn, and pulled into a nearby motel.

A teenage girl booked them into a single room. They paid cash in advance as they planned to be gone well before dawn.

"Okay, guys, one bed or two?"" asked the young girl, as her father had taught her, but giggling as she did.

Francois thumped the counter. "Listen, princess, do I looks like I wanna sleep with—"

Eric jumped in quickly, pulling Francois back. "Easy, man. Two beds, please. One key."

As she would tell the OPP the next day, she thought one was cute, sort of. Tall, with intense blue eyes, black hair that fell over his face, and a slight accent, perhaps Swedish or German. The other "bozo" was shorter, with red curly hair and bad breath. Yuck!

Within minutes, Francois and Eric were back on their bikes. Heading north, they entered the village of Sheguiandah where they turned left down the Town Line Road, cruising slowly as they consulted a folded map, and took note of an old farmhouse high on a hill to their right. It had a porch along one side, facing a large yard, and beyond that a row of bushes, mostly sumac already tinged with the red leaves of fall. A dog slept near the porch.

"That's Adler's place," Eric noted with a thumbs up. "The full-sized Audi and BMW are there, so they gotta be home."

They knew Max and his nephew lived alone in the old Howard place, and had already spent considerable money on new utilities and beds. A local woman came in daily to cook and clean, and her husband came once a week to do the gardening. And there was a guard dog, a Great Pyrenees named Milo. The bikers kept going, but turned back about a kilometer away, took another quick look at the farmhouse and nearby homes, then cruised back to the highway and turned in at a restaurant in a park. They talked a little but quietly, so that the three other diners and the waitress could not hear what they were saying. They left about an hour later, heading back to the motel where they settled in for the night.

Shortly before four in the morning, they gently closed their room door and walked their bikes to the highway before firing up the motors. At the village, they turned down the side road again, cruising slowly before pulling off behind a grove of trees just around a bend from the farmhouse.

Eric opened his saddlebag, took out a small package wrapped in newspaper, and walked around the trees and up the lane to the farmhouse. Francois bent low, skirting the sumac row. The house was dark and silent; the only movement was the Great Pyrenees on the porch who began to stretch, but, as expected, didn't bark. As Eric moved closer, Francois circled around before sweeping down from behind, unnoticed by the dog. Moving quickly, Eric unfolded the newspaper package of burger and placed it in front of the dog. Milo sniffed for a few seconds, looked around as if to get his master's approval, then began to eat.

Francois emerged from the shadow of the sumacs. Silently pulling out a freshly sharpened hunting knife, he grabbed the dog's head and mane from behind, and before Milo had a chance to yelp, quickly sliced his throat, left to right. Blood gushed out over the meat and newspaper page, then turned the thick hair on the dog's chest into a matted red mass with streaks dripping down both forelegs. Milo's terrified eyes bulged and stared as his body slumped.

No lights came on in the house as Francois and Eric stole away, picked up their bikes, and walked the five hundred meters back to the highway before turning on their motors. Once on the highway, they headed north into Little Current, then jogged right onto the swing-bridge over the North Channel and onto the mainland. At the junction of Highways 6 and 17, they turned west toward Sault Ste. Marie and throttled up.

Back at the farmhouse, Max and Franz slept on, unaware of the tragedy. Ola, their housekeeper, arrived promptly at seven to prepare their breakfast. This day, however, breakfast would be delayed as she stumbled over Milo's lifeless body lying in its own gore near the porch. She screamed into the cool morning air.

Max, the first to stir, grabbed a robe and hurtled down the stairs, through the kitchen, and onto the porch. He was struck dumb, shaking his head in disbelief as he stood over Milo for a minute before helping Ola to her feet.

Ola broke into his thoughts. "I'll make coffee, Mr., I mean, Herr… Oh dear, I'm not myself. This is awful...who would...oh, poor Milo...oh…"

Franz joined them, bending over the dog for a closer look, then noticing the blood-soaked paper. Biting his lip as he pulled himself upright, he glared at his uncle. "You and your savages! They don't want us here! They're crawling around out there; they won't be satisfied until we leave."

Max settled down by the dog, rubbing his hand along the back of Milo's neck.

"Savages? Yes, Franz, a cowardly savage killed my Milo, but it was not one of *my* savages, as you call them."

"No? Then who, Uncle? Whose savages?" Franz replied. "Where's Ola with the coffee? Bury your damn dog!"

Franz turned to go, but Max stood suddenly and grabbed him by the collar of his bathrobe, forcing him to look again at the slaughtered dog. The early morning light from the east was still faint.

"You can read German as well as I can, Franz. Read the paper under Milo!"

"No, some Indian brought it here."

"You preposterous fool. Read it!"

Franz shook off Max's grip, and squared his shoulders before turning and facing Milo.

"As you wish, then. Yes, of course, this is about me, Uncle. The paper, it's German, from Munich I think, and if I can make out the date properly, it's only three days old. Let me get a better look."

"No," said Max, pulling his nephew up. "The police will want everything undisturbed. I must call—"

"No police, Uncle. No more questions; no nasty little Canadians digging at us."

It was Max's turn to step back, shaking for a moment as he reached inside himself to put words around the raw taste of revulsion that brought bile into his mouth.

"Look at Milo, Franz! Look hard at what you have done."

"He's just a dog," Franz hurriedly interjected. "Thousands of dogs die every day, killed by cars, or just put to sleep when they get too old. People even kill them for food, like any dumb animal. Bury the beast. What's to worry?"

Max now had regained the cold austere look that came across his face when he wrestled with difficult decisions.

"What's to worry about, Franz, are you and your cowardly friends. If they can kill a dog like this, slit its throat in the middle of the night, then they can kill anybody for any reason. I cannot sit back and ignore who you have become anymore. My generation has too many memories of doing nothing. You are no longer family."

Before Max could finish, an OPP cruiser pulled up beside them.

"Just checking houses along here, sir," said a uniformed officer. "I'm OPP Constable Tindale. A neighbour reported two bikers went in and out of here this morning, probably four-ish. He got up for a pee and saw them pull their bikes from behind a tree. Anything out of order, sir? … Oh, my God, is that your dog? Jesus...pardon me...I'd better call this in, sir."

Constable Tindale made the call, then pulled out a blue tarp from the trunk to cover Milo's body. "The crime scene team will be here shortly," he told Max and Franz, "and I expect we'll need statements especially from Mr. Dietrich here. Do I have your name right, sir?" he asked, looking at Franz. "Good. I'm only a patrol cop, not a detective, but everyone in the detachment has been advised that your life might be threatened at any time. The paper under the dog's head looks German to me. Any idea what it says, sir?"

"Not really," scoffed Franz, his face visibly pale. "I need to—"

"FRANZ!" shouted Max. "This is not some prank. You, our hotel, everything has been violated. For your mother's sake at least, tell the officer what you can read.

Franz turned away to the porch, and asked Ola for coffee.

"Franz!" Max repeated, his frustration mounting as he tied his robe tighter. "Tell the officer what you can see."

Finally, Franz nodded, pulled back the tarp enough to read the top of the newspaper spread under the meat. "Just the headline. That's all I can make out."

Tindale was taking notes. "Hmmm. That's all? So, Mr. Dietrich, what's it say? Time is critical here. Others could be in danger. Our traffic cruisers are already checking the island and, I suspect, beyond. I know this is a difficult moment, but we do need to know what that headline says, and one way or another, we will find out."

Franz stood up and stiffened. "The headline, then. In German or English?"

"English for now, sir. We'll get a full official translation later when the newspaper can be recovered."

"If you insist. I'm the target, you know that already. The headline says: 'Missing Witness Sought in Biker Killing.' "

Police checks picked up the bikers' trail from the ferry to the gas station to the motel and the diner, and finally to the man who got up for an early morning pee. Then almost nothing. A truck driver reported that two bikers almost cut him off when they turned west from Highway 6 to Highway 17, blasting through the intersection. From there, the trail was dead, the police saying only that "investigations are continuing."

The reports did not mollify Fergus, who was furious, mostly at himself for not saying more to the immigration inspectors in Toronto. "Stupid" and "naïve" were only two of the words racking his brain as he explained to Mary the significance of Milo's slaying.

They said little to each other during the day, focusing instead on the mundane tasks of weekly house-cleaning and gardening. Fergus warned that Franz might well turn on her. But Mary refused to take any extra precautions. Instead, shears in hand, slashing furiously at the dead-head hydrangea blossoms, she repeated, mantra-like: "The bikers slit the wrong throat."

Mary's vehemence stunned Fergus. What the bloody hell? The shears! Get them away from her; don't let her hurt herself.

Not a hope! Fergus was half a heartbeat too late. Before he could finish the thought, Mary kicked away the hydrangea stems, fell to her knees on the damp earth, and manically began executing every flower and shrub around the west side of the house. Quickly, the garden was in ruins.

For one frozen moment, Fergus stood there, hands twitching at his side. Fight or flight decisions like this had always been defining moments for Fergus. Flight was always the easiest. When he left Boston rather than answer his draft call, he told no one in his family and took an overnight train to Canada. Even when his wife died, none of his family came to Toronto for the funeral or even sent a mass card. Just one phone call: "You've crapped in your own bed too often," said his older brother who had worked underground on the Boston subway and helped support the family after their father died in the Korean War. "So lie in it!"

There was no time now to worry about Boston. Fergus managed to wrest the shears from Mary, and led her back into the house where he first calmed himself with deep, gulping breaths, and then ministered to her. Tea helped, so did a sleeping pill, and by early evening, Mary's breakdown or seizure or obsessive compulsion or some other dysfunction he couldn't fully comprehend was over, at least for the time being.

Chapter 8

An hour later, Fergus crept up the creaky farmhouse stairs, and checked on Mary. He heard nothing out of the ordinary, only her shallow breathing from under the thunderbird-design quilt she had pulled up almost over her head. Her day clothes were scattered though, unlike her methodical habit of putting everything in its proper place

Downstairs again, he slid a half-eaten shrimp casserole into the microwave, then turned on the computer while he waited.. A dram of scotch first, as the evening felt chillier than usual. He called up one website after another, but time dragged and jumbled images of Franz ate into his consciousness, beginning with the presumptuous young man in the Dresden airport. The microwave sounded its all-clear, so he got up, pulled out the casserole, stared at it, and came to the conclusion that sometimes leftovers were just leftovers – calories, not metaphors for his own existence. Just eat.

As he ate, his subconscious posed another question: What did Mary know that he didn't know?

It seemed obvious to him that if Mary was paranoid about Franz, perhaps to the point of self-destruction, and if the Germans were trying to intimidate Franz, then Franz might well try to protect himself against both Mary and the bikers. As much as Fergus was tempted to pack his bags and run away again, back to his solitary life in Wiarton, he came to the conclusion, with just one dirty casserole dish and one dirty fork staring back at him, that he couldn't pretend she never existed. He accepted that her pain had become his pain, just as the soldiers who did go to Vietnam ended up fighting for their buddies, not for the great causes and charlatans. Screw them, he decided. Mary's war had become Fergus's war.

This war had its own domino theory, which he accepted. Native culture on isolated islands like Manitoulin, as he was beginning to understand, would either grow or die. The Ojibwa would survive as proud people or be marginalized as sideshow Indians for tourists. That was a blunt assessment, Fergus knew, but it weighed heavily on Mary. Many here held to an old prophecy that the Ojibwa would be blessed with the emergence of a new generation – Mary's generation – which would find a sacred way that long had been lost.

The simpler question, the only one Fergus could deal with at this point, was whether Mary herself could survive. It might have been the scotch, or the stress of the day, or perhaps his age, but suddenly Fergus felt tired. He gave way to the urge to flop into his leather recliner chair, his only real piece of furniture. He slid easily into a nap, but it provided only short relief, as his subconscious kept running over what he did know, beginning with the bikers. According to Matt Peltier, the usual biker sources in Sudbury said they had heard nothing.

As Fergus slowly emerged from his nap, he remembered that Franz had shown no indication of going back to Germany. He also recalled hearing that Franz was often seen with a young native man, a typical rural teenager who liked to roar around the back roads in an old pickup. The kid lived with his grandmother, who wanted the OPP to intervene.

Still half asleep, Fergus mused that drugs were probably involved, given Franz's own habits. Mary had already told Fergus that Franz was fascinated by the darker side of Ojibwa culture: the curses and bogeymen, myths that still frightened some people here. Franz was already pushing for a Bearwalker Bar in the hotel, complete with neon images around the walls and ceiling of large bears shape-shifting into human form.

"Wha...what's going on? Oh, it's you, Mary."

Mary, now more awake than Fergus, had slipped silently into the room and gently touched his arm to stir him.

"Just me, Fergus. At least I think it's me, not that wild woman out there. I really lost it, didn't I?"

Fergus sneaked a quick look at his watch, and realized he'd been napping for almost an hour. Mary had been out for almost three hours.

"Yeah, woman, you were really out there. But first things first. Hungry?"

She smiled back at him with her own memories of gentler times.

"Your miracle food, sir. Scrambled eggs, toast, and tea. Okay?"

"Five minutes. I think we have eggs. Then we need to talk."

"Oh?"

"After you eat."

"But—"

"Set the table while I perform my culinary magic. Then we talk."

Fergus found enough eggs while Mary puttered around, forcing herself to check her email – nothing urgent that needed attention – then seven minutes later followed him, plate in hand, to the wooden kitchen table where they usually ate breakfast.

"So, Fergus, the eggs need a little more salt, but I thank you. Really. Can we talk now?"

"Flat out then," said Fergus as matter-of-factly as he could, sensing that she could blow up again. "Stay away from Franz. He's a jerk; we all know that. Come back to Wiarton with me."

"Wiarton! Just like that. Run away. Hide out in that cave of yours. Let that little bastard win?"

"It's safer, Mary, just for a few months until he's sent back to Germany. Then we can—"

"No, Fergus, no. Let me borrow your gruesome word. No bloody way. I have to see this through, the whole of it – not just the hotel, but why I'm here. I know this is weird to you, but I'm here for reasons that are monumentally more important to me than Franz, or even Max."

"The old man?"

"Like you, a bit. So we're staying. Both of us."

Fergus knew when he was outmatched. "Two conditions, then."

"I thought what we had was unconditional."

"Stop playing word games, Mary. It's… Just consider what I have to say as strongly worded advice. Okay?"

"Get on with it then."

"First, stay away from Franz as much as you can, particularly in public. The police tell me that he wants OPP protection because he's claiming you're threatening him."

"What?"

Fergus knew immediately that his advice was not going to be easily absorbed by Mary. She had stopped eating, elbows forward on the table. One hand was jabbing at him..

There was no doubt in Fergus's mind that he had to get to the heart of his warnings quickly and succinctly.

"In legal terms, you may be a hair away from uttering a threat. Remember your run-in with him yesterday in Little Current where you told him to watch his back after your public rant about his parentage."

Mary let out a breath, and finally dropped her fork to the plate.

"I did, didn't I? But he's such a sleaze."

She sipped at her cold tea.

Fergus, still cautious, rose and grasped the back of his chair.

"Sleaze, he is. But let me borrow a word from you. He's also provocative, and will try to bait you. You told him that natives have their own special way of getting rid of bad people. Or that's what Franz is alleging. Now let me make my real point. If anything happens to Franz, if the bikers in Germany or wherever come after him again, the cops will have to go after you. Get it?"

Mary was wide-eyed now, hands folded over mouth, as the implications of what Fergus was saying sank in. Fergus moved to her side as she began rocking in her chair.

At first, he could only hear her moan and then, very softly, she spoke to him. "Oh, my God, I *am* losing it, aren't I?"

Neither spoke for a moment until Fergus took her by the hand and led her to his big chair. He pushed a hassock in front and sat facing her.

"Which leads me to my second point. You need professional help. What happened in the garden was downright scary for both of us. Your blow-ups with Franz have been growing – first in Dresden, then the Munich and Toronto airports, and now Manitoulin. Yes, yes, you're the victim; I understand that, but he's also touching something deep inside you that's fuelling your anger."

Mary didn't reply for a few moments.

"No, Fergus. That took courage to tell me, but we both know I don't have time to go to Toronto or even to Sudbury to speak with a shrink. Perhaps when construction is fully underway and plans are set and—"

"No way, Mary, we can get help. Call the husband-and-wife medical team we met back at the Ojibwa Cultural Centre. He's a family doc, and I think she's a psychologist or psychiatrist. I've also been told that she's an ex-nun who was posted around here for a while. Remember her?"

Mary sucked in a deep breath, then looked away before she answered. Fergus's heart rate picked up as Mary squeezed his hand.

"Don't push me, Fergus. You're pressing too hard. I need some room to find—"

"Find what?"

"My own way, Fergus. Yes, I know them. Noel and Don Callaghan."

"So you know them. Why in bloody hell didn't you just tell me? What else are you holding back?""

"Fergus, please focus. This is reality time for me. Certainly, I know I need help. Oh, God, I'm not an idiot. But my world, my mind, are falling apart faster than I can patch them up. I'm not sure yet how I know them... I mean her."

"Really, you knew her all this time?"

"Yes and no. She...she's a large white woman, tall; perhaps she must have reminded me of someone, that's all I remember. Can we leave it? If I get time, I'll call her. Okay? Satisfied?"

"Oh, wow, this takes getting used to. But, hell no, I won't be satisfied until you see her professionally, as they say. Can you?"

"I...I already have."

"Seen her?"

"Yes. Briefly, one afternoon. This week. Found her office and walked in. No appointments, no answers yet, so don't push me. I need my own space on this. Can you accept that?"

Fergus was too tired to press the issue. He led Mary to the bottom of the stairs, anxious to get her back to bed.

"For the moment, yeah, but don't let it go. You really scared me today, Okay? And hey, I forgot something. Conall sent me an email tonight asking whether he can send us a present, even if we aren't getting married."

"Did he now? You Irish astound me. Will it wait until morning? I just want to cuddle with you a little, just cuddle. Coming up?"

He did. They hugged, arms wrapped tightly around each other for a good and caring moment. But just as he was dropping off, he heard Mary answer her cell phone with a brief response: "will do," or something that Fergus couldn't quite make out. Call over, Mary arched over his shoulder to kiss his forehead, muttered something about security problems at the hotel site, then gathered up her clothes and went downstairs. Sleep overtook Fergus again, and he didn't hear her Jeep rumble out of the driveway, only registering when it returned about an hour later.

Chapter 9

Mary's side of the bed was empty, and Fergus could only wonder whether she had again taken flight into the early morning mists, like an out-of-body exodus into another world. Fergus was not the spring-loaded type, whose consciousness quickly snapped into place, and he couldn't tell whether he was still groggy from a night of interrupted sleep, or if something strange was happening.

His left shoulder ached, and his bladder called. He sat up in bed, wondering if this was the moment when Mary had finally left him. Sometimes, increasingly so now, he realized that it was often easier to love her than to like her.

They'd had a good romp, but he also believed that romps should end before reality set in, and someone got hurt. At times, he was sorely tempted to go back to Wiarton and sit in the shadows. But bloody hell, not this morning, he told himself. She needs me. So damn Franz, and damn the bikers, wherever they are. I stay.

He usually saw their home as a sanctuary. To the east, just around the white clapboard house, dawn's first light was barely visible. This morning would be different. Neither he nor Mary had had much sleep the previous night before she'd been called back to the hotel construction site just before midnight to check out a security problem. She took her advisory role with the German hotel project seriously, even in the dark of night when she was hesitant to go out alone. Especially on Manitoulin, with its old stories of evil creatures hovering just beyond the campfires.

Returning home an hour or so later, she had awakened him without words, first with her hands, then her tongue. He still savored her enveloping presence, the heated intensity, the grabbing and the clinging, nails digging in, hips surging urgently, almost trying to hide herself in him. Her tears flowed in the crook of his neck, and the denouement lasted several minutes.

Then suddenly she had rolled over, quiet and composed and still. She rose again just before dawn, but Fergus was used to acknowledging her need for space. At one point, he thought he heard her voice, but that, too, became part of her ritual cleansing, where she scrubbed herself so hard in the shower that it sounded painfully abusive.

Suddenly there was no time for worrisome reverie. Fergus was startled, eyes flying wide open, as he heard a car hurtle down the lane and run over a sprawling clump of high-bush cranberries. Then he felt his pulse jump when he saw the OPP cruiser screech to a stop. Within moments, he heard an officer banging at the door. He hurriedly pulled on the jeans and sweater he grabbed from the chair beside their bed.

Terrifying images pounded him. What the... Cops! Bloody Christ, where's Mary? Fergus rushed downstairs to check on her things. Laptop? Yes. Boots? No. Jacket? No. He glanced at their combined working and living room with the long trestle table. Nothing missing, just Mary. He looked out the window. No, the big Jeep she drove, she'd taken that with her.

His dog, Brendan, a large white and black Landseer related to the big Newfoundland breed, picked up his anxiety as revolving red and white lights from the OPP cruiser shone through a kitchen window. Two officers, one in uniform, the other plain clothes, emerged.

"Dr. Fraser, it's the OPP. We need to talk to you!"

The uniformed officer again pounded on the oak panels.

Fergus froze, not breathing for several moments, emotion and memory frantically colliding. *Was Mary hurt?* he wondered. Did she miss the big curve at the sandpit?

Staff Sergeant Matt Peltier stepped back from the door, and saw the light in the kitchen window.

"Fergus, where's Mary? Get her up and out here. Now! This is serious. Don't make this difficult."

Fergus began breathing again. He hurriedly crossed into the hall beyond the kitchen, stepped into his rubber boots, and opened the door.

"Sorry, Fergus," apologized Peltier, hands on hips. His height, well over six feet, and erect bearing, had always intimidated Fergus. "There's been an incident near her work site. Mary may be able to—"

Fergus, jarred fully awake, jumped in.

"An incident? What kind of incident? Mary, she's okay?"

"I can't answer those questions, Ferg. That's why we're here."

"It's barely dawn, Matt. Are you going to tell me what's going on? What in the name of sweet Jesus has Mary got to do with this? Can't it wait 'til morning?"

"It's not the middle of the night, Ferg, and we haven't had any sleep either, so before I really get testy, get Mary up and out here. Now!"

"She's not here."

"Not here?"

"Yeah, she's does that sometimes. Just goes."

"Just like that, eh? Goes where?"

Something visceral told Fergus not to connect the dots between Mary's morning flight and the police visit. Let her run with the wind before the thunderclouds. Give that to her unconditionally.

"She didn't say, Matt."

"Oh Lord, Rich," Matt blurted out to the other officer. "She's run on us."

Fergus jumped in. "Run from what?"

"Got any coffee in there, Ferg? We'd better come in."

The two men stared at each other. Fergus finally nodded his head and stepped inside as Peltier turned to his partner, Detective Sergeant Rich Sawicki. Ferg barely knew Sawicki.

"It's your show, Rich," Matt said, "but I'll advise Dispatch that Dr. Fraser's not here and advise all units to watch for… Ferg, Mary still driving that big Jeep Wagoneer? What year?"

Fergus nodded again. "'93, blue, I don't remember the plate number. You know all that anyway."

They were silent while Fergus made coffee and reached for three mugs straight from the dishwasher.

Matt took Fergus aside. "I'll only say this once, Ferg. Everyone knows we're friends, and that Mary's special to a lot of folks. I'm just here, well, to smooth things for everybody if I can. This is serious, buddy, damn serious, so just co-operate with Detective Sawicki, and make this easier for all of us."

Sawicki, impatient with the buddy approach, moved to assert control.

"Were you here all night, Mr. Fitzgerald?"

"Yes. With Mary."

"Was she here all night?"

"Dammit," Fergus looked again to Matt. "Slow down. You can't just barge in here, our home, and poke into what we do at night. It's personal, private. Or can you?"

Sawicki moved into Fergus's face, almost nose to nose.

"It may be personal, Mr. Fitzgerald, but it's no longer private. For starters, we noticed bloodstains on the door handle as we came in. Fresh, too. We'll need to—"

"Blood? Whose blood? Jesus… Will you guys listen to me? I told you, Detective, she's not here."

"We need to check the upstairs rooms."

"You can do this?" asked Fergus.

"With a warrant. That'll take a few hours, and we will be securing this place. Another cruiser is on its way to control access from the road."

Fergus again turned to Matt. "What in hell are you doing to...? You know us, you know Mary, you—"

"Not this morning, Fitzgerald," Sawicki interrupted, breathing in sharply. "This is how we investigate. No assumptions, no favours. By the book. Got it?"

Fergus continued to stare.

"Get dressed, Fitzgerald," Sawicki demanded. "You're coming with us to the detachment. We need a statement, so make this easy, man, at least for her sake."

But Fergus was loathe to leave the home he and Mary had created.

"For her sake, you say. Why for her sake? Just tell me that."

"She could be in danger. There appears to have been a killing last night. That's why we're here. I can't tell you much more, not now anyway, but it's possible she's either involved, or can help us."

Fergus slumped into a chair, spilling his coffee as he did. He looked around for a sweater or jacket as a chill came over him.

"Who's dead?"

Sawicki turned to a uniformed constable, Al Kirkland, who had just arrived. "Better check the office first."

The call was made. "ID just confirmed, sir. By his uncle, Maximillian Adler."

Fergus took a step back. "Franz is dead?"

Rich sucked in his own breath before turning around to face Fergus.

"About five hours ago, Mr. Adler's security guard reported he had discovered a body on the hillside overlooking the work site. Death doesn't appear to be the result of natural causes. Nor was it robbery, at least as far we can tell."

Fergus struggled free of his own mental cocoon. "Franz, that's who is dead, Matt?"

Peltier first looked at Sawicki, and then answered. "When Rich and I did a preliminary search, his wallet was still in his jacket with the appropriate licenses.

"His uncle has now confirmed Franz Dietrich as the deceased, and our emergency response team has taken over the site."

"Oh, wowoooooooooh," moaned Fergus. "The little bastard is gone. I should have… God, this is sheer hell. How? Good Lord, why? A biker hit?"

"That's why we want to talk to Mary. Obviously, the bikers will be of interest if we ever find them, but we need to know how Mary fits into this. For starters, she and Franz, they had a nasty history of their own. We both know that, Ferg, so what can *you* tell us?"

Chapter 10

What could Fergus say? Too much had exploded in the first fifteen minutes of his day, leaving only the unavoidable acknowledgment that his Mary, with her wondrous mind, had grown angry enough to kill Franz. The thought first walloped him like a load of buckshot, because he knew she had said that she would. Mercifully, Fergus's investigative-reporter mind fired back with its own questions: Could she really kill like that…or did the bikers get to Franz first?

Brendan whined and bumped Fergus's leg with his head.

"You'll have to wait a sec," Fergus cautioned Matt, who was visibly frustrated with the delay. "Brendan needs to be let out; it's his usual time. Okay?"

He smiled, sensing that Brendan's bladder might buy him some time. Grateful for the interruption, he led the dog away from the officers and into the yard. Brendan trotted over to the front right tire of one of the cruisers, where he lifted a leg.

While this pleased Fergus, Matt threw his hands in the air. "Jes… Ah shit, Fergus, I'm serious. Stop stalling; we're all going back into Little Current. About Mary, she's gone missing, and we probably have a murder to deal with. Make this hard and we'll have to… Make a choice, man."

Fergus did make a choice, sort of. "I'm not stalling; Brendan needed a piss. Or do I need a lawyer to look after my bloody dog? So you're thinking Mary did it, is that it, Matt?"

"Slow down, Ferg. We just need to—"

"Bloody hell, Matt, get your own act together. First, you tell me to stop stalling, and now you tell me to slow down. What's it going to be? Do I have time to take a piss myself?"

Detective Sergeant Sawicki stepped in front of Peltier to answer. "You're playing us, Mr. Fitzgerald. I don't know why, but enough crap. You're coming with us."

"PLAYING YOU?" Fergus yelled back at them, louder than at any time in his muted life. "Jesus, man, you've got more balls than brains. You're too bloody much. First, you guys tell me to keep Mary out of the crossfire between that little shit, Franz, and whoever the hell the heavies are in Munich. Then you let a couple of bikers – at least that's who you think whacked that dog – come onto the island unnoticed, and if it *is* the bikers, then you don't know where the hell they are. You couldn't protect Franz, and now I can't even take a piss."

The phone rang.

"Don't answer that!" said Sawicki.

Two more rings.

One more ring. "Matt, better grab that."

"No bloody way," said Fergus. "It's my house and you haven't…" He lunged for the phone.

"Hello."

"Be careful with what you say, Fergus, but don't lie. You may be at risk yourself."

It was a woman's voice, one he did not recognize.

"What the, who are…?"

"We met at the Cultural Centre."

"We did?"

"Are you alone, yes or no?"

"No."

"We thought as much. I'll call back in about fifteen minutes to tell you where Mary is and what is happening to her. Can you wait for my call, yes or no?"

"Perhaps… Yes."

"You're a good man, Fitzgerald. I know you can do this! " Before Fergus could hang up, Rich Sawicki grabbed the phone. No caller ID. He pushed *69 and heard several rings before a teenager answered with an expletive. He explained that Fergus's call must have come from a local payphone.

"So, who called?" Sawicki demanded impatiently. "Was it Mary?"

"No, Detective, it wasn't Mary."

"You're on thin ice yourself, Fitzgerald. Again, one more time, was it Mary?"

"No, I told you already. Why should it be?"

"I'll ask the questions here. If it wasn't Mary, then who was it?"

"Don't push me, man, not in our home. I'll bloody well ask whatever bloody questions I want."

Peltier interjected, now openly angry at his friend. "Home? Fergus, get real! You're just baggage passing through."

Again Sawicki took charge. "Let's stay with the case. Once more, Fitzgerald, who called?"

"I don't know," deflected Fergus, getting control of himself again and choosing his words carefully.

"You don't know? That's your answer?"

"Yes. I really can't say any more. No names were given."

"Okay, we'll play it your way. Did you recognize the voice?"

"Vaguely familiar."

"Vaguely familiar, Fitzgerald! That's all?"

"That's all. I'm not going to guess, if that's what you want."

"Enough. We're taking you into the detachment. Constable Kirkland—"

"And miss the best part?"

"Miss what, Fitzgerald?"

"The call back in about ten minutes."

"You want us to wait here? Regular little morning coffee klatch."

"No, we could look for Brendan."

"You're jerking us around again?"

"No, but I may be able to tell you more about Mary when they call back. That's what I was told."

"Constable, go look for the damned dog."

The phone rang again, and Sawicki moved quickly to block Fergus.

"Yes?"

"May I speak to Dr. Fraser, please? Dr. Mary Fraser?"

"Who's calling?"

"The *Sudbury Star*. We've been told there's been a killing near the hotel project on Highway 6. Can you help us, sir, to clarify a few things? I've only got a few minutes."

"No, not at this time. Who told you to call here?"

"That's none of your business. This looks racial, so perhaps Dr. Fraser could shed some—"

"She's not here, and this line is OPP business, so this chat is over."

"Just like that. Really? The German consulate, our readers—"

"You got it! Just like that." Sawicki disconnected the call.

"It's been almost twenty minutes, sir," Kirkland said, "since the first call came in."

"We'll wait, Constable; that's what cops do. Hold on. Fitzgerald, you got a second phone, a cordless?"

"Beside the computer, next to the speaker, in the other room. Get it yourself."

"Constable Kirkland, get it. We haven't much time."

The phone finally rang again, and they stared at each other before Fergus answered. "Fitzgerald here."

"Sorry, we took longer than expected. Assessments always do."

"Assessments? What's going on? Who is this?"

"Is there a third person on this line, Fergus?"

"Yes."

"Who? Police?"

"Let me handle this, Fitzgerald," Sawicki broke in. "This is Detective Sergeant Sawicki from the Manitoulin Crime Unit, and I recognize your voice, Dr. Callaghan. "

"Ah, you get a gold star then, Detective. But sorry, this is a confidential call about my patient. Which means, of course, that I'll decide when we talk to the police. Fergus, are you still there?"

Fergus gulped and paused, needing time before he could speak.

"Slow down, both of you!"

Sawicki and Fergus glared at each other, each refusing to let the other take the lead in the conversation with Noel Callaghan, the psychologist Mary and Fergus had bumped into a few months earlier at the Ojibwa Cultural Centre. Sawicki had had frequent battles with her about access to her patients – disagreements, really, because he had come to respect her instincts about people; she seemed to be able to feel things most folk couldn't. He knew that her professional colleagues had long appreciated that she was unusually sensitive to hidden psychological stimuli.

Rich got on well with both her and her husband, and in the way of small towns, they had invited him several times to their comfortable home overlooking the North Channel. For an ex-nun, Noel Callaghan was not a bad cook, Rich had always thought.

Dr. Callaghan broke the silence, and made another effort to direct the three-way call and its colliding conflicts.

"Rich, let me turn to you first. I don't know yet what happened to Mary Fraser last night, and even if I did, I couldn't tell you, not now anyway. Perhaps never."

"Never? Okay, we're all short of sleep, Noel. So what can you tell us then? I'll make my take on this clear, so we can keep this professional. Okay? This probably is a homicide investigation."

"Oh! Well, then, I understand your urgency. Still..."

"Still what? A man is dead, and Dr. Fraser may be, ah, able to help us."

"Again, I appreciate your position, Detective, and most certainly I will try to accommodate your interests...at the appropriate time."

"Appropriate time? Who do you think you…? We have our time limits, too, Doctor, and they are closing in quickly. We now have a full crime scene team at the site, probably more than a dozen people. Tracker dogs, too, and the coroner from Little Current is coming to examine the body. The press is already calling; it could be racial, and I expect the victim's uncle, Max Adler, will be putting pressure on the German consulate in Sudbury and perhaps Foreign Affairs in Ottawa. So where is Dr. Fraser, or do I bring all of you in for questioning and possible charges of obstruction?"

"Patient confidentiality still trumps all of that. You're missing a layer. Fergus, are you still there?"

"Yes,...Dr. Callaghan, I'm here."

"We're all feeling some stress, Fergus. You will understand, and you, too, Detective, when I say that Mary, like too many other native women of her age, is currently overwhelmed by stress from massive traumatic flashbacks, increasingly so since the Dresden trip. Do you understand what that means, Rich?"

"I'm sure you'll tell me, Doctor."

There was a long pause at the other end of the line. Fergus and Sawicki exchanged anxious looks until Fergus could no longer deal with the silence.

"Fergus here. Understand what, Doctor? We're talking about my Mary. Do I get her a lawyer, or let you and Sawicki tramp through our lives?"

"Unless the police want to charge her with something, she's still my patient, Fergus, and at this point, I don't want her talking to anyone except a qualified professional therapist. She's too fragile."

Another long pause. This time Rich took the lead.

"We just need to ask her a few questions that may help us all, and let you get on with your diagnosis and treatment."

"You're still missing the point, Rich. I respect your position in this, but I won't know whether Mary can even understand your questions, let alone remember what has happened to her over the past couple of days, at least until we receive the results back from Sudbury."

"Sudbury? You've taken her to Sudbury?"

"I haven't. My husband has. They'll be there within the hour."

"I'm stopping them. I can't look the other way, and you damn well know it. If nothing else, Dr Fraser may be a material witness. Moreover, she could be in danger herself. She threatened Franz several times, both here and in Toronto, and she fled her home without explanation to Fitzgerald. If you want my opinion, Fitzgerald, get a lawyer."

"Rich," replied Noel, "you know my professional credentials, so I don't have to run through them. And it's my blessed opinion that she won't be any use to you until we get her stabilized and assess her grip on reality. If you want to hold her, or look at my notes, then you'll need a court order. Or—"

"Or what?"

"Or we can trust each other for a few more hours. Holy Mother of God, surely your people can work the crime scene while the docs at Northern Care in Sudbury assess whether Mary has any grip on reality. She's repressing something. I don't fully understand it yet, but I do know that it's so severe she's shutting down."

"I hear you, but it's not my call. I need to consult with the Crown. Noel, give me the contact numbers in Sudbury to confirm this. Fitzgerald, you'd better get a lawyer… Fitzgerald, you still on the line?"

"Yes, dammit! What the bloody hell? You two are cutting some sort of deal, and I still don't understand why. But I'm the one who's told to get a lawyer. Explain! Now! FUCKING NOW!"

"Easy, Fergus, easy. You're hurting and confused and—"

"Don't *easy* me, Noel."

"Okay, Fergus. First, Rich, are you still there?"

"Yes. Go on."

"Good. Listen up. If I'm going to decode this for Fergus, then you either hang up or accept what I say as pure speculation and off the record. Choose which way and please, please, don't tell me you have to bounce this up the line."

"Tough lady. I'll listen, but were you ever a Mother Superior?"

"No, not my fantasy, but I once wanted to be a bishop with the bully pulpit. Off the record! I need to hear you say it!"

"You really are a tough br…woman. All right, off the record."

There was another short pause while Noel gathered her thoughts and weighed how much she could say. Take a chance, she concluded.

"Fergus, what I am about to say is preliminary, based on two brief meetings with Mary, yesterday and again early this morning. We both know she is having considerable difficulty with childhood abuse that occurred before she was adopted. She has scars, both physical and emotional, that have not been healed. Agree so far?"

"Yes. Go on."

"Something is triggering flashbacks. I don't yet know what. It could be anything, but the vivid memories are making her at times angry, but increasingly withdrawn."

"And? Last night?"

"Two hypotheses. I repeat, speculative on my part."

"Finally! Which are?"

"The most benign theory is that her flight this morning had nothing to do with Franz's death, but is part of her accelerating breakdown."

"Or?"

"Or she was somehow involved in Franz's death or at least was a witness. If so, the accumulation of stress and flashbacks would overwhelm her ability to deal with these…ah... issues, and so she called me. Let me repeat, though: There is no clear evidence she was there or was involved."

"Rich here. But the timing suggests otherwise."

"Could be sheer coincidence, Detective."

"But she did say something, Noel, and the fact you are rushing her away tells me she could be involved."

"Rich, Fergus, it's my best professional judgement that she is so traumatized at the moment it is possible she no longer clearly knows what happened last night. All the legal warrants you could serve will not help me to distinguish between what, if anything, happened last night and what happened to her forty years ago as a child."

"Forty years?" interjected Sawicki. "You're really stretching this. Too far, even for—"

"Not too far. Ask your own medical advisors. In effect, Mary is caught in a terrifying nightmare and desperately needs time and help before she can help us, and more importantly, herself. That's all I can tell you."

"One more question, Noel. Okay?"

"If you must."

"You're giving me the clear impression that you know a heck of a lot more about Dr. Fraser's past than you're letting on."

"Of course, I did see her this morning."

"No more lectures on confidentiality. Did you know her before she came back to Manitoulin with the Germans?"

"This is too soon… All right, I may have known her as a reserve kid."

"'May have,' Doctor? Is this more than a professional case you're protecting?"

"What are you implying, Detective?"

"Implying? Nothing. Just a straight-up question. Yes or no, do you have a personal interest in Dr. Fraser that predates your claim to professional confidentiality?"

"Just this, then. Yes, I knew her as a reserve child whom I cared for as a nurse about forty years ago. That's all I am saying for now."

"That's all?"

"Trust me, Rich. I still can't tell you what really happened this morning."

Before Rich could break in again, Constable Kirkland waved him to the door.

"Sir, I just took a call in the car from the crime scene guys. They've found something you should look at. Very strange."

Fergus, all energy suddenly drained, slumped against the kitchen sink until Matt Peltier came over and started to pat his back, but then stopped short.

"Come on, guy," said Matt gently. "We'll need your statement. I'll drive you to the office myself."

Chapter 11

Later that morning

Fergus was driven home from the Little Current detachment just after nine o'clock, and had settled in for only a few minutes before the phone rang. Still, he let it ring three more times.

"Yes, who the hell else is this?" he answered.

"Is this Fergus Fitzgerald?"

"Who'd you expect?" Fergus demanded, as he began to recognize the raspy voice.

"Easy, buddy. Just doing my…you know. You've done this kind of call yourself. It's Isaiah Steen at the *Expositor*. Can you help me?"

"Help you? I can barely help myself. Look, can this wait? Oh, hell, let's get this over with. I know the drill. You call the cops first?"

"Not much there. Just who the dead guy is – a Franz Dietrich. Caretaker found him; crime scene closed; they're still investigating. So how soon can I talk to your Mary?"

Fergus paused. He didn't know Isaiah well, just from the usual shoptalk at the *Expositor* office in Little Current, but he was known as a straight shooter who could keep a confidence.

"Mary's...ah...Mary's…out of town on medical leave and…"

"Anything serious, Fergus? I mean will she be back soon?"

Fergus paused again, not wanting to sound evasive but not wanting to encourage any premature suspicions about Mary's sudden flight.

"Too soon to say. Just...ah...just woman problems that...ah...need attention. Talk to ya later."

Fergus stood in his kitchen, alone now save for the dog, Brendan. His statement at the OPP detachment, largely a repeat of what he had already told the police, had not taken long. Then Matt had driven him home, but without saying anything to him.

Fergus didn't even notice that the coffee in the chipped Wiarton Willie cup was cold. For a moment, he fondled the bottle of his favourite Cragganmore, took out the cork, breathed in its smooth scent, then sighed and put the cork back in – awkwardly, though, as his hands still trembled. But his mind was fighting back: Jesus bloody Christ, Peltier stiffs me, and now I'm screwing around with a reporter. Get a grip, man. You're no use to Mary, or even yourself.

The trouble was that he couldn't sort out whether he was talking to himself, which he often did, or hearing another voice. Stress did that to him, or just as likely, it was his sensitivity to loneliness and silence that let him hear strange things.

Deal with this, his inner voice whispered, an older voice that he sometimes heard, but from a face he never saw. Find some answers. Fergus felt as if he was in one of those "thin places," the mystical refuge of writers that lay between reality and possibility. Who in bloody hell will drive me? he muttered to himself. Ain't nobody else here. Mary always winced when he slipped "ain'ts" and the like into his speech.

At least take a shower. He had dressed hurriedly when the police came, and there had been no time since for his usual morning ablutions. While he didn't always take time to shave, he sometimes thought of a warm shower as a baptismal place: old skin and sweat replaced with a new life and the exuberance of new ideas that flowed – magically, he thought sometimes – from the relaxed and refreshed recesses of his mind.

Shower finished, he dressed quickly, same old jeans and sweater but fresh shorts and shirt, and marched quickstep to the computer in the great room, where he planned to make notes and break the big problem down into manageable bites. He booted up the computer, then shut it down just as promptly. Think this through, idiot. Think like a cop. If Mary is really in trouble, then the OPP will be back with search warrants, and will most likely seize the computer.

Damn her to hell, his mind raced. She brought the bloody carnage into our bedroom. Like we were on fire. Oh, Lord, forgive me, I enjoyed it, too.

He looked around the room, and focused on the whiteboard attached to the wall beside Mary's desk. She had kept track of the hotel's construction schedule and her own to-do list, preferring the easily erasable jottings to post-it notes that she found messy and too confining.

Where to start?

He began to write in his own shorthand style left over from his reporter days. *Get it down quickly,* he thought, *and then think about it.*

To Do:

Save Mary

1. Objective: Keep cops from tunnel vision and from going after Mary as only available suspect.

2. My role? No badge, no gun, no authority. So? Do what I do best. Ask questions. Keep prodding until the story makes sense. Work the phones.

3. Where's M? Who knows where she is? What Sudbury hospital? See and/or talk to her? Call the Callaghan psych. Where do docs fit into this? Why was Mary so spooked when they met at the cultural centre?

4. Where are bikers? Doubled back to MI? Easy boat ride from north shore of mainland to western island, Gore Bay, wherever. Check OPP/RCMP. Motivation. Yes, but why kill F. once they had left a trail from his home? Weird. Third party?

5. Whose blood on door? Not mine. Mary's? Relevant? Did she cut herself with shears? Any prints?

6. Where's coroner's report – time, cause of death, etc? Create timelines, etc.

7. What did she do at hotel site? Acct for time away. Ask M. who called her from site? Where's her cell phone?

8. Why was F there? Was Max?

9. Where's her Jeep? Ask OPP.

10. Worst case: Mary charged. Needs good lawyer. Off island or local? Don't rush this. Am I at risk?

11. Mitigating factors: good woman vs. sleaze. NB: Why was F. there?

Fergus stepped back, pondered his scribbling. He came to the conclusion that he'd rather take Brendan for a walk than start his calls and get told to butt out. Too soon for some of these questions anyway, he concluded, but he felt better for the mental exercise. Will I need Matt? No, call Sawicki. Pay the price.

"Out, I know. Just ask Rich to get back to me when he has a chance."

"Yeah, Fergus Fitzgerald. He's got my number. Thanks."

At the hotel site, the police were definitely pragmatic about the body in front of them. Sawicki, as the ranking crime specialist on Manitoulin, was anxious to come up with his own take before the OPP's case managers arrived from North Bay in about an hour. Waiting for him next to the tarp-covered body was a younger detective, Chris Marston, recently moved up from the OPP's highway patrol.

Marston pulled back the tarp.

"The German's dead, that's the easy part," he observed. "He's not going any place until the IDENT team gets here. But look at this. Weird!"

Sawicki rolled his eyes. "Not yet, Chris. Slow down. Coroner here yet?"

The younger officer's enthusiasm was less than infectious, as Rich struggled to override his worry that there could be other bodies here, a routine concern at crime sites. A meeting had already been called with the crown attorney from Gore Bay to determine how to gain access to Mary Fraser, and to decide whether her doctors were obstructing the investigation.

Marston tried once again to get Sawicki's attention. "This case could get messy."

"Constable, let's build some context. Where's the coroner? Dammit! Where is he?"

"Right behind you," explained Dr. Barb Charlebois, one of three island doctors rotating as coroner, as she emerged from the shadows. "I got the call."

"Sorry, I wasn't ignoring you. I was expecting George Gay."

"Yeah, I know, you fish with George sometimes. Guy stuff. Not this morning."

"Ooh, you Toronto types. Always in my face. So?"

"Touchy, aren't we, this bright morning? So I hear you've been to the Fraser place already – Mary Fraser's and that writer friend of hers."

"You heard WHAT?"

"Wow, you really are touchy today. Hmm. Let's just say I hear things. Social call for morning coffee, was it? So what'd she say?"

His anger rising, Sawicki felt like telling Charlebois to butt out. "She wasn't there."

"Okay, forget I said that," replied Charlebois, sensing she had gone too far. "Gone, eh? In the middle of a murder investigation. Curious, to say the least. You know where, or even why?"

"Doctor, we both have jobs to do, and yours doesn't involve Mary Fraser."

"Point taken. But really, Rich, we all know she had several run-ins with the vic."

"Okay, no leaks to the media then. Understood? She's had a mental breakdown of some sort, and has been taken to Sudbury for assessment. That's all I can say for now."

"How convenient."

"Oh yeah? There's nothing convenient about this. Look, let's get back to work before the guys from North Bay run over us. God knows, perhaps even the Mounties will want to take their own look at this. And the German police. Hold the judgments. There're layers and layers here."

As he and the coroner bent over the body, Sawicki wondered about Franz's all-black, stealth-like clothes. Stealth? What was the victim doing here in the first place?

"Man, you should try decaff," Charlebois joshed.

"Just look at the body. And yeah, I was expecting George. Sorry."

"No prob." Charlebois lifted up Franz's arm and looked at the head wound. "I can pronounce him and sign off on the paperwork, and then do the burial certificate when you're ready to bag him. Judging by the blood clotting and early rigor in the lower extremities, I'd say he died between midnight and two this morning."

Marston tried again to get Sawicki's attention, but was ignored as Sawicki bent over to make his own observation and take notes. Franz lay crumpled face down, legs twisted in a muddled heap. At first glance, most of the damage looked external, the skin lacerated at the back of his head with jagged edges along the split. Not much blood either.

"The victim was hit from behind. My preliminary assessment is that he died from a blow to the back of the skull," Charlebois said, looking up. Both the detectives and the doctor had seen violent trauma like this before. None of them had cared personally for Franz, with his nasty reputation. If there was any judgment, they probably would have concurred that the island was better off without him. Still, personal feelings aside, they had to deal with the few irregular blood splatters that held other meanings.

"Homicide? Accident?" Sawicki asked, bending down for a closer look at the young German.

"Once you guys are through with him," said Charlebois, writing on her clipboard, "you can ship him to Sudbury for the post. We'll know more then."

"But?"

"It's a crime scene, all right," she said, lifting and turning the victim's head. "Look inside the impact lacerations. More extensive bruising. Those pieces of skull bone are the impact point, I'm quite sure. The pearly-white part, Rich."

"And underneath?"

"Brain matter. He took a hard blow, hard enough to penetrate the grey matter from the cerebral cortex and then into the white axons."

"Hit from behind?"

"Or from the side as he was turning. Here, take a look yourself. His legs are twisted, and his body shows severe bruising on the upper chest and forearms. No other bones broken, and no damage to his face. Hardly an accident either. I suspect the post- mortem will show more."

"Defensive? A struggle of some sort then?"

"Yes, definitely so. Murder, manslaughter, whatever – that's your call. But he didn't do this to himself. Somebody worked him over, certainly, with a blunt instrument of some sort."

"Die fast, or what? We need to build some timelines."

"Depends on the force of the blow, Rich. Death in these cases is either sudden or occurs in about two hours from brain hemorrhaging. Given how we found him, face down, I would say death was sudden. Blow sheared some axons – the brain's wiring system, to you – and he probably lost consciousness instantly. No sign that he tried to crawl away. Or was armed. Merciful, in a brutal way. Lucky, too."

"Lucky? He gets his brains bashed in and you say he's lucky?"

"Could have been in a vegetative state for a long time if he had lived. I repeat: Somebody really wanted to kill him. Add up the physical evidence so far: small wound, deep penetration, which means he was hit from behind with a *lot* of force. Brain-dead almost instantly. That part's easy. The big questions are *who* and *why*?"

Sawicki straightened up and turned to Marston. "Any sign of a weapon or weapons yet, Chris?"

"Can't do much until we get more people here, sir."

"Good man. And now we just stand in the mud waiting for the nitpickers from North Bay. What about the warrants? Can you clear them with the JP at Gore Bay, Chris, or will we have to go to the faceless wonders in Newmarket?"

"Could be this afternoon, sir, if we get lucky. But first, you gotta take a look at this over here. Really weird, even for this place."

Sawicki responded, stepping over a pile of concrete-forming boards and rebars, and stooped down behind two trash barrels. Charlebois followed, being careful to step exactly where Sawicki did.

Marston pulled out what initially looked like an old blanket or coat and a pillow of some sort.

"Is that what I think it is?" asked Sawicki.

They all moved into the shadow, where even city-bred Charlebois recognized what Marston was holding, in spite of the bloodstains. "That's a bearskin," she exclaimed. "Big, black, claws and all. Pretty tattered. Somebody did... Where's the head?"

"Here," said Marston, pointing behind another pile of scaffolding. "It's been severed from the body, but somebody's beaten its snout and eyes as well. The hide is obviously not fresh, but the damage may be new."

At the farmhouse he was renting, Max wished the transatlantic call to his sister in Germany had not connected so fast that it seemed to be mocking distance.

"*Ja, ja* Christa. This is Max, *Ja*, calling from Canada. *Bitte*, let me get through this. It's awful. Are you alone? Werner is there? *Gut.* Yes, it's about Franz. Trouble with the police again? No, *es tut mir leid*, your son, he's dead… I'm coming home as soon as I can."

Finally, in Sudbury

"Where am I? Who are you? I'm so dry. Can I have something? Oh, where..." Mary Fraser struggled to reach beyond the fog in her head, but the last thing she remembered, and only vaguely at that, was Noel putting her in the rear seat of the Callaghans' forest-green Subaru wagon. She had no recollection at all about leaving Manitoulin, winding past the string of Espanola's mill-town shops and then east along Highway 17 to Sudbury. Consciousness did return, fleetingly, when the wagon exited through a grey rock cut into the city, finally stopping at the Northeast Mental Health Centre. It was an old, red-brick, rectangular building, tucked away in a side street behind the newer, modern buildings of Laurentian University.

"Drink all you want," said Don Callaghan, passing a plastic bottle of water behind him. "Let me find the right door, and we're there."

Mary jerked up, eyes wide with terror, and threw the bottle back at him. Don managed to keep the car in the right lane. Noel had warned him that Mary might become confused and abusive if the trip took too long and the sedative wore off.

Mary was hunched over now, head almost touching her knees, hands pulling frantically at the collar of her yellow turtleneck sweater. "THERE? DON'T WANT TO GO THERE!" she screamed so loudly that Don's ears hurt. "No, no, no, it was all dark, wasn't it? Just one light and too… Please, please. Can't see me. Yes, yes. That's what I want. Must clean the mud off. Dirty, dirty. Oh yes. Must get clean… Who are you?"

"You won't remember much for a while," said Don. "Memories will come in and out. You've been through a lot, so I gave you a shot of Ativan to let you…relax a little."

Mary shrank into a corner of the back seat as a sliver of reality sneaked back. "Who are… You're a doctor?"

"Yes, I'm your friend. Noel Callaghan's husband. We've met before, back on the island. Yes, I'm a GP, and I've arranged for you to come here."

Looking out the car window, Mary saw a woman in a blue smock with one shoulder bare, crying with a hand over her mouth, staring at the car as it neared the institution's front door. Then she noticed a youngish male, slouching, head down, tagging along beside an older, humpbacked woman. Back against one wall stood a security guard.

Memories flashed: running down a hill, screaming, trying to wipe blood from her hands. Then leaving, boots caught in the tall grass. Fergus? Another woman? Driving down a dark road, almost out of control.

"Why is that man staring at me? Does he have a gun?"

Don Callaghan felt his seventy plus years for a moment as his knees creaked and his bladder needed relief.

He opened Mary's door, unfastened her seat belt, and gently took her hand.

"Easy, Mary, easy. There are no police here. That man over there in the uniform, he's here to protect people. There're good people here, and I've made arrangements for you with the director, an old friend. You are important, though, my dear, and we have a private room with a view waiting for you on the fifth floor."

He did not mention the OPP cruiser that had silently caught up with them about a half-hour west of Sudbury, and had tailed them onto the hospital grounds.

Mary followed him inside to the reception area and the elevators. She saw another patient in a pyjama top and jeans who looked up for a moment, and nodded at her with a weak smile.

Don searched for a nurse. "Noel will be here as soon as she clears up some things in Little Current. Do you understand that?"

"Yes, I think so. Will I be here long? I have work to... Where's my laptop?"

"Not to worry, Mary. My understanding is that you'll be here only a couple of weeks."

Increasingly awake and alert now, Mary stiffened. "Something happened last night, didn't it? I can't see it all, just colors and noise, but that's why I'm here, isn't it?" She remembered his name. "Don, yes, that's who you are. Yes, Don, Noel's husband, the older man. Tell me what happened. Tell me, dammit."

"I don't know. None of us do."

"Does Fergus know where I am?"

"Yes, Noel told him."

"So you're leaving me here, with these people, whoever they are. And then what?"

He squeezed her hand as a reception nurse approached. "Time will take care of that, Mary. Now indulge an old man who must find a bathroom."

Chapter 12

Still at the crime site an hour later, Rich Sawicki was in no mood to indulge Fergus, let alone return his phone call. Though he wouldn't say so out loud, he wondered why Fergus didn't run back to Boston or wherever he came from. He would never understand the sensitive balance between the native and white communities.

There were times, particularly this morning, when Sawicki wished he had been born native and not white. He knew, for instance, that when he looked at clouds, he saw just clouds, the usual meteorological range from low-level cumulus gatherings of popcorn puffs to the high-flying strands of wispy cirrus. Native officers, by contrast, didn't just see the superficial. "It's Manitou's voice rising on the winds," Peltier, part-native himself, had often told him. "*Animikeek*, the warning of an approaching storm, isn't just a weather advisory; it's a metaphor that's deeper and foreboding in its meaning."

All Sawicki knew this morning was that he felt unsettled, because he now had three potential suspects – Mary and the two bikers – who might or might not be related. And, within the hour, he had to report to the OPP's case managers when they arrived from North Bay to monitor and direct the investigation. Definitely not something he was looking forward to because, like most folk here, he equated Manitoulin's isolation with the freedom to live his own life with only limited intrusions.

His immediate needs, though, were more basic.

"Too much coffee," he barked at no one and every one. "Anybody arrange for food? We could be here all day with the usual flurry fuck of looking busy."

A young constable approached. "For you, sir."

"North Bay already?"

"No, the duty guy in Little Current."

"Can it wait? Just tell them to handle that B and E themselves. They can—"

"You better take it, sir. They sounded pretty excited."

"Sawicki here. So, what's happening?"

"Just doing our job, Detective, just driving around town."

"Constable, so you've found an illegally parked car. Give the nitwit a ticket and move on."

"Yeah, it's illegally parked in a handicap space. Badly parked, too. Front wheel up on the curb. Skid marks. Must have been going fast."

"So write the silly bastard up. You can write, can't you?"

"We ran the tags and—"

"Who, for God's sake? We're into—"

"It's Dr. Fraser's Jeep, and it's parked outside the Callaghan clinic."

"That's solid?"

"Solid, sir. Double-checked before I called you."

"Holy shit. Well, Constable, well done! One for the patrol grunts."

"Thought you'd like to know. There's more."

"More?"

"Well, it looks like blood on the door handle. Not much, but it's visible."

"Well, well, well. Which side? Driver's?"

"Yep. Not sure about the back seats. Too dark there. So, do we take swabs and start dusting for prints?"

"Hold it, don't do anything yet. Just tape it off and stay with it until you can get it towed into the compound. I'll tell Marston to get the warrants and whatever."

"Been a lot of media calls to the office. Can we mention the Jeep and the Fraser woman?"

"Slow down, cowboy. This your first murder investigation?"

'Oh, yeah, sir. This is the big one."

"Just tell the reporters we're making progress and will make a formal report later today."

"That's all?"

"Just keep it tight, Constable. For starters, we're not close to making an arrest. The Fraser woman is only a possible suspect, a person of interest, at this point. She's had altercations with the victim before, and she's taken flight. We don't even have her fingerprints in the system."

"But—"

"No buts. Just slow down. Okay, take a bow for good work, Constable. Ya done good. We've got her car and someone's blood. That will tell us something. So go by the book. Don't screw around with potential evidence or the Crowns will chew our asses, and not just mine. Just do your job, guy. Gotta go."

Rich walked away from his team, pushing his hat back, rubbing one eye and wondering where Mary Fraser was taking them. First the bikers disappear, and now her. This is fucking stupid, he told himself. And what a shitty waste of a good person. Fraser, not the German. No, no maybes or grey feelings. Ultimately it comes to a black or white world, guilty or innocent. Nothing more. Either I do my job, or I turn it over.

Meanwhile, the dead dog story was going nowhere. At least Sawicki's end of it. The actual dog charge, cruelty, was relatively minor, but the possibility of intimidation and obstruction charges in Germany were more important, and thus all-out Canadian co-operation was imperative. The security cameras on the Chi-Cheemaun's car deck showed the two bikers as they tied down their machines in front of the stern ramp. Licence plate images were fuzzy, but cameras in the stairwells leading up to the cafeteria produced a clear look at the bikers' faces. Ferry security made the images available to all involved police investigators in Canada and Germany. The Hamilton cops thought the swarthier biker might be a local with a long sheet of assaults and related drug convictions.

The motel was checked. Mug shots were shown to the young girl at the front desk. She thought, but was not positive, that one biker really was from Stoney Creek, a Hamilton suburb. None of his family or bike club members knew where he was at the moment, and without fingerprints, there was no conclusive evidence linking him to the dog killing. The German CID and Interpol were checking out the second biker, who had been active in Germany after emigrating from Bosnia, where he had taken part in the ethnic cleansing. The room had not been used since the bikers left. Sawicki's investigators suspected the pair was professional, probably hit men for hire who swabbed down the room before they left.

As expected, the police found nothing at the restaurant, which had a high traffic turnover. Moreover, the waitress who might have served the bikers had left the island and returned to Alberta without leaving a forwarding address. There was no evidence the bikers had tried to cross into the United States at either Sault Ste. Marie or Thunder Bay. Routine highway patrol checks from Thesalon on Highway 17 north to Chapleau and Timmins produced nothing. Sawicki believed the bikers' best bet would be to hide out at a pre-arranged hunting camp where they could switch their bikes for a pickup with building materials. From there, they could head northeast to Timmins and then into the Rouyn-Noranda region in

Quebec. The Quebec Surêté, the provincial police force, had been alerted. But Sawiciki was still faced with a bigger, thornier question: Why would the bikers first want to intimidate Franz, and then return to kill him?

True, Franz's death did send a lethal warning back to any other potential witnesses in Germany. With Franz dead, the murder trial in Germany would be delayed, but officials there were still interested in who set up the dog killing, and in possibly laying obstruction and intimidation charges.

Sawicki looked at his watch. Within a few minutes, the OPP case managers would arrive from North Bay, and want a verbal report on the usual checklist: crime scene security, time lines, coroner's initial determination, physical evidence, warrant status, witnesses, preliminary list of relevant contacts, possible suspects. Damn, he didn't have the warrants yet..

"Marston, we gotta talk," he shouted. Marston hurtled over a pile of concrete-forming boards to reach him. "Rich …ya…gotta come over here!"

"No, Constable, you come here. I call, you come. Your priority now is warrants. Get on to it."

Marston kept pushing "Trust me, Rich. You gotta see this, now!"

Sawicki stood firm.. "Oh yeah? The warrants, Chris. Push the JP."

"Done. I'm waiting for a callback from the justice of the peace at Gore Bay. If he's available, I'll get the warrants to him by noon. But really, ya gotta see this quickly before—"

"Make it quick then. Company's coming, and soon."

"Just follow my footsteps."

"What did you think I'd do? It's not my first—"

"Whatever…"

The two officers followed a narrow path, just a line of grass and weeds that had been stamped down, for about twenty meters, then stopped. Ahead of them, a piece of scaffolding lay in plain view: grey cold metal, indistinguishable from materials found at thousands of other work sites, nothing sinister about it except for a big blob of blood and glutinous matter at one end and what appeared to be a bloody smudge at the other. Red splotches were spattered on the immediately surrounding grass.

Both officers bent down to examine the piece of metal.

"Good call, Chris," said Sawicki, pushing aside some graceful stems of St. Anne's Lace. "You find this?"

"Nah, Kirkland did. He saw the reflection off the metal near the path."

"Good eyes, that guy. Notices stuff."

Marston took the hint. "Could be, eh?"

"Could be what?"

"Our blunt instrument, Rich, the weapon."

"By the book. Why?"

"Post-mortem lividity sets in within a couple of hours."

"Which means, Chris?"

"This is where the victim died. He wasn't dumped here."

"Good. The coroner agrees with you. Sum it up, Chris!"

"Can do! What we have so far is a homicide victim, identified as one Franz Dietrich from the Dresden area in Germany. Coroner suggests he died early this morning of massive head wounds inflicted by a blunt instrument. Won't know for certain, though, until the IDENT guys finish their photo work here, and until the post-mortem in Sudbury. Also, we have a piece of scaffolding with possible prints in what appears to be blood. Possibly the murder weapon, but we won't know until the forensic guys in the Sault do preliminary blood work. DNA, of course, will take much longer, but they should be able to compare blood types from the corpse and scaffolding quickly."

"You know about the Jeep?"

"Yeah. I got the patrol report, too. So how's this add up? Colleague of the victim takes flight sometime after the homicide. She's a university prof doing consulting work for the vic's uncle, also German, who is building a hotel here. Fraser's companion, the Fitzgerald guy, at first didn't know where she went, but her vehicle was located in Little Current outside the office of a psychologist, Dr. Noel Callaghan, who in turn shipped her off to a mental care unit in Sudbury. Could be a coincidence, but what appears to be blood was also found on the door handle of Fraser's Jeep. It was parked illegally and is being towed to our compound for preliminary inspection. Fraser is at least a person of interest, as the late Mr. Dietrich made a complaint last month that she had threatened him. She was warned, but not charged. The customs guys at Pearson Airport in Toronto reported a similar confrontation between them."

"Good so far, Chris. Just so we're on the same page, what's your take on the biker involvement? Separate incident, or related?"

"Can't say at the moment, until the two heavies are tracked down. I assume North Bay knows as much as our detachment does at the moment. Obviously, at least to me, they've gone to ground in northern Ontario, which has a lot of ground to get lost in. They'll surface, but when or where?"

"Okay, Chris, good summary. Weird though. Like that old beat-up bearskin we found near the Dietrich body.

So what's really going down here? A cult killing or just a couple of drunks or hopheads wailing at the moon?"

Sawicki backed up a couple of steps and hunkered down on a pile of loose lumber, suddenly tired from lack of sleep and the complexity of a case he couldn't sort out in his own mind, especially with the bearskin adding a mythic layer he couldn't comprehend.

"The bearskin…yeah, unusual," replied Marston. "Sure as hell, somebody was trying to scare somebody. May be impossible to get prints, though."

"Yeah, definitely intriguing. That's it, Chris?"

"For now, anyway. Oh, just one more thing. Sorry, I almost forgot."

"Forgot what?" asked Sawicki, slowly pushing himself up.

"The Crown called and wants a briefing. He sounded pretty on edge to me. The drug unit in Sudbury, it wants in, and so do the feds. Lots of folk covering their butts on this one, eh?"

"Crown calling back, Chris?"

"Not this guy. He wants you to call him. Want me to look after it for you, drive over to Gore Bay?"

"No, you stay, Chris. You brief Robitaille."

"You're leaving? I'm missing something? Just because you know Fitzgerald."

"So? Personal relationships can't be helped on a small island. Just do your job, or move on. The case team is coming up the hill."

The two officers waited silently until the case managers from North Bay joined them.

Sawicki stepped forward. "Inspector Robitaille, good to see you. You know Detective Chris Marston? Good. You can reach me back at Little Current. More paper to move."

With the morning's paperwork finally out of the way, Sawicki decided he could no longer avoid returning the call from Fergus Fitzgerald. The more he thought about what had happened to Mary, the angrier he got. Fergus could have prevented this; Mary was too good a person to be caught up in this murder.

He slammed down a phone book on his desk. "Too many losers who can't handle life," he snarled.

"Who? Me?" asked a startled clerk.

"God, no, not you. Just a guy I'm dealing with. Another righteous son-of-a-bitch American who comes up here, buys a dream-catcher, takes in a powwow, gets mushy about native rights, and moves on."

Three minutes later.

"You called me," said Sawicki.

Fergus paused before answering. "We should talk."

"Talk? You're good at that, Fitzgerald."

"Words, yeah, Rich. That's all I am. Bloody words."

"So some say. I got work to do."

"Your guys tapping this call? I thought I heard something."

"No, Fitzgerald, storm coming. So, you want to come in?"

"Little Current, your office? Tempting. Let everyone see us."

"But?"

"Not yet, Sawicki. I'm not ready. We do this alone. Face-to-face, whatever."

"What is this? High Noon in Little Current?"

"I thought you guys didn't have a sense of humour."

"What guys? Cops? Natives? Anybody who isn't Irish?"

"Delete that. Stupid words. Okay?"

"You want me to forgive and forget? You could've stopped all this at the Toronto airport. I read the intelligence reports. Oh, no, not you, Fitzgerald. So now you want help. That's rich."

"We've got one thing in common. Right?"

"That's why I called you back. So who's on first?"

"Mary Fraser."

"So, we gotta get her home."

Sawicki paused as he looked out his office window at the bending treetops. The once-distant thunder seemed closer.

"It doesn't look good, Fergus," he said slowly, almost inaudibly. "I have to be honest with you."

"Beyond a reasonable doubt?"

"Not yet. Forensics will take time, and we both know that Dietrich had other enemies. But so far it all points to her."

"She could be charged. Really?"

"Yes, really, Fergus. Look, man, you're pushing me… Hell, I shouldn't even be talking to you. But…but, yeah, we could be wrong, but worst case, yes. Strong motive, opportunity, and a potentially incriminating blood trail."

"No witnesses, though."

"Not yet, anyway."

"What do you mean, Rich? Not yet? That sounds ominous."

"Hell, Fergus, we can't even assume there's only one body on that hill, let alone no witnesses. More cops on the scene. We're bringing in a plane for an overview. DNR's coming with tracker dogs. This will take a few days."

"DNR?"

"Department of Natural Resources. Usually their dogs are used to find lost hunters or old folks who wander off."

"Bloody hell. Alzheimer's and guns."

"It's a bloody world, Fergus. Can you get to your point? Why did you call me?"

"I need help big time, and I don't know where to start. Got time for coffee?"

"You want my help?"

"Yes. No. Not like that. Reload. Mary needs your help. Can you handle that?"

"Just between us then?"

"Of course. You've got a job to do."

"I can live with that. Down by the west harbour. You know where. Half an hour."

"Okay, but no guns."

"You bring the coffee, then. Double double."

"Fattening."

"So? I'll bring the Criminal Code, Fergus. There's a section you should know about."

Chapter 13

Later that evening

For about thirty seconds, Fergus felt like a New Age warrior out to save his woman: a glass of scotch in one hand, the Criminal Code in the other, and the comforting satisfaction that he was about to check off three priorities from his whiteboard. Find Mary – check. Find the Callaghans – check. Find a lawyer – check.

The trouble with drinking good scotch like his beloved fifteen-year-old Cragganmore was that the second glass seemed more beneficent than the first, so smooth that it had almost no bite – austere even – and magnificently long when taken in slow sips. Deceptively so, however. Fergus was apt to become a morose drinker when left alone with his fey instincts that the world would always break his heart.

First off, he knew if her 'Dr. Mary Fraser' persona were still intact, Mary would bristle at being called "his woman," or anybody's woman, for that matter. Hug me, love me, just don't own me, she'd say. Second, he confessed to himself that he was a reluctant white knight, and still battling the urge to withdraw from the battle and settle into his own guilt.

There had been a time when he'd been content with the life of a recluse, back in Wiarton, where he had sanctuary and no sudden intrusions. Not here now. Gone. The growing gloom felt more like a shroud. He spent a few minutes looking at the Criminal Code, but soon gave up trying to concentrate on the small print, with its sections and sub-sections and sub-sub-sections – way too complicated for a man who liked his scotch neat.

He reluctantly roused himself. He knew their small garden needed a fall cleanup, but what the hell, he thought, let the flowers flop where they are. Mary's job anyway. Not mine. Ain't that a hoot? Just walk away. Mums and marigolds are pretty hardy. Let them die where they are. Nature's way. She'll never know, so why bother. Shh! Or what the Ojibwa believe: Somebody always knows when I've been naughty and not nice. *He'll* know. Manitou, too. Jesus Murphy, *I'll* even know. So fucking what? Too much fucking scotch. Get a grip, man. Try again. No more, no more scotch. For now, anyway.

Two hours later, sort of

Click

From: **Fergus Fitzgerald <Brendan@bmts.com**
To: **Conall Fitzgerald <Famtrack@corknet.ie**
Subject: **self-exorcism**

Relax! It's only a metaphor. Self-exorcism, that is. No flagellation or renouncing Satan and all that. Weird, I know, so humor me. Obviously, there is part of my subconscious talking to me, stirring feelings that still well up. There are moments here when I suspect that life on Manitoulin is more subconscious than conscious, isolated from the mainstream with a spirit world that lies just under the surface of everything.

But Mary's at risk now, and the Criminal Code is bloody poor comfort in a quiet, lonely house. At least it will frame my thinking when I meet with the lawyer tomorrow. It's becoming clear now that Mary could be charged and probably remanded for more psychiatric examinations.

Still, I will get to visit with her first, before she's formally charged and taken to court.

There is some good news. According to Dr. Callaghan, the psychologist and ex-nun who knows much more about Mary's early life than I do, the treatments at the Sudbury clinic are beginning to help. Not a cure, she stressed, but Mary is responding to the medications. If so, then can she recall what happened to Franz, or whether she was alone or why she went there at all? And if she did go there, when did she arrive? The gist of Mary's situation, according to Dr. C., is that trauma has been piled upon trauma, much too much to deal with. Repression takes over and shuts down Mary's conscious memory, too. I've barely eaten or rested since the police first came.

'Nuff whining, bloody hell. I've had too much of that. Whatever. At least I can get back to the Criminal Code and the sections about assessment orders. If I understand this correctly (the type is awfully small), she can be held involuntarily for only 72 hours in the Sudbury hospital where she now is. If she's charged, she could be transferred to a forensic detention centre in North Bay for the Crown to do its own assessment as to whether she's fit to stand trial, and whether she is criminally responsible. This could take up to 30 days. At that point, she goes back before the judge in Sudbury with the assessment report. What then? It gets complex, but these are all the variables I can handle at the moment.

Question: If I accept all this, then why I am still so pissed off? And I am; I confess that I'm mad as hell. The Germans have a word that seems appropriate here – *gotterdammerung*, very Wagnerian, self-destructive, twilight of the gods, that sort of thing. Mary, Max, and Franz all made choices that blew up in their faces. So what's left for me? Bless me, Father, they screwed up and I do the penance. In a pig's eye.

The reality here is that she is going to be charged, probably with murder or manslaughter, and the prospect of losing her tears at my soul. It's out of Sawicki's hands, now that his superiors have taken charge. He didn't say much when we had coffee. Just gave me the Criminal Code, pointed me to a couple of sections, particularly 672, about mental disorders and non-criminal responsibility. I think the citations are right. Then he went back to work in Little Current. A peace offering, I guess.

Be well, friend. Must pick some flowers for Mary before they die. And a bunch for my own table. Brighten up the place.

F.

Chapter 14

The next afternoon

"Rich, do we have a case yet?" asked Matt. He and Sawicki were in Matt's office in the OPP detachment in Little Current, and both knew where the evidence was heading, or at least where they believed it was heading. Rich picked up the stress behind the question, but ignored it, remembering Peltier's sensitivity about Mary Fraser.

"Up to you," responded Rich, wondering how much he should share with Matt. Keep it vague, he decided. "We hope to get the first fingerprints in a few hours or so, but the DNA blood work will take a week. The warrants are coming through, though, and we'll be hitting the Fraser home…well, soon."

"Any problems?"

"Shouldn't be, Matt. Her sudden flight gives us cause to go in."

"Anything else? Any witnesses?"

"Haven't talked to anyone yet who saw what happened. Lots of questions from the victim's uncle. Know much about him?"

Matt, frustration beginning to show, jumped on the question. "Oh Christ, can't forget Max, eh? If you insist then. Adler, yeah, Max Adler. Elegant type. Met him once. Talked about security issues and native stuff. Interesting old guy; says the Allies killed his parents, bombing raid someplace. Dresden rings a bell."

"That's him. Well, anyway, Adler is convinced she did it. Feels pretty guilty himself. Give me a sec to check my notes... Yeah, here it is: 'I terribly, terribly regret that I assigned Franz to work with that witch. It is uncommonly rude of me to say so, but she has been trouble from the start.' Adler leaves for Germany today and told me he's not sure he wants to come back."

"Oh yeah," said Matt. "No more euros. Anything on Dietrich?"

"Officially, he is, or was, clean. No outstanding warrants here or in Germany. But the German police and Interpol want to be kept informed."

"You still think bikers could be involved in the hit?"

"Tempting. Big international conspiracy. But get real. Let's stick with the facts we know."

"What about the facts we don't know?" replied Matt skeptically as he leaned back in his chair. "So what if it looks like a coincidence? We've asked the Quebec police to run checks and talk to their snitches. The trail, it's cold, and so far there are no forensic clues: no blood, no prints, nothing that says they were there."

"Point taken. Accessories then? Hired or used the Fraser woman?"

A constable knocked, then opened the door to the office. "Call for Rich from the IDENT guys in the Sault. Want to take it in here, or outside?"

"Take it here, Rich," Matt offered.

Both officers knew the call was crucial, given that Manitoulin, as a rural detachment, did not have the resources for a detailed forensic workup. The IDENT squad from the Sault had already taken away the bloody piece of scaffolding, the fingerprints lifted from the crime scene, and the impounded Jeep.

Unfortunately, results here usually took days and weeks instead of minutes. Still, the team was tapped into ViCLAS, Canada's Violent Crime Linkage Analysis System that examines comparative data on all major crimes. Neither Mary nor Franz showed up in the ViCLAS database, but the intelligence guys from the OPP's Resource Management System had picked up the occurrences and strip searches at Pearson, and later in Little Current. Patterns were beginning to form.

Sawicki finished the call, checked his notes, and went looking for Peltier.

"Nothing conclusive, Matt, but we're looking in the right direction."

"Just tell me."

"The Fraser woman. Sorry."

"Yeah. Rich, I know it's your call, but dammit, I need to be kept in the loop. So?"

Sawicki threw Matt a cocky grin, and flipped open his notebook with one finger that, almost, remained pointed at the ceiling.

"One of these days, Rich," said Peltier, "I'm not going to laugh at that."

"Okay then. The visuals show us lots of reasons to hurry."

"Oh?"

"Two items of interest. First off, the prints in the blood on the piece of scaffolding and the Jeep came up clear. Relatively easy reads, but the lab boys backed them up with the lasers. They had to use the fuming chamber on one, with cyanoa…never get this right the first time..."

"You're some scientist for a crime scene dick, Sawicki. It's cyanoacrylate, crazy glue to you. The fumes raise prints on non-porous surfaces, like metal. So?"

"One print each on the scaffolding and the Jeep door come from the same finger. But—"

"But we don't know whose finger yet, right?"

"I said there were two items of interest. No, we don't know and won't know for a few days whose body was waving those fingers. But Fraser's prints are in the system, and photos are being couriered to us as we speak. Wish faxes weren't so grainy. Probably here tomorrow."

"She's done time?"

"Yes and no, Matt."

"Gimme the 'yes' part, Rich."

"Not a major crime, but appears she got caught up in a tree-hugging protest in the eighties when she was living with a Haida artist in the Queen Charlottes. Married to him, but lucky for us, kept her own name for professional reasons. The RCMP did her prints and mug shots, then kept her in a cell overnight with a dozen other natives and Greenpeace types. She was released the next morning when the logging company involved worked out a compromise with the local chiefs. No convictions registered."

"Perhaps. You're jumping fast, Rich. I know it's not my case, but, man, it's gotta be airtight. Anything else?"

"Couple of things, but nothing substantive so far. One other print on the scaffolding. Unidentified as yet, probably from one of the construction workers. Or a biker for that matter. Could take time to check everyone out. And a lot of traffic went through there from the village."

"So we may have a witness, an accessory, or, and I hope not, another body someplace. Basic one-plus-one. Never assume there's only one body. Kill once, and the second is easy. The hard fact, though, is that we still have only one possible suspect."

"Yes, it's Fraser."

"No one else fits, Rich. Who would have thought this could happen when she came here? Before I call the Crown, do you need anything?"

Rich paused. "Just some time to sort out the weird stuff."

"The bearskin? What do you think? Strange games?"

"Or kinky Germans, Matt. And all we have is some blood, which we've sent for DNA analysis. No prints."

"Media will love this zoo. Oh yeah. Big bad bear scares—"

"Not going to feed them that. We got a nice little murder here, probably drug-related as you say, so let's not drag out all the weird stuff. Hold it back and see what pops. Okay with you?"

Matt nodded.

Later that afternoon

Finally, the police talked to the media at the OPP offices, and immediately wished they hadn't.

"Is this a racial killing?"

The first probe came from *Sudbury Star* reporter Louisa Ledingham, whose Haweater parents still lived in Manitouwaning, a Manitoulin village. "Many First Nations people are not thrilled by the prospect of a powwow hotel, particularly since it's being built near old burial grounds. Is racial intimidation one of the leads you're following?"

The MTV camera team put on its lights.

"Louisa, you're on dangerous ground even asking that question at this point," Rich answered quickly. "And I would be an even bigger fool if I tried to speculate. At this time, we have not talked to anyone who witnessed the attack on the victim. Our forensic people have taken away considerable material for analysis."

"So you have leads, eh?"

"First impressions."

"Fingerprints then. Whose?"

"I will not comment upon specific pieces of evidence at this time. We don't even know whether there was only one or several people on that hill when Mr. Dietrich died."

"Possibly several people are involved? The bikers perhaps? Any word on them?"

"We are doing all the routine checks. A number of police agencies are involved, but nothing conclusive yet."

"Are you checking out Dr. Mary Fraser, a colleague of the victim?"

Rich struggled to keep a stony face. "We are talking to everyone who worked with Mr. Dietrich, plus we're consulting with German officials."

The reporter from the *Manitoulin Expositor* jumped in.

"It's not that I don't appreciate the good work you're doing, Rich," said Isaiah Steen, brushing aside his thick hair, "especially with the people around here pushing one way or another, but one question. Okay?"

"Sure, fire away."

"Well, just this. Let's tighten the focus, so we don't get this wrong. Have you identified a person or persons of interest so far?"

Sawicki looked quickly at Peltier, who arched an eyebrow. Both knew that a person of interest was often only a hair away from being identified as a suspect and likely to be charged. Mary Fraser could fall into that category, but Rich first wanted the fingerprint match in his hands. He also did not want to lie.

"We have not spoken to anyone at this time."

"Not spoken to anyone?" countered Isaiah, measuring the words slowly. "Still looking for someone specific, then?"

"Like I said, we're talking to a lot of people. Routine investigation."

The reporters didn't quite buy the brush-off, and leaned forward. The TV lights remained on. Louisa decided to up the ante. "Sounds like something is about to break, eh?"

Rich bristled. "That's your speculation, Louisa."

His evasion didn't work, and a radio reporter picked up the scent. "I tried to interview Dr. Fraser myself today, but she's not available. Haven't been able to reach her companion, the Fitzgerald man, either. Do you know where they are?"

"They're both busy people who travel a lot."

As Rich anticipated, the radio reporter jumped back in. "Was this some kind of hit?"

Rich knew he had to wrap this up.

"If this was beer night at the Anchor, we could sit around and dream up all kinds of theories. That's not what I do, and I encourage you to be patient. When we make an arrest, you'll be the first to know. Now, no more questions."

Chapter 15

The next day, just before noon

At first, Fergus was not impressed with Michael Balfour, whom he thought looked like a small-town fuddy-duddy, better suited for wills and real estate deals than hard-nosed criminal law, and certainly not the lawyer to keep Mary and himself out of jail.

Their handshakes were perfunctory and decidedly weak, more out of courtesy to their hostess than to each other. Noel Callaghan was introducing Fergus to the Callaghans' personal lawyer. Fergus instinctively trusted the Callaghans as a support team without really knowing why. He simply accepted them as serendipitous angels, as his mother might have said. Not that either looked particularly angelic to him, Noel being far too brusque and direct for that, although her husband could be as affable as required. They were meeting in the Callaghan home in Little Current for drinks and lunch, both of which were generous and comforting.

Michael Balfour, or Mike, as he was known informally in spite of the three-piece suits he preferred, understood his role. When asked about a client who had particularly sensitive issues, he generally pursed his lips, stroked his pencil-thin moustache and bushy eyebrows, straightened his regimental tie, and grinned. He had had no experience with murder cases, but he did appreciate that his presence provided privilege if the OPP wanted to question Fergus and the Callaghans as to who knew what and when. When he accepted the luncheon invitation, he reminded

Noel that all client/solicitor discussion would be deemed confidential, including information gathered in anticipation that Mary could be charged and eventually tried.

The Callaghans' news was not encouraging.

"I saw Mary briefly in Sudbury this morning, Fergus. She's still in locked-door isolation."

"What's happening there? Is she in danger?"

"No, not at the moment, Ferg. A couple of days in isolation are pretty routine in these cases. Preliminary assessments, suicide watch, adjusting her meds – that sort of thing."

Fergus looked down at the basil-tomato soup Don Callaghan had placed in front of him. He swirled his spoon around the earthenware bowl, but did not eat. His glass of white wine stood untouched.

"Suicide?" he finally blurted out, his questioning voice rising sharply. "Has she said anything about what happened, about me, about—?"

"Easy, Ferg, easy," responded Noel hurriedly, as she reached across the table and lightly touched his hand. "All she has told me so far... Mike, this is privileged. I'm protected, right?"

Balfour wiped a thin line of soup from his lips.

"Noel, we've done this before. No change in the law."

"Fergus hasn't, Mike."

"Understood," confirmed the lawyer. "Everything you hear here today, Fergus, is confidential. The police may press you, perhaps even threaten you with obstruction, but you have a right to discuss Mary's situation with counsel, whom you have retained on her behalf. Big decisions ahead."

"I agree, Mike, but please, one step at a time," interjected Noel quickly. "Let's not get too far ahead of ourselves. As I started to say, everything Mary told me this morning unfortunately suggested that she was there when the German was killed."

"You think she did this? Smashed in Franz's skull?"

"I'm not the police, Fergus, not even a reporter. Psychologists don't interrogate."

"But she spoke to you?"

"Briefly, random phrases, unconnected. She's been medicated to counter the anxiety and depression, and to help her sleep. It is possible she still can't recall what happened yesterday morning because her mind is still fighting to repress whatever she saw or did."

"Did?"

"I can't explain that, Fergus, not yet. My notes are sketchy, but it's apparent that she was involved or thought she was involved."

"Just tell me, Noel."

"Okay. Mary repeated several times phrases like 'I tried to, I tried' and 'she wanted.' Finally, there was one phrase she kept repeating: 'I didn't know, I didn't know.'"

"Who's 'she'?"

"She didn't say, and I didn't press."

"Bloody hell! There may be a witness, and you let it drift away, just a little chat between the girls and—"

"FERGUS! Oh Lord, now I'm shouting, too. You're hurting, you're in obvious pain, perhaps shock, but I won't—"

"Don't play Mother Superior with me, Noel. I could damn well lose Mary, and if that doesn't scare you, then why are we here?"

Don Callaghan and Mike Balfour stopped eating, trying to absorb the emotional confrontation. The only sound came from the living room where a CD was playing Gershwin's "They Can't Take That Away from Me."

"There are things you need to know about Mary and me," Noel said to Fergus, her shoulders rising as she breathed deeply to calm herself, "that may have legal complications for all of us."

"Oh? She told me she knew you when you were a nun, Noel, not much else."

"That's it? Nothing else?"

"An old Toronto friend, now working at the *Sudbury Star,* said you left religious orders after you went to the States for post-grad work. Then later, I forget when, you came back to start a psych practice. That's when you met Don. That's all. So?"

"You need to know more, Fergus."

"Can't Mary tell me herself?"

"In time, I hope she can. But for the moment, we need to protect you."

Fergus rose from the table, leaving his soup untouched. He did take his wine with him, and crossed to the bay window overlooking the trim back lawn. He didn't think he was being rude; he was restless and had always liked to walk around when his mind was racing. Part of him felt as if it were moving in harmony with the Callaghans' two hound dogs frolicking on the back lawn, endlessly circling a large maple whose leaves were already beginning to fall.

Returning to the table, Fergus sharpened his focus. "So, why do you need to protect me, Noel? Lord, don't we have enough victims already?"

It was the lawyer's turn to intervene.

"The point we're all dancing around, Fergus," said Mike deliberately, "is why Noel sent Mary to the Sudbury hospital just as the police came looking for her."

Noel and Don remained silent but stole furtive looks at each other, knowing what was coming and fretful over how Fergus would handle this.

"She needs treatment, that's obvious," said Fergus. "I did my own Google search on repressed trauma last night when I was alone".

"Of course, you're right," said Mike. "Nevertheless, the critical issue here, Fergus, is legal, not medical. What the OPP and the crown attorneys will be asking is whether Noel aided and abetted Mary's flight simply to get her away from the police. Put it this way: Did the Callaghans knowingly obstruct the police?"

"Jesus! The cops already know that Noel met Mary as a child on a reserve. But surely it was coincidence that Noel met Mary again, wasn't it, Mike?"

"Possibly, but difficult to substantiate."

"Come on. We all know she needed help."

"Indeed, Fergus," the lawyer said, clearly determined to override his client's protective reasoning. "Look at it this way, the way the police will. Mary was whisked out of here suddenly and just before dawn. Remember, also, the cryptic phone calls Noel made to you. The OPP can access your telephone records, and those will *not* be privileged."

"Really? Just like that? Just bloody well take over my life, what's left of it, and turn it inside out?"

"Yes, really, just like that. This is a worst-case scenario, but that is what the police are paid to look at: the worst cases. They will be talking to you again, most likely with a warrant to search your house, even confiscate your computer. Our role today is to make certain that you do not knowingly mislead them."

"Legally, that could entail what?"

"Perjury, Fergus, perjury. A crime for which you could do time and put everyone else at risk. Do you understand what I'm saying, why we're here? This ain't, if I may put it bluntly, a free lunch."

Fergus sucked in several loud breaths, exhaled forcibly, and then turned to the Callaghans. "Don, is there more wine, or do I need to get my own bottle? I sense you have more to tell me."

"Of course. First, though, Mike's point is valid, theoretically speaking of course, good counsel that he is. Now, perhaps a malt instead?"

"That would be nice, as my late mother would say. No ice, though."

Noel watched silently as her husband retreated to the sideboard. She rubbed a hand across her forehead and hair, now silver-grey and pulled into a bun behind her neck. Her glasses, quite plain with half-lenses, hung down on a silver chain.

"There is another level to this, Fergus, some of which you know, about Mary and me a long time ago."

Fergus thought back to the first time he and Mary had met the Callaghans at a native art exhibit in the Ojibwa Cultural Centre. Mary had taken one look at Noel and fled, no explanations, either then or later. Fergus had seen Don and Noel exchanging a few words, but he couldn't hear what was said, and was far too embarrassed to ask. If Mary's flight then had bothered the Callaghans, it hadn't prevented Noel from taking Mary on as a patient now, and, as the past few minutes had illustrated, even at considerable risk to herself.

"Yeah, Noel, it's bloody well time I knew what happened. There's a whole other world of hers I don't know about and can't even see. A few fleeting shadows, but she's kept that part of her life so secret that I have to either love her unconditionally, or not at all."

No one said anything so he went on. "Perhaps there's no other kind of love – real love, that is, not some sloppy, self-serving romanticism. Yeah. Nothing held back. It can be a wondrous, beautiful thing. Oh, my God, yes. But with all this OPP shit – pardon my bluntness – it's hard to love only one side of a person."

Fergus's eyes began to moisten as he spoke, as his body and soul finally gave way to the emotional ache inside him. A lump welled up in his throat, so large he barely managed to get out, "Sometimes, sometimes, there are too many Marys to love."

Noel knew she had to build on this point.

"'Too many Marys,' Fergus – that says nothing and yet everything. You obviously do love her; otherwise you would have ru… chosen another path. My turn to talk now, and yours to listen. We owe you that."

"Finally. Go on."

"When I was a nun back in the late fifties and early sixties," said Noel, hands now folded on her lap, almost like a penitent, "I was asked to make a school visit to a small Ojibwa reserve along the North Shore. I had trained as a nurse in Nova Scotia and sometimes was invited into schools here when abuse was suspected. Much has been said and written about the abuse suffered by native children in residential schools. Many *mea culpas*. That was real, very tragically real, but not much – at least until recently – has been said about abuse on the reserves. Rape and incest and mutilation were not rare back then, but it still isn't spoken about much because some people see it as the natives' dirty little secret: particularly the incest, not only by the fathers but by brothers and uncles as well. Mothers looked on, usually powerless."

Fergus struggled again. "You know all this, Noel? You've seen this, the dirty little secret, as you call it?"

"Not the acts, but the wounds. Oh yes, the wounds that burn forever, it seems." She paused, but then moved on quickly. "That's why I'm here. Life was changing rapidly for the church in the 1960s, and when I began to ask too many questions, I was sent to St. Louis University in Missouri for my psych master's. My thesis was on sexual abuse involving native children."

"My, my," said Mike wryly. "Quite stimulating for a nun in those days. Not quite the chaste, safe world of the convent."

Noel countered. "Strange how life works out, though. Given my first taste of freedom as an adult, I decided one morning to kick the religious habit, and apply for a doctoral fellowship at Berkeley, all on my own. Fieldwork for my dissertation brought me back here, and I eventually settled down to practice. Oh, Lord, I was so tempted to stay in California – warm weather, no snow – but that was not who I was. I couldn't be just another expert. In the end, I knew that one day I would come back here. Sorry, I'm away from my point. Excuse me."

"Yeah, of course, but my Mary, when did you meet her? Conferences?"

"Not like that, Fergus, no, no, nothing so civilized. We first met back when I was a nun, when she was about five or six. She was incredibly bright, even then. But her behavior was erratic, and she sometimes came to school with visible bruises. Eventually, her teacher learned third- or fourth-hand that she was being abused. Sometimes, in cases of abuse, aunts or grandmothers, who couldn't or wouldn't interfere directly, would tell somebody who told somebody outside the immediate family. I was asked to do a physical check. It was not pretty. Somebody – I believe her father, if I recall the details correctly – butted out cigarettes on her left hip if she cried. The burns were red and raw with signs of infection. Horrible! So horrible, I still have problems understanding how a father could do that to a child."

Fergus listened silently with his eyes squeezed tight, barely breathing.

Noel continued, "I don't know whether the burns came after or before the genital penetration. I gather the scars are still there?"

"Yes."

"At least we were able to get Mary out of her abusive environment. By that time, the late fifties, the Canadian government was reviewing its residential school policy, and began to make some young natives available for adoption. I'll shorten Mary's story, but rather than include her in the pool of children available for adoption, I was able to place her with my sister in Peterborough who had just had a miscarriage, and was told she could never conceive again. So your Mary became Mary Fraser, loved and cared for and well educated."

"But you didn't stay in touch. Why?"

"No, and I regret that now. My sister died shortly after Mary entered Trent University, ten or twelve years after the adoption. By that time, I had rejected my old life for a while, and, like most Californians, was totally self-absorbed in the new me. Age of Aquarius, the sixties – it was some trip. Did it all. No letters home, not even Christmas cards. But in the end, I couldn't escape my own life story, so I came back. Couldn't stomach Vietnam and Nixon either."

"Best I jump back in," declared Mike, sitting up straight again. "If the Crown decides to play hardball with us, they might allege that Noel's decision that Mary needed emergency treatment was biased or influenced by her early history with Mary. In effect, they could argue that Noel was protecting a friend, indeed a niece by adoption, and not just a walk-in client."

Fergus caught the drift now. "Where does this leave me, Mike? What do you advise me to do if Sawicki comes calling again?"

"Don't lie, but try not to say anything. He can't tie you to the murder, but if he gets pushy, tell him you're calling me. We still have rights in this country."

"Rights? We'll see," snapped Fergus. He turned back to Noel. "But aren't we forgetting something?"

"What, Fergus? I've tried to tell—"

"And you have, Noel. I'm grateful, truly, but you said earlier that Mary referred to a woman. Who is she? Where did she come from? Witness? Accomplice? The real murderer? Who the hell knows? Does anybody bloody well care? Bloody hell, do we just go tell the cops they got it all wrong and to give Mary back to us? Shit, we sit here, drinking wine, enjoying decent music and food, and let that slide by like inane table talk?"

His explosion shocked the other three. Noel hung her head, and folded her hands for a moment to give herself time to gather her wits. Mike sat back and furrowed his eyebrows so deeply that one long line of hair cut across his forehead. Don looked puzzled.

"Okay, Fergus, take a breath," nattered Noel. "Mary's my friend – closer than that really – but I'm also her psychologist, and the rotten truth is that I don't know. She began life with a horrific trauma, day after day, and was powerless to stop it. And, God help her, now she's involved in another awful trauma. If there really is a mystery woman, is she Mary's birth mother who stood by and watched the abuse of her child? Is she my late sister? Does she come from Mary's art world? Was she with Mary on that killing field? We don't know right now. That's why we took Mary to Sudbury, and it's going to take time to reconstruct what's in her head."

Mike Balfour sensed Fergus needed time to absorb what had just been said. He eyed Noel's chicken and mandarin salad, waiting on the sideboard. "Noel, would you like me to serve?"

She nodded, but fretted that much of Fergus's mind was still running in circles, like the two dogs out in the yard.

Fergus knew he had more questions than answers, and wondered whether he should back away again. Just leave – no judgments, no complications, no commitments – go back to Wiarton, write for beer money, and pray that death would come suddenly one night. Tempting. But he also understood now that comfort was not always equated with companionship. 'So, on balance, what should I do,' he asked himself. 'Toss a coin? Leave life to chance and chaos? Leave Mary in a cell someplace rotting away in her nightmare?'

Mike Balfour had eaten only a few bites of the salad before a disturbing thought dulled his appetite. Good food and Gershwin's soothing music notwithstanding, he was profoundly worried that the events of the past thirty-six hours had left the Callaghans teetering on a precarious fault line that might indeed take away the good life as they knew it.

"As your lawyer, and most importantly your friend, I simply cannot sit any longer without speaking my mind," he summed up. "Noel, I'm not blaming you for taking Dr. Fraser away to Sudbury. As always, you're one of the most compassionate and competent people I know. But you may not be able to save her without risk and damage to yourself, and most likely to your husband and Fergus as well. In the end, Manitoulin may not forgive you, let alone Mary."

His outburst silenced the others. Don rose, crossed the room, and turned off the stereo.

"Let me not dance around this, no lawyerly pontificating and obfuscating. Simply put then: Yes, we all know we live in a small town, not quite two thousand souls in winter, on an isolated island in northern Ontario. Like most of the folk who were not born here, we admire the rootedness of the early white settlers and their descendents who survived the first winters eating hawthorn berries, which is why they were called Haweaters, by the way. Such terrible, terrible times they had. But there is another side to the Haweater tradition that's divisive and edgy. We've all felt marginalized at times, not quite full citizens."

The room was still silent, and only Don sipped at his wine. Noel and Fergus pushed back from the table, sensing that Michael's main point was yet to come.

"The more serious side of this is the subtle racism between the Haweaters and the First Nations – the natives, the Aboriginals and their own sense of place and traditions. Yes, we all share the ceremonial powwows and our youngsters all play hockey together and that sort of thing. But there are deeper, darker moments when the differences cannot be ignored."

Noel could not hold herself back any longer. "Michael, please, get to your point. Quite frankly, you're alarming us."

"Just this then, Noel. The murder of a white man, whatever we think of Franz, by a native woman will sorely test the island's fragile sense of balance. However this works out, our lives may not be as comfortable as they have been. In the end, we may be forced to leave the island and live elsewhere. Or stay and be shunned. Now I suppose I should finish my lunch."

Chapter 16

Sudbury, two days later

The wind picked up, and a single yellowed, withered leaf twisted, then tumbled to the ground almost unnoticed, save by Mary Fraser. She sat, as she had for hours now, facing her window, passive, numb almost, fixated on the fading autumn, and too weary to remember why she was in the Northeast Mental Health Centre.

Food trays came and went, almost untouched, nurses checked her vitals, and a nice older man in a white coat came in to talk. She barely had strength to answer, even when she wanted to. Yes, I was a professor once. Art. Where? A lot of places. Toronto? That seems right. No more, please. Not now. Can I go to the bathroom, Sister? Please, please. I don't want to soil myself.

Then her mood would quickly change with a different, faster emotional upswing that put her into hyper-alert consciousness. "People are coming to see you," the nice man in the white coat told her. 'Why?' she asked herself. 'Where are they taking me now? Just to talk? Okay. Yes, I can do that. Goddammit, I'm a university professor. You can call me Doctor, too. I'm not like them out there, smoking those pitiful cigarettes. Stupid people; stupid, stupid slackers. That's why they're here. So they can sit around all day in their pyjamas. Like that one by the door, with the young man at her elbow. Go on, you fat, ugly cow, hang down your damn head; you should be embarrassed to be here. I'm Doctor Mary Fraser, and I bloody well earned my doctorate, world class. I'm… So why am I here with them?'

"Oh God, Fergus, you scared me. Don't do that."

"Do what, Mary? I just—"

"Come up on me like that, touching me."

"I'm sorry. I didn't mean to frighten you. I just, I needed to be here."

Mary had been unaware that Fergus, Noel, and Mike had driven in from Little Current that morning. Noel wanted to test Mary's recall, and arranged for Fergus to visit her alone, without warning. Now Mary turned away from the window to face Fergus, hugging herself, arms clasped tightly in the ancient chenille housecoat Noel had brought her. Mary preferred her housecoat, although it was not in style anymore. But it was warm, and she liked to let her fingers run over the soft ribbing, with its well-worn, orderly texture of highs and lows. My clan totem, she thought, some great soaring bird with strong, wide wings and golden chenille feathers that hold me until night's end.

As Fergus wrapped his arms around her, he noticed that Mary smelled differently than at home; the light jasmine scent from her soaps and lotions was missing. She had no toiletries of her own yet, so she showered with the hospital soaps and shampoos.

But she was emotionally able to reach out, and Fergus felt good. Clarity came for a few minutes as she rubbed his shoulders: not clarity about what had brought her to this place, only an awareness of what was happening to her in this room that was almost a cell with its small single bed and a bedside table for her things, but no newspapers, books, or TV yet, and all behind a solid steel door with an observation window.

Fergus sensed that it took all her energy to ask one question.

"Can I go home with you, Fergus? Just take me home. I hear things sometimes…"

Noel and Mike told Fergus not to raise any false hopes.

"Tell me what you hear. I want to listen."

"There's a bit of poetry that creeps back when I try to sort things out."

"Sort what out?"

"Not much, yet. I still see things, all blurry and bright. Not those things."

"Oh? What other things, Mary?"

"One moment, I can't feel anything. Just that I'm here, in this chair, detached from everything out there. I can't care about them anymore. I'm not the good little Indian girl trying to please everyone. And then, suddenly, I'm frightened of everything. Sometimes, I just crawl back in bed, face the wall and…"

"There's a fine line between fear and forgetting, Mary. You used to tell me that."

"No, no, no, Fergus. Not anymore. I can remember it. Yes, I can...I think. Where is it?"

"The poetry?"

"Yes. Don't interrupt me, or I'll lose it again. That woman, from Wiarton or near Owen...Owen… Well, Marie Knapp says… Yes, yes, I've got it: 'It isn't a fine line after all. There is no line.' She's right. She sees it. I'm just one person, even if I can't feel it all the time."

Fergus sensed that the poetry seemed to ground her, a fragment of memory that her consciousness could cling to. She even tried to comfort him a little, patting his hand. "It's okay, Fergus. Did you bring Brendan?"

"Yes, he's in the car."

"That's nice. I can see her, too, sometimes."

"The poet, Marie—?"

"No, no. Not her. The other her."

"Oh? What is she telling you?"

"Nothing. She just watches."

They sat silently for a few moments. Fergus held her again, and this time she snuggled close to him, almost hiding under his arm and shoulder. He smoothed her hair, not praying in any formal way for mercy, wondering if they would ever sit or lie together in their own bed.

"Sorry, Mr. Fitzgerald," interrupted the nurse, "but you're wanted in the conference room, the lawyer says. Anyway, it's time for Mary's meds."

Mike and Noel were waiting for him with a copy of that day's *Sudbury Star.*

"It's started," said Mike. "The finger pointing."

"Mary's been charged?"

"Not at this moment, Fergus, but read this, the paragraphs I've marked."

The story ran three columns across the bottom of the front page. Its headline was a simple and declarative one, the usual way the *Star* played killings, particularly from out-of-town places like Little Current:

German Hotel Exec Murdered

There was no picture with the story, but the subhead had an edge:

OPP Mum on Leads, Native Missing

The top of the story was straightforward: the basic who, where, and when stuff all attributed to Detective Sergeant Rich Sawicki. The only reference to motive was that robbery had been ruled out because the victim's wallet and papers were found undisturbed in his clothes. Then cautiously, obviously trying to avoid a public dressing down from a judge, Louisa Ledingham's report deftly began linking the murder to Mary.

> *While Detective Sawicki said police have not yet talked to possible suspects, they have seized a Grand Wagoneer Jeep, believed to be owned by Dr. Mary Fraser, a colleague of the victim. The vehicle was discovered yesterday morning in Little Current by an OPP patrol unit. Nearby residents said the vehicle was quickly secured with standard crime scene tape and later towed to the OPP compound.*
>
> *Later, they said the Jeep's license was Ontario ARET*753. It was then traced to Dr. Fraser through a local dealer who services the Jeep. The vehicle had been illegally parked in a handicap zone outside the office of Dr. Noel Callaghan, a local psychologist.*
>
> *Neither Dr. Fraser, an art historian who teaches at the University of Toronto, nor Dr. Callaghan was available for comment yesterday. Dr. Fraser, a non-status Ojibwa who is considered to be one of Canada's leading experts on native art and symbols, was retained earlier this year by the victim's uncle, Max Adler from a suburb of Dresden, Germany, as cultural advisor for the hotel project now under construction at Sheguiandah.*

"There we have it, Ferg," said the lawyer. "Time for us to get ahead of the curve."

"Slow down, for God's sake," responded Fergus, struggling to catch up, still staring at the article and its impersonal tone. The reporter in him should have expected the page-one coverage, and there it was in cold, black, unforgiving type. One person's life, nailed down in three paragraphs that could be read and re-read, clipped and filed.

"Noel, help me here," Fergus finally blurted out, growing steadily angrier. "Mary's in there, across the hall. She barely knows my name, let alone whether she killed anyone. And the *Star* drags her name into this."

"She's sick, Fergus," said Noel. "Really sick, which means that you have to focus on her and not on the *Star*. She needs you."

"Oh yeah, Noel. The jury's already in. Sweet Jesus, why don't they just haul her over to the Sudbury rink, hoist her over the centre-ice scoreboard, and let her drop? Stompin' Tom can sing something merciful-like. 'Hang down your head, Mary Fraser, hang down and we'll all have a good cry.' God, where does the bloody *Star* get off?"

Noel closed her eyes to Fergus's violent images, rubbed her jawline, and stared at the floor. Then she went around the coffee table, and quickly knelt in front of him, simply there to focus his attention.

"Fergus, listen to me," she asked softly, half rising from her knees, balancing with one hand on the floor. "It's time, my friend, to stop feeling sorry for yourself, all wrapped in that damn Irish guilt. Just move on. Forget the *Star*. It's doing its job, so you do yours.

"There is no doubt in anyone's mind here," Noel went on. "My own professional opinion is that Mary suffers from PTSD...sorry, post-traumatic stress disorder. She's shut down because that's the only way she can deal with the horror in her life, first as a child and now with Franz's murder. There is no pill that will quickly sort it out for her. It will take time. Lots of time. Right now, her mind will bounce around, numb much of the time, but then suddenly hyper-vigilant, responding quickly to everything."

Noel's clear and orderly words calmed Fergus enough that he could put the paper aside.

"You're right. *The Star*, it's not the problem. I've been a reporter, and everything in that bloody piece is in the public domain. God, if she had only parked down the street. Oh shit, why can't we leave her here, give her the help she needs, and tell the cops to bugger off until she's well?"

"My turn, Noel," said Mike. "My reading of the *Star* piece is that Rich Sawicki came close to saying outright that Mary is a person of interest, and that when more pieces, probably fingerprints, fall into place, they will charge her. Murder, manslaughter, I don't know which at this point. But it could come soon. Sawicki knows his job and won't wait once he's convinced. Perhaps tomorrow."

"That soon? She's not ready. She's weak, confused."

"Two points, Fergus, and then we must discuss what to do next."

"One point or two points?" said Fergus. "Whatever... However many bloody points ya need, Mike."

"Stay with me, guy. You do love her, so it's time to reach out. There's no one else. Can you do that?"

Fergus exhaled, got up and locked his hands behind his neck. The tension eased. Noel stood behind him and rubbed his shoulders lightly.

"Yeah, I'm here. Still here, wherever here is, someone said. Just tell me."

"Good," enthused Mike. "First point: If Sawicki thinks the cops have a provable case against her, if he believes she killed Franz, then he will take her into custody immediately. It's their job to keep killers off the street and let the courts sort it out."

"So she goes to jail until trial, Mike, some miserably cold bucket of a cell with bars and a stainless steel toilet in the corner?"

"Not necessarily jail. We have one shot at this."

"Which is?"

"Rich Sawicki gave you a copy of the Criminal Code for a reason. He wanted you to look at Section 672 which covers NCR remands."

"NCR?"

"Not criminally responsible. If the cops charge her, as we think they will, then we can ask a judge to remand her to a forensic detention centre for thirty days."

"That's better than jail?"

"Much better care. Professional staff, perhaps even native counselors."

"Cure her?"

"No, not in thirty days. But it will buy us – and Mary – time."

"For what? Will I be able to see her? Will you see her?"

"Not so fast, Fergus. There are risks."

"Risks?"

"There is a quid pro quo involved," said Mike. "If we want the Crown and police onside when we ask for an NCR remand in lieu of a bail hearing, then we'll have to give the cops access to Mary and her records."

"Just like that?" snapped Fergus. "We ask them over, eh? 'Hey, Rich, wanna go for a beer?'"

"No other way. Mary has to be able to tell us what really happened to Franz and, more importantly, who the woman she keeps referring to is."

"And tell the *Star*, too? They'd really love a mystery woman."

"In time, Fergus, in time," Mike cautioned. "Think 'reasonable doubt', not headlines. It could be the real murderer, or an accessory – perhaps her mother – or a relative, but it's all locked in Mary's head and she's lost the key."

Chapter 17

Little Current, The next day

Too bloody long, Fergus muttered to himself as he woke, rubbing the sleep out of his eyes. Mary's shrinks will take way too long. So? So, I gotta unlock my own head.

He had only a groggy memory of what had happened at the Sudbury mental hospital, but a vague sense of direction had seized him. If he understood anything about his own mind, it was the power of his subconscious to unscramble and make sense of information overload. Translation: Sleep on it, and trust the night shift.

"Think reasonable doubt," Mike had advised. Bullshit, thought Fergus. Leave the tunnel vision to the cops, and reserve the right to challenge easy answers. She's my Mary, not theirs.

"And stop feeling sorry for yourself," Noel had added. More bullshit. No, she's right. So fuck the guilt trip.

Fergus stripped buck-naked and headed for the bathroom, and the stimulation of a warm shower. Somewhere between finding the right water temperature and reaching for the soap, his synapses began popping, and messages crowded into his consciousness. Remember your whiteboard, dolt! What hasn't been answered yet, or explored, or whatever? Franz, yeah, the little bastard. Frame the question: Why was Franz at the hotel site in the middle of the night? Christ, did the bikers drag him there? Or did somebody else, maybe the second woman Mary babbles about?

No answers, of course, but the reporter in Fergus told him that questions were more important now than answers. But where to start?

Ablutions finished, he made coffee, enough for himself now. He found the sweater he had flung over a chair the previous night. Warmth had left the house, along with Mary and their usual routines.

The coffee helped, and he began to move slowly to his own beat. His sense of time seemed to have moved up another notch, not just clock time, but also the run of things that mattered. It was colder outside, and a faint squall line of snow had blown in, although barely heavy enough to last in the midday sun.

An hour or so later, Fergus forced a wan smile at the drugstore clerk as he tore off the receipt for a prescription, and neatly folded it into his wallet. No one said anything to him. One woman did touch his arm briefly though, smiled knowingly, and then walked away. Judging only by her broad, weathered face, she most certainly was native, and probably old enough to be his mother.

He was grateful for her concern, however unspoken, as most folk found it difficult to look him in the eye. They didn't appear angry, just embarrassed for him and not knowing quite what to say, the way some people are when they go through a funeral reception line, worrying whether it's morbid to look into an open casket. The streets were not crowded. All the tourists were gone. Fergus looked for the rented Ford Focus – the police still hadn't returned Mary's Jeep – and a chance to pop one of the anti-reflux pills Don Callaghan had prescribed to ease his heartburn and chest pains. "No, your heart's fine," Don had confirmed, "but the stress is playing havoc with your stomach. Call me if it doesn't help."

As he walked eastward, Fergus spotted a cluster of townsfolk near a sidewalk planter and tried to hurry past.

"Coffee with milk okay?"

The voice belonged to a familiar face: Isaiah Steen, a reporter he knew from the *Manitoulin Expositor*. When deadlines weren't looming, they occasionally had coffee or a beer, and mostly talked about books and writing.

Before Fergus could answer, Isaiah jumped in to explain. "It's for Cheryl at the office, but I can get her another coffee later. So how's it going? Time to chew a bit?"

Fergus usually enjoyed the sweet serendipity of chance meetings, particularly with Isaiah, in a small town where lives crossed frequently. Still, he didn't want to fuel more speculation about Mary.

"Yeah. Can't stay long, though. I have to get home. Brendan's probably cross-eyed by now...if he hasn't already peed on the floor. Quick coffee, though. Thanks."

They sat side by side against the low wall that shaped the municipal planter outside the *Expositor* office.

"How's Mary doing, if you don't mind me asking?"

"Hey, I can't go there. Not today, okay?"

"Sure, Ferg, just curious. Haven't seen her recently and—"

"And what?"

"Well, you know what folks are saying. Can you tell me where she is?"

"You had to ask that, didn't you?"

"Hey, you know where I work, and you'd be asking the same question about my wife if she had cop problems."

Fergus jerked upright. "But it's not Linda, Isaiah. It's Mary, and it's damn hard to sit here…and…"

Talking became so difficult that Fergus couldn't finish the sentence. Instead, he pushed himself away from the wall, turned abruptly, and planted himself almost in Isaiah's face.

"Christ, now even friends are questioning me. So bugger off!"

Isaiah, though shaken, held his place against the wall, not sure whether to push Fergus away or take a chance and listen.

"Man, I know this is hard, but I wanted to… C'mon, you know the drill, Ferg. We'll give you a chance to explain Mary's side of things. You know where this is headed."

"You want to turn the tables, put yourself in my shoes, right? Okay, shitface, put me in yours. Let me ask one question. Just one. Okay?"

"Just one? No reporter ever asked just one question."

"Trust me."

"Trust a fucking reporter?"

"There's nobody else here. One question, Isaiah."

"On the record?"

"Yeah, bloody yeah. Most questions are more telling than answers. My question out front – no hedging, no hiding behind informed sources, everyone's on the same page, let history judge. On the bloody record. Okay?"

"God, where's my pen. Always missing…here…go on, ask."

"Just this, Isaiah. What in hell was Franz doing at the work site in the middle of the night? Nobody seems to care about that."

The question stumped Isaiah, and he quickly parsed its implications. Not once had the police mentioned Franz, other than to report his death. Curious oversight? Or were the police diverting attention, and if so, why? Lord, no one here is even planning a memorial service for the late Herr Dietrich – just bag him and ship him back to Germany, postage due. All of which looped back to Mary, and why –

don't forget 'allegedly,' Isaiah reminded himself – why she killed him.

"So, Ferg, you want me to look at the victim, is that it?"

"Just a question. Gotta get home."

"Dammit, man, you're worse than Sawicki. You're both jerking me around, like something's going on between you two that neither of you wants to mention. Something smells. Yeah, it smells. And yeah, we need more on Franz, but I damn well want to know why."

Fergus shook his head, eyes down, crushing the empty coffee cup as he stepped back. He tried to walk away but bumped into two pedestrians. Said sorry, twice.

Isaiah took a step sideways along the wall. He became increasingly convinced that Fergus was trying to say something to him, but couldn't find the words. His reticence was unusual, even curious, as Fergus normally was more than willing to share his intriguing breadth of interests on almost anything. So, at the risk of misjudging what he had just heard, Isaiah tried again. "Methinks you're trying to tell me something about Franz. Is he part of the mess?"

"Okay, okay," replied Fergus slowly "We all are, we all did it."

Lighten up, Isaiah told himself. Don't spook him; don't shut him down. He took a deep breath. "So, Ferg, we're all butterflies, bumping into each other and setting—"

"No butterflies, Isaiah. I should have kept Franz away from Mary."

"They had to work together, didn't they?"

"I had the chance to stop him, and I didn't. Give him a chance, I said, and they did."

"Who's they?"

"At the airport in Toronto. The immigration guys."

Isaiah was now writing furiously, wishing he had brought his tape recorder to catch the nuances. There was no time to stop. He had to let the good stuff flow.

Fergus knew that, having mentioned the interrogation at the airport and having revealed his own sense of guilt, he could only go forward. He had asked his question on the record, which meant everything that followed would be, too, unless he struck a new deal with Isaiah. More shoppers straggled by, but took no notice of the two men.

"Immigration! At the airport, Fergus? So what happened? Back up a little."

"I'll tell you, but can I go off the record for a moment? Okay?"

"All right, but you can't take back what you've already told me."

"Agreed. Just this, then. I can tell you part of what happened, but not for attribution."

"You're cautious."

"I don't know the whole story, that's all."

"And if I get it confirmed elsewhere?"

"Then it's your call. But no direct quotes."

"Other than what you've already said."

"Okay. The rest is background."

"So what happened?"

There was a long pause before Fergus answered.

"Franz had been coming on to Mary in Germany. One moment, he's playing the gracious host – nothing's too good for us – then the predator shows up with absolutely no remorse. He could be a real sleaze."

"None? Like it's all a big game?"

"Not for Mary. She can be feisty, you know that, but it turned ugly when we landed at Pearson."

Fergus told Isaiah about the blow-up between Mary and Franz that had triggered the strip search by officials in Toronto. He also added what he had been told of Franz's activities in the German drug trade, and of the reluctance of the Canadian officials to allow Franz into Canada, based on the briefing from Interpol.

"Was he active here? I mean, was he dealing?" said Isaiah.

"God, the bikers came looking for him, so anything's possible. Was he dealing personally? I think so, but I can't confirm that."

"I can check on that, but tell me this."

"What? I do have to go."

"Why – and this is personal – why do you feel so guilty about this? Franz is, or was, Max's nephew and responsibility. The immigration guys, and presumably the local OPP, knew about Franz, so why are you taking all this shit upon yourself?"

Fergus walked to the other side of the planter to gather his thoughts. An old mantra came back to him from his youth when he actually went to confession: "Bless me, Father, for I have sinned most grievously." Then he turned back to face Isaiah and the moral judgment of a friend.

"When I came to Canada from Boston in the seventies, no one questioned why I didn't want to fight in Vietnam for a war that I didn't believe in. A few called us draft dodgers with a bit of a snarl, but we were accepted. It was that simple, and I began my life again."

"That simple, eh? The Canadian way. Blame it on Canada!"

"That's not what I meant. You're bloody twisting this and—"

"Then get to the point! Get it over with. The way you tell it, Franz was a slimy piece of work, a twisted psycho of some sort who probably fed off other people's misery. But that's not the whole story, is it? Again, face it, man, what do you feel so damn guilty about?"

Fergus finally looked directly at Isaiah. Much as he would have liked to head off home and take a pill, he knew the time had come to find relief in this street-side confessional.

"When the immigration interrogators asked me about Franz back in Toronto, I could have prevented this mess. 'No, no,' I said, quite nobly. 'Give him another chance,' I said. Now I'll never know what would have happened if I had said more. He's dead, and Mary's… Oh Lord, what a mess. Forgive me, Father."

Decision time.

There were only two OPP cruisers at the crime site, inside the tape that flapped in the breeze. Only Sawicki and Peltier were there.

Collars up, they fidgeted, not quite certain what to do next, now that the case managers and forensic teams had gone back to North Bay and Sault Ste. Marie. Both knew the decision to charge Mary began with Sawicki, even though he could be overruled by their superiors.

"Peut etre," said Matt Peltier, standing by to provide a second opinion, if needed.

"What?"

"Perhaps, Sawicki. Perhaps she did it, and perhaps one day you'll learn some French."

"Someday, someday, not today Matt. So, do I—"

"Charge her now, Rich, or let it ride until—"

"Fraser and that sneaky doctor of hers take off again, and we're left explaining to the media and the brass why we needed more time."

Matt turned away and walked down the hill. Part of him was glad that it was not his job to make the call. Back away, he told himself, and let Rich do his job. But there was a deeper part of Matt that said Sawicki was missing something, that other theories could be possible. Should we wait until Mary's head clears and she can tell her side? What's the drug angle? Biker hit? Or do I just like her too much?

But all he said aloud was, "We always need more time, and we won't get DNA confirmation for another week. But you get to wear this."

Sawiciki didn't blink. "If I don't, others will, and probably from North Bay. And soon."

"That's the way it plays?"

"No other way!"

Sawicki was aware the time had come to earn his stripes.

"You know, we got a warrant to take another look at the Fraser home."

"And?"

"More blood marks on the front door handle and frame. With her prints."

"She does live there," Matt said. "So?"

"But I don't think our victim lived there, too."

"Your meaning?"

"The forensic team also picked up blood residue around her bathroom, using a luminol scan. Blood from both places matched the victim."

"Hard call with no witnesses, Rich, but you're making your point. Too many coincidences to ignore."

"Which leaves us with a preponderance of evidence that points to only one person."

"Wanna wait for the DNA?"

"Not this time, Matt. No doubts. We've tracked Dietrich's blood, his type anyway, from his head to the weapon to the Fraser car to her house. Okay, she had reason to fear him. No, delete that. I'll set up a meeting with the crown attorney. Better check first that Fraser hasn't run again."

Rich made the call, and a meeting was set at the Little Current OPP office just before noon. Peltier looked away as he ducked under the yellow tape.

"All set?" Sawicki asked, pumped up again. "Time to move on, then."

Little Current OPP offices, Later that day

"Chris, is the Crown here yet?"

Detective Marston responded quickly to his boss. "No, but we got a call from…" He flipped rapidly through his notes.

"…from Michael Balfour, a local lawyer. He wants to meet with us and the Crown. Crafty old guy, I'm told."

"Can he wait?" asked Sawicki.

"Wouldn't recommend that, sir."

"Can't you ever get to the point?"

"It's about the Fraser woman; he represents her. Balfour also wants to bring Fergus Fitzgerald and the psychologist with him to Gore Bay."

Chapter 18

Next morning, the drive to Gore Bay took unexpected turns and bumps even before they left Little Current. Without explanation, Noel had insisted they get on the road an hour earlier than planned.

Nothing more was said, not even the usual morning banter, until Fergus turned on the car radio for the CBC news, more out of habit than anything else.

"Do you mind?" Noel said sharply. "I need to focus on Mary and McTavish."

From the back seat, Mike, ever the diplomat, jumped in to soothe feelings. "We'll get through this. Hey, did I tell you how I beat McTavish? He—"

"I'm not supposed to do this," she bristled, ignoring Mike completely. "Not professional, not this way."

Whatever she meant by 'not this way' caught Fergus's attention. "What? You want to cancel? What's so bloody unprofessional?"

Noel took in a long breath before answering. "My journey with Mary has been too long. There's no distance any more. None."

Mike didn't probe, and was anxious himself that their gamble could fail and that Mary Fraser would end up in the Sudbury jail by nightfall. And so they drove quietly for another ten minutes, before the highway dropped steeply into M'chigeeng, formerly known as West Bay, the First Nation community where Fergus had first met Noel at the Ojibwa Cultural Centre.

Noel lifted her head with a quick shake, squared her shoulders, and gave Fergus more instructions. "Well, since my life has come full circle, take the next left."

"Full circle? Back here?"

"Yes. And back to Mary."

"This is why we left early?"

"Yes, Fergus, now left again. There, behind the tall pines, please."

"At the church? You're sure? Visit a church? This is not like you, Noel."

"Stay in the car, if you want. It's… I need to do this."

"No," Fergus replied emphatically.

"No?"

"No, Noel, I'm coming with you."

Mike Balfour opted to stay in the car, re-reading his files and the Criminal Code.

Fergus had been here several times previously with Mary. She was comfortable in this church, able to put aside her usual academic appraisal of its motifs and icons, instead being quietly grateful that her life could come together, at least for a few minutes.

Before them sat Mary's sanctuary, unique in that it had a traditional Catholic name – Church of the Immaculate Conception – but with the shape of a thirteen-sided tepee. With only a short steeple and much of the building buried below ground level, it seemed closer to Mother Earth than to the heavens. Fergus recognized the usual Stations of the Cross on the inside walls, but he was more taken with a sense that he and Noel were standing in a traditional fire pit where Aboriginal people listened to the Great Spirit. The air still held remnants of the smudging ceremony that had proceeded last Sunday's mass. Even the tabernacle was in the form of a small tepee, and four large dream catchers – red, yellow, black, and white – faced the altar to protect all races.

The church's baptismal font rested on the back of a large wooden muskrat representing the Anishnaabeg story of Creation after the Great Flood. Fergus was comfortable with the imagery, knowing the story well from Ojibwa writers like Basil Johnson. It told of the time when the water creatures persuaded Waszhask, a little muskrat, to bring up some pieces of soil from under the water, and life began again.

Noel bypassed the baptismal font and the other Catholic icons, preferring to gaze up at a carving of the Thunderbird, the ancient native symbol of transformation and vitality.

Fergus knew enough about native spirituality to believe that if Mary Fraser had been raised as an Aboriginal, she might well have belonged to the Thunderbird clan, full of energy and innovation, but eruptive, too, and overpowering.

Noel first turned to the east, and then full circle.

"You're praying, Noel, is that it?"

"Perhaps, Fergus. I don't know if I am. It's been so long."

"We're hypocrites, you know, just being here."

"Judge for yourself, Fergus. Me, I need to be here."

"In this church or whatever it is?"

"Not necessarily here, but it helps."

"Helps what? Helps you?"

"It helps me find Mary. I need to sense the child in her again, here in all the crosscurrents that scarred her innocence. That's what we're fighting for."

Gore Bay

Just over thirty minutes later, Calvin John McTavish sat rigidly at the end of the conference table in the courthouse jury room, and solemnly presented his opening position as crown attorney on Manitoulin Island.

"Let me make this absolutely clear," he said, moving his eyes from Noel Callaghan to Mike Balfour and then finally settling on Fergus. "Anything you propose means nothing, absolutely nothing, until I agree." Rich Sawicki, at his side, said nothing, having discussed the case with him yesterday by phone.

Another pause.

"I am not a social worker or a therapist. My mission is quite simple: Uphold the law and punish the guilty."

There was another pause before Mike Balfour spoke, straightening his tie as he did. "Of course it is, Cal, and we respect that. You have serious responsibilities as Crown, which is why we're here today. May I ask first how your new son is doing? Your wife is an incredible woman, teaching your children at home. My, my, that must make it five, no, six—"

"Mr. Balfour, my family is fine, but we do need to move ahead. Detective Sawicki has already briefed me, and I must say that the case for your client does not look promising."

The prosecutor's summary did not bother Noel as much as his manner did, coldly stoic and devoid of compassion. So far, Calvin John McTavish was exactly what Mike Balfour had told her to expect: a somewhat small man, given to dark blue suits, crisply starched white shirts, and subdued ties. No apparent sense of humor, conservative, and rigidly dogmatic. Might have made a good bishop, she mused. Her training told her to look for the flip side of his personality. Mike had told her it was common gossip that McTavish had been assigned (some said exiled) to Manitoulin eleven years earlier to round off the rough spots in his personality. No one doubted his intellect and diligence, but the senior Crowns in Toronto believed he needed time to develop some social graces and to learn to restrain his quick-draw, often black-and-white judgements about everyone who got in his way.

Noel could not resist testing her assumptions. "So, Mr. McTavish, sir, you think Dr. Mary Fraser is guilty, do you? Just like that?"

"Mrs. Callaghan, the—"

"*Doctor* Callaghan, please. My doctorate is from Berkeley and—"

"Oh, yes, Berkeley, California, the well known university with its hippie lifestyle. Most curious. I've heard about you, the ex-nun who went over the wall."

"Noel... Cal... please," interrupted Mike Balfour. "We need to get back to the Fraser file."

Noel settled nervously in her chair, and McTavish fiddled with a pencil before re-aligning it squarely against the single pad of yellow paper in front of him. Rich Sawicki remained silent.

"Thank you, Mr. Balfour. My day is very busy and I am due in court in thirty minutes, sooner if possible. So?"

"Just this, then. Three points for your consideration. Please, take the time you need."

Mike was slowing the pace as Noel has advised during their strategy planning earlier with Fergus. They had made it clear to Fergus that the biggest hurdle was simply getting Cal McTavish to listen to the proposal, and so they came well prepared. Using a simplified form of one of her basic personality assessment tools, the Myers Briggs Personality Inventory, Noel had laid out the battle plan for what she called McTavish's classic profile of an introverted, reflective person who preferred concrete information, accepted conflict as normal, and liked to focus on task-related action. They agreed that their best strategy was to present their ideas sequentially, give McTavish lots of time, and emphasize the benefits to him. But Noel confessed she was worried this frustrated little man didn't trust psychologists in general, and her in particular. "He assumes that we're too empathetic and forgiving."

As agreed, Mike continued to take the lead, and they all noticed that McTavish's body language seemed slightly more relaxed, hands spread in front of him, palms almost facing upwards.

"Well then," said Mike, "we start with the assumption that you are preparing to charge my client arising from her alleged involvement in the death of Franz Dietrich. You don't have to reply to that, as this is only an informal conference, not a hearing."

Sensing their silent agreement, Mike continued. "I'll move on to our first point: Mary Fraser is an exceptional person caught up in a tragic situation with a young German ne'er-do-well. She is a world-class scholar, while he lived on the edge of the drug trade. She brought great promise to her fellow Ojibwa, and he, as I understand, brought more drugs to the island."

McTavish raised his right forefinger, and pointed it directly at Mike.

"What you say is true, Mr. Balfour, except that Dr. Fraser certainly didn't choose her friends or colleagues wisely. She could have returned to Toronto at any time. Instead, we must consider the motives of an older, sophisticated woman working closely with a young man, a stranger in this country. Who tempted whom the night of the murder?"

"The problem, Cal, ah, Mr. McTavish, is that as far as we know – and correct me if I'm wrong, Detective – only two people know what happened at the construction site, and one is dead and the other, my client, is now a patient in the Northeast Mental Health Centre with almost no memory of what happened. Classic PTSD: She is currently being treated for post-traumatic stress disorder."

"So you say, Mr. Balfour. If you were so confident of the diagnosis, why didn't you advise Detective Sawicki here at the start? Or was Dr. Callaghan trying to hide something? From where I sit, her role is far from innocent."

The small conference room became quiet. The battle lines had been drawn. Noel ignored Mike and their carefully planned strategy, and suddenly pitched herself into the fray.

For all her training, Noel was not prepared to leave the accusation unchallenged. Strategy be damned: Her mission had suddenly become too personal for her to remain professionally detached. "You are a well-educated person, Mr. McTavish, and the Crown's representative in the pursuit of justice, so surely we can make the assumption that you accept that PTSD is a disorder recognized by most senior and discerning psychologists in the western world."

McTavish was speechless, as much taken aback that the verbal assault came from a woman, as by her implication that he didn't keep up to date.

It was Fergus's turn to calm Noel.

"I hope you will excuse our passion, Mr. McTavish," said Fergus, knowing when to grovel a little. "It's been a devilishly exhausting time for all of us, and, well frankly, sir, we think we have a proposal that will meet your needs and ours as well."

Noel, appalled by her own loss of control, nodded her agreement, worried that she had destroyed whatever chance they had to help Mary.

And with good reason. McTavish was livid and tight-lipped. Sawicki leaned across the corner of the conference table as the Crown hurriedly began to shove his writing pad into his briefcase. They exchanged whispers before McTavish grinned and put the pad back on his desk.

"Fifteen minutes, then, and get to the point. Mr. Balfour, if you will, sir."

"Well, my, my," replied Mike. "Yes, indeed. Our points, in order: Dr. Fraser is an internationally respected scholar and important to her people, the Ojibwa. We believe her conscious memory has been seriously impaired, both by the long-repressed trauma of childhood incest, and more recently, by the violence of whatever she saw when Franz Dietrich was murdered. We accept that your evidence strongly suggests that she was involved. How involved, and indeed why, as your own questions imply, none of us know, except Mary Fraser herself."

McTavish countered, "Is this what you're about? Incest charges, Mr. Balfour? How does this relate to Dietrich? Are you claiming mitigation as a defense?"

"Yes, Dr. Fraser had been abused as a child," said Mike. "But, no, that's not why we're here, at least not at this time."

"Your proposal, please."

"Thank you, Mr. McTavish. Dr. Callaghan and I, with the full support of Dr. Fraser's companion, Mr. Fitzgerald here, are prepared to give you and the police access to Dr. Fraser in Sudbury as well as to her case files."

Noel and Fergus nodded in agreement.

"And in return, Mr. Balfour?"

"Just this: If and when the OPP charge Dr. Fraser, as it appears likely they will, then you and I will jointly seek to have her remanded to the North Bay Forensic Detention Centre under Section—"

"Section 672, Mr. Balfour. I do know the code. An assessment order to determine whether she is fit to stand trial or is criminally responsible. NCR. Clever! I must warn you, however, that she could end up with an indeterminate sentence in a maximum-security institution. You're aware of that?"

"Of course. One way or another, Mary Fraser's life will not be restored until we unlock the trauma that has shut down one of the brightest minds in Canada. There's one more thing."

"Now what? I must go."

"You did say we had fifteen minutes. If Detective Sawicki agrees, can she be charged, taken to a Sudbury court, and transported to North Bay without any jail time in Sudbury? It's not usual, but it can be done. It's in everyone's interest to heal her trauma, not add to it."

"Not the usual drill, Mr. Balfour. I agree with your theory, but the reality of your proposal is much too problematic."

"But it can be done, sir, if Detective Sawicki and his team can coordinate the charge and court appearance with the availability of a bed at the assessment centre."

The phone on McTavish's desk rang. He grunted something into the receiver and hung up.

"I must go. We'll get back to you after Rich and I review your proposal. Interesting logic, but a judge awaits."

The OPP office, Little Current, Later that day

"…and that's how it went, Chris. Gutsy move."

"Will McTavish go for it?"

"We'll see tomorrow," said Sawicki. "Not his style, though, to deal like that."

"So how did you get him to listen after the Callaghan hissy fit?"

"Not to be repeated. Okay?"

"Sure."

"I quietly reminded him that we work in a small town, and that his wife and Noel Callaghan play bridge together sometimes, and sometimes the woman-to-woman chatter gets quite intimate. Need I say more?"

"He went for that?"

"Yeah, Chris, and then I told him we've been getting some informed media calls about Franz Dietrich and his drug business. A lot of questions are being asked about why Dietrich was let into the country at all."

"Newspapers, TV... So? They don't run this case. They don't pay our salaries."

"No, Chris, but they can ask embarrassing questions. They've been on to the elders and band councils, who are demanding answers."

"Then you better handle this bunch of call backs yourself, sir.

"Shit! More from the media, Chris?"

"No, the regional drug squad in Sudbury, and our brass in Orillia as well. Even the RCMP is monitoring this. What I hear is that there's more Ecstasy around Sudbury and even some reports of a rave on Manitoulin."

"Has a joint task force unit been set up yet?"

"Budget problems, I gather, but a JFU is being discussed. The OPP's own Biker Enforcement Unit wants to hit a new Hells Angels chapter in Sudbury, and even the Sudbury regional government is drawing up an anti-biker bylaw. If Franz was dealing here, then our guys want to know about his sources and how the shit came, in because the bikers are active in Germany, as we know. Damn, we got enough problems already with booze, and now this."

"That's all, I hope? We may have to roll tomorrow."

"Not quite, sir. The Sudbury guys want to talk to Max Adler."

"From Germany, Chris?"

"Probably, but from wherever. Mongolia, if necessary."

"Just get 'im then. Neat old guy, but he has a lot to answer for."

Chapter 19

That evening, Fergus did his best to resurrect his normal life, begging off dinner with the Callaghans. At home, he tried to phone Mary at the Sudbury hospital, but wasn't allowed to speak to her. He put a dish of leftover pasta in the microwave, and stepped outside to check the mailbox at the end of their lane. Slow day. An unaddressed flyer for used tractors from a local dealer. Tossed. For Mary, one credit card promo, pre-authorized for $10,000. Platinum, too. Tossed. For himself, only a note-size letter with no return address, just his name hand-printed on the envelope. Curious. So what to do? Toss or open? Eat first, of course, Fergus decided, because the pasta was ready. Red or white wine? Red.

Later

From: **Fergus**
Fitzgerald<Brendan@bmts.com
To: **Conall**
Fitzgerald<Famtrack@corknet.ie
Subject: **strange mail**

Dammit, here I am apologizing again. Seems to be all I do these days. I'm in a dither about an intriguing letter that arrived today.

It was postmarked Espanola, a mill town on the mainland about a half-hour's drive north of here. At first I put it aside, as I've been getting some nasty letters and calls about

Mary. No signatures or return addresses, only some quite crude, mean-spirited, and judgemental comments.

This letter felt bulky, though, so I opened it to find one sheet of paper and $500 in cash. Not a check, but one $100 bill, two $50s, and the rest in $20s and $10s. Only two handwritten sentences of explanation:

This is for Dr Fracers lawyer She didnt do it

The spelling and punctuation are exactly as I received it – no possessive apostrophe on Mary's name, for example. You can work out the rest. Either this letter was written by someone without much education...or perhaps by someone who is deliberately trying to cover his tracks.

What to do about this? I'm well aware that the mood in Little Current is starting to change, now that the local media is focusing more on Franz and his role in the drug trade. Finally, bloody finally, the various cop shops are taking a comprehensive look at Franz and his suppliers. My own sources tell me that he's been on their radar ever since he arrived. Lots of other questions, too. Where has Franz been getting his front money? Uncle Max? And where are those bikers who killed Max's dog?

One reporter told me that the chiefs and elders are putting pressure on the cops to clean it up. Booze has always been the drug of choice around here, so much so that the island's alcohol-related crime and health problems are way above provincial averages. Demographics are part of it – low income and high unemployment, etc. But the cops shut down at least one sizable marijuana grow op – estimated at $1 million plus in street value, by the way. Finding the grow op was accidental, though, because the island is crisscrossed with side roads, isolated beaches, and empty barns. Now the synthetics like Ecstasy are slowly moving in, and there have even been reports of a rave someplace.

So, where does Mary fit into this? I have never seen her do drugs, though I suspect that, like most persons her age and education, she at least smoked up when she was younger. Lord, who didn't? I don't smoke, so I couldn't inhale. Tried weed a couple of times, but it almost made me sick. Seriously. Still, the cops and the local crown attorney clearly believe she's involved somehow, because all the physical evidence points at her. We expect she'll be arrested and charged soon. As I told you a couple of days ago, we haven't heard whether the crown attorney (a truly pompous little prick) will support our recommendation that Mary be remanded to a forensic detention centre for assessment.

I suspect the letter I mentioned won't help our case. Although the money certainly will, if Mary ever goes to trial. If she does, I'm prepared to re-mortgage my home in Wiarton to cover her legal bills.

The broader meaning of the letter intrigues me. Somebody believes, or says they believe, that Mary is innocent. If so, the writer either is compassionate or is feeling guilty enough to help. Mary, in her limited lucid moments, has referred to a "woman" who so far is unknown to us. Nor do we have any idea what her relationship is to Mary and, bear with me, where the relationship is even from – Mary's childhood, her birth or adopted mother, somebody at Trent or University of Toronto, or the woman on the far side of the moon, for all we know.

Let me know what you think. I'm so close to her tragedies that it's bloody impossible to be objective. Had she not been abused as a child, would any of this have happened? You take my meaning. True, we might never have even met. That's not what bothers me. I can't get past the nightmarish images of incest, by her father and perhaps others. It's not rare, incest that is, in native families, but was incest always there, or is this another side effect of their treatment as sub-humans? I suspect the latter, just like the British treatment of the bog Irish a couple of centuries ago. We're all more civilized now, or are we? Mary still has scars on her hips, so raw that these images remain and remain and remain. My faith dims that we can ever rise above the old rages.

I've rambled on way too long, but these email epistolaries do help me clear my head and at least organize my thoughts. There's an old quote from D.H. Lawrence that has always intrigued me, and now seems particularly relevant in this context. He seemed to believe that a man and a woman were equal in love when they "met like two eagles in mid-air," free and proud. Something like that. There were moments when Mary and I fit that definition, but now there's a third bird, perhaps a predatory hawk, bearing down on us. Take care.

F
***

From: **Conall Fitzgerald<Famtrack@corknet.ie**
To: **Fergus Fitzgerald<Brendan@bmts.com**
Subject: **missing link**

And you take care, too, cousin. You're a good man, if a touch thick at times. Interesting mystery letter you describe, and forgive me if you already realize this, but you should take it to your constabulary as well as your lawyer. I've had a jar to mull this over and have come to the inescapable conclusion that the letter raises the possibility that a third person either took part in the murder or is in a position to know what really happened. Or they feel sorry for you and the burden now on your shoulders. Some kind folk are like that, bless their souls, and will probably be leaving a pot of stew on your doorstep.

On the other hand, if the letter comes from a sense of guilt, as you suggest, then you have to ask why the writer feels guilty. Who knows? There may be fingerprints or sweat smudges on the letter that can be traced. I suspect the money has changed hands too often to provide a lead, but ya never know. Very, very interesting, and at the least, the letter does raise some reasonable doubt, as the barristers say.

Couple of related thoughts, now that you got me thinking. Terrible thing that. Anyway, if you do give the letter and money to the police, get a receipt. Your lawyer will probably arrange that anyway. Inspector Morse, the TV copper on the BBC, would probably want to know whether the currency is old or new and are the numbers in sequence. And another thing – what's the handwriting like? Just trying to help.

C.
***

From: **Fergus Fitzgerald <Brendan@bmts.com**
To: **Conall Fitzgerald <Famtrack@corknet.ie**
Subject: **update!**

First off, thanks for the advice. I'm off to my lawyer, right off as you might say, and then to our police. And we will ask for receipts or whatever the proper procedure is for such things. Some of the bills look pretty old and crumbled, much the way I feel most days. Yeah, the handwriting, legible but shaky, almost childlike or old.

Some more news. My lawyer called to say that we have another meeting with the crown attorney here in Little Current – and at his (the Crown's, that is) request, too. No word yet as to whether he will join our recommendation to remand Mary for assessment to the North Bay Forensic Detention Centre. It's about a four-hour drive northeast from here and is attached to a regional psychiatric hospital where she'll get decent care. The care is what we're gambling on, even though it's a medium security facility – locks and chain fences. But I doubt the Crown would come all this way just to say no. Still, he's a strict law-and-order guy, fair, I'm told, and not given to personal favors. If he does say no, Mary ends up in jail pending a bail hearing, and probably stays in jail until trial at least. If he agrees with our proposal, she'll be taken quickly from the hospital in Sudbury, held briefly in a holding cell in the courthouse, and then sent before a judge for a remand hearing. Thanks for staying in touch.

F.

Chapter 20

Superior Court, Sudbury, Two days later

"No, no… Please, I'll be good, *mamam*… No… *Gashi!*"

Fergus shivered, and his resolve to behave himself almost froze as he listened to Mary's soft whimpering in the prisoner's dock at her remand hearing. If nothing else, he must stick to his lawyer's advice to hold his tongue once the heavy courtroom doors had closed. But it was almost too much to bear to hear Mary reaching out for her *gashi*, her tribal mother, with the terrified cry of a woman suddenly turned child.

There was nothing he could do to help her. Nor should he even try, especially not at this time when bad was good and mad was even better. Or so Mike had said, as he warned Fergus to forget 'nice', to forget who Mary once was. "Just for today," he'd said, "okay?" And Fergus had agreed. The plan was simple: Convince the judge that Mary was not criminally responsible for whatever she did. Better she be roaring crackers than coldly sane.

This made faultless legal sense, Fergus knew, but he was still profoundly shaken when he entered the Sudbury courtroom in mid-afternoon and saw Mary. She was not the proud, feisty woman he'd first met in Wiarton, the woman who had taken a strip of hide off him for writing a smart-alecky column about her art classes for native kids. "You're in my no-fly zone," she had told him then, "so no cheap shots about my kids. Earn your beer money someplace else." Almost bloody miraculous, he thought, that we could move beyond sarcasm, put aside our protective shields and became so fond, so very fond of each other. So different, yet so much alike. And he remembered her healing graces that night when she had quietly sat him down, and breathed smoke and strength over and into him. Smudging, she had called it, an ancient native ritual and my gift to you.

Here, however, in this great hall of justice, he could not even light a candle for her, let alone a braid of sweetgrass. Even as a reporter back in Toronto, he had hated going to court with its feeling of grim finality, a sombre place with a funereal sense of a life lost, or at least misplaced.

Like today. Only a few hours earlier, Mary had been formally charged with murder by Detective Sergeant Rich Sawicki, quickly booked at the OPP regional detachment in Sudbury, and then brought to a holding cell in the courthouse. She would be called into court later.

Louisa Ledingham and Isaiah Steen, reporters' notebooks in hand, were waiting in court, and a Sudbury TV crew was stationed outside. Two detectives from the JFU drug squad were sitting in, just in case Mary said something about drugs. A young clerk from the German consulate in Toronto was also there.

Fergus still fretted about the mystery letter, now turned over to the OPP with the cash. A few fingerprints had been lifted, but no matches were found in the system. "That letter won't help Mary today," Michael Balfour advised him before the hearing. "Later, perhaps. Don't screw up our strategy and make the prosecution think we're jerking them around. McTavish may even believe you wrote the letter yourself."

But Fergus could not dismiss this possible link with the mystery woman Mary had talked about. Find a way to join those dots, he thought, and perhaps there would have been no need to arrest Mary. Did we – hell, let's face it, did I – give up on her too soon? Police and guards and now a judge rule her life. What's left of her academic freedom? Publish or perish. Ha, some irony. Yeah, just perish now.

His introspection ended abruptly, pushed aside as the judge entered. Fergus was relieved, at least for the moment, when he saw that Mary's handcuffs had been taken off. From his seat on the first row of benches, he forced a smile toward her, but Mary only stared blankly back at him. A court official in a blue uniform moved to stand behind her, tapped Mary on the elbow and motioned for her to stand.

Fergus held his breath as Mary abruptly turned and brushed aside the court officer's arm, with the angry, defiant look of an unruly child trying to pretend she was not frightened. She was, Fergus sensed, very much alarmed, and rapidly losing control as the officer's pungent smell touched off a deeper fear in her. When another officer moved to pin her other arm, Mary panicked and screamed one long piercing "Noooooooooooo!" She turned toward Fergus and Noel, and cried, "No…no… Don't do this, don't do… I'll be… Oh, oh." Suddenly, she pulled her arms free, and sank back into her chair, cringing into the corner with her knees up.

Thus began Mary's bail hearing in Sudbury's Superior Court. Madam Justice Rita Stroud had reluctantly agreed to hear the case, even though she was uncomfortable with the deal struck between McTavish and Balfour. Yes, there were defensible reasons for the arrangement, but from long experience, she knew this kind of accommodation would draw unfavorable attention. Every criminal lawyer in the region would almost certainly want the same treatment: off to the forensic detention centre for an assessment. Easy time.

"Ah, Mr. Balfour!"

"Yes, Your Honor?"

"Do you need time to get control of your client?"

"May I have a minute to consult with Dr. Fraser's psychologist, Dr. Noel Callaghan, who is—?"

"Better still, Mr. Balfour," Justice Stroud interjected sternly, "why doesn't Dr. Callaghan speak directly with Dr. Fraser. You either calm Dr. Fraser or I'll remand her over for custody here and now until she's able to behave."

Mary appeared to understand what was happening and where she was. She tried to smooth her hair, tugged at the top of her tracksuit, and then slowly, gasping a little, found the energy to speak.

"It's okay, I can do this. I'll be good. I promise I'll be good. Sometimes things scare me and I remember… Oh Lord, why am I here?"

Justice Stroud wondered to herself whether Mary was a superb actress or had unintentionally made her own case that she was mentally unstable. More likely the latter, she concluded, but she was still intrigued as to why Cal McTavish had agreed with the assessment recommendation. Strange winds from Manitoulin.

"Mr. McTavish, Mr. Balfour, you've entered a joint recommendation that I remand Dr. Fraser for a thirty-day assessment in a forensic unit," said Justice Stroud, looking over her half-moon glasses and holding up their briefing papers. "You are still in agreement, I trust?"

The two lawyers glanced at each other and nodded.

"Very unusual, gentlemen, almost a precedent. Two lawyers who can't or won't speak, and yet are in agreement with each other."

McTavish and Mike knew when to keep quiet, Mike in particular stifling an urge to tell Madam Justice that she was more than capable for speaking for everybody in the court.

"Very good, then. Your briefs, along with the preliminary assessment from the Northeast Mental Health Centre, plus the appropriate warrants, are hereby entered into the records of this proceeding. The agreement states that there are reasonable grounds under Section 672.12 of the Criminal Code to raise a question of whether the accused is unfit to stand trial because of mental disorder. Then, gentlemen, you won't mind if I question Dr. Fraser directly?

"Mr. Balfour? No? Good.

"Mr. McTavish, the same? Excellent.

"No objections, for the record. Let me explain a point of law, also for the record. As Dr. Fraser is charged with an indictable offense, murder, in this instance, then this hearing must be held before a superior court judge – which I am – and not a justice of the peace. NCR cases, by their very nature, are complex, drawing on both the Criminal Code and the Mental Health Act, and thus require broader judicial experience than most bail hearings can offer. So bear with me, gentlemen. In the end, it is this court that must be satisfied there are reasonable grounds for a Not Criminally Responsible assessment."

Having established the ground rules for the two lawyers, Justice Stroud turned toward Mary and changed her tone to one that was calmly reassuring with no sudden highs or lows in her voice. "Dr. Fraser, a few questions. Don't be scared, my dear. I'll try not to frighten you. Do you know who I am?"

Fergus held his breath, but smiled when Mary looked at him. Noel squeezed his hand tightly under her purse.

"I think so," said Mary softly.

"Can you speak a little louder so we can all hear you? It's important. Dr. Fraser, do you know who I am?"

"You're a judge, I think," said Mary again. "You dress like a judge, all black with that sash. Yes, you're a judge. I knew a judge once. A man. He had a moustache."

"Thank you, Dr. Fraser. Do you know why you're here?"

"Somebody's dead. Yes, I remember that."

"Do you know how that person died?"

"No...no...no...noooooooooo!" Mary's response was at first soft and pleading; then it rose with great gulping pauses. "Sometimes I...I see blood," she paused again, still gulping for air. "And then somebody's...somebody's hurting me...and I can't move...and it hurts again, down here. It hurts...it hurts..."

Mike Balfour stood up quickly. "Your Honor, I object. Surely you must realize the fragility of my client's composure. Please, in all humanity, Dr. Fraser needs help, not more interrogation. She's clearly regressing again, and it's possible she's confusing several events in her life. If your line of questioning continues, however valid and within your rights, as I acknowledge, then I fear more damage will be done and we may never unlock what is in her head."

Startled by the challenge, Justice Stroud had no idea how to respond. Mike was still standing, barely able to control his anger. Give in here, she thought, and I let the lawyers run my court. Do I deny the objection and risk censure if Fraser never recovers and the case remains open? Hmm. Let me throw it back to Cal; let's see where he really stands.

"You may have a point, sir. But this court has to be sure. Mr. McTavish, do you agree with Mr. Balfour in his objection?"

"This is a most complex case, Your Honor, relying on subjective assessments that may—"

"Mr. McTavish, you are an officer of this court. Yes or no? Do you join with Mr. Balfour's objection that the court's questions may do more harm than good? Don't just nod your head, sir. We want your words for the record. Yes, or no?"

Calvin John McTavish drew himself up. He still wondered if the Fraser woman and Dr. Callaghan had concocted a witches' brew that had twisted his common sense. But he also realized he would look like an even bigger idiot if he changed his mind. And, in reality, what was a thirty-day delay? More time to build a stronger case. And to obtain the DNA results.

"Yes, Your Honor. I agree with Mr. Balfour. As you yourself noted, he has raised a credible point of concern about the ultimate outcome of these proceedings."

"I take that as a yes. Very well then, gentlemen. We are agreed. Dr. Fraser, you may sit if you like. This won't take long. Dr. Fraser, I am remanding you to the Forensic Detention Centre at the North Bay Psychiatric Hospital for up to a thirty-day assessment under Section 672.11 of the Criminal Code to determine whether you are fit to stand trial and can participate in your own defense, and whether you could have appreciated the nature of the act of which you are accused. One other thing. I have also noted that you appear to have taken flight after the alleged offence, and therefore I am ordering that you be kept in a double-locked facility during your assessment. When the assessment is completed, you will be returned to this court. Court is adjourned."

Fergus could only blow a kiss to Mary as she was led from the court through a side door. He knew that she would be transported to North Bay almost immediately by the OPP, and that he would not be able to see her for several days. He also noticed that Cal McTavish had crossed the middle aisle in the courtroom and was speaking to Noel. Their words did not carry, but the exchange appeared contentious.

Later, when he caught up to Noel and Mike, he asked what Cal had wanted.

"That infuriating little man," said Noel, trying to retain her composure. "He's so petty and—"

"We already know that, Noel. What more is he looking for?"

"A lot more, Fergus. If the assessment review comes back that Mary is fit to stand trial, he'll want his pound of flesh, nasty and vindictive as that may seem."

"He'll go hard after Mary?"

"That's a given. Unfortunately, there's more than that. We've embarrassed him. Rita Stroud sensed that, too, so she went after him, tried to turn him.

"Mike was eloquently brilliant as always, but if Mary goes to trial, McTavish told me he might lay obstruction charges against me, and possibly you."

"Bloody hell! He couldn't, could he?"

"Fergus, let me put it this way. There's a thin line between justice and vengeance, if a line exists at all. My experience is that it takes a wise and humble person to find the difference within himself- or herself. Can Cal McTavish feel that shading in his own soul? I'm not sure."

Chapter 21

North Bay, Three days later

Fergus was miserable as he drove through the cold autumn rain to North Bay.

Staying on course was a challenge. Noel Callaghan and Mike Balfour had given him emphatic instructions that his first visit with Mary was a working trip, and not merely a compassionate reunion. "Be subtle," they had both told him, "but find a path into her mind."

Oh yeah? There was nothing subtle about the way he felt as he passed through North Bay. Deep within himself, he doubted whether Mary would ever be able to explain how Franz was murdered. At least the detention centre, eleven kilometers north of the city, did not look sinister or foreboding, but rather more like a university campus with roads winding through stands of birch trees.

By the time Fergus worked his way through the administrative processing, he fully appreciated that a forensic detention centre really was a jail, mercifully more humane than the bleak regional bucket in Sudbury, although inmate movement was still restricted, and doors still clanged shut behind him.

She was sitting alone in a meeting room, holding a watercolor as he entered. The earphones from her CD player blocked out the sound of his approach. He observed that, blessedly, she seemed calmer than she had since this latest nightmare had entrapped her. The anti-anxiety medications were working.

"Oh, Fergus, you're here. Can you hear this?"

She handed him the earphones, and he recognized the music they'd shared so often in their old farmhouse. The big, sensuous voice of Barbra Streisand purred before stretching into the higher notes, and then the lower register of Neil Diamond, just as romantically resonant, came through.

Mary closed her eyes and almost whispered, "It's so right, isn't it?"

Without any explanation, Fergus felt what she was saying.

"You don't bring me flowers anymore," Mary sang softly to him, head down.

"Yes, I do," said Fergus and handed her a bouquet of yellow and orange marigolds, picked from their garden on Manitoulin that morning. "Glorious, aren't they? We planted them so late, I didn't think they would bloom but they did."

However thoughtful and given out of love, the flowers had been an item of discussion with Noel before Fergus left. "Find a way to break through her sense of isolation and powerlessness," advised Noel. "Don't let her wallow in more anger and confusion. She'll be sitting alone, with her first-class, well-educated mind, transported from the Sudbury court in cuffs and shackles, routine but also traumatic. All her personal clothes will have been taken away, and she'll be wearing a two-piece orange sweat suit. At night, she'll sleep in a six-bed ward with who-knows-whom snoring beyond the curtains. Given all this, the flowers will remind her of the outside world, petal by petal, with their life and beauty."

Mary did indeed welcome the flowers. She held them to her cheek.

"This will be hard for you, Fergus," Noel had warned him. "I've talked this approach over with Mike Balfour and he agrees. Engage Mary's mind, so the healing can begin. Getting her into the detention centre was only an interim step. You can talk to her frankly, if you think she's responding well. No, don't mention the letter and the money you received. We don't want her talking to others about it. We may need it later, if only to argue reasonable doubt. If Mary mentions the other woman, be gentle. Don't push so hard that her mind wants to shut down again."

For the first few minutes with Mary, Fergus stuck with to casual, non-threatening questions.

"Food okay?"

"Not bad. It breaks the monotony."

"Treatment?"

"Lots of talking, with the predictable medical and psych tests: MMPI and that stuff."

"MMPI?"

"My recall's better now. Noel would know this: the Minnesota Multiphase Personality Inventory. God, I'm down to this. Don't they know or care who I am? Like my new outfit? Bugger them, that's what the others say. Leave the lights out and let me sleep."

Fergus had come prepared for an outburst, not the exact words, but the emotionally propelled frustration. "When Mary gets angry, and she will at this stage," Noel had told him, "just hold her for a few moments and then get her to build on the anger. Bring her into the legal strategy. And goal number one: Get me onto Mary's therapy team."

Fergus knew he had little time left, so he reached across and stroked Mary's hand. "Your skin's so dry," he said.

"I don't have any lotion here," she explained. "Can you—"

"Of course. From home. It's still there."

"From home. It's hard to imagine what that means anymore. I know the concept, but I can't visualize it. The links, the synapses, are gone."

"Remember this, then, Mary. There's another Streisand song that touched you."

"If I can, Fergus."

"'I Don't Break Easily.'"

"Oh, you sweet man, my Neil. That wonderful sound, pure Streisand. But look around, Fergus – this room, these outrageously ugly orange sweats. I did break, didn't I?"

Fergus knew he had to pull her back from self-pity. "Gently," Noel had said, "Don't trigger another flashback."

He needed a moment to frame his answer. "No, my love, no. Hold on to this, instead. The winds blowing through your life are strong, and you have to bend with them sometimes, like a Tom Thompson painting: a Georgian Bay evergreen, hard-rooted in the Shield. You didn't break, and what's more, I need your help."

"There's a devil in you, Fergus."

"Oh?"

"And oh, this moment feels good. Your devil, Fergus, he's Irish and he's literate. You must be part Ojibwa. What can I do?"

"For yourself, really, just this: Noel wants approval to share your files with the staff here."

"My files? My confidential files? Just turn them over to the doctors here, let them know everything that happened, everything I said to Noel? That's what Noel wants? To let them pick me apart?"

"Noel can be here to help and protect you, if you want her. This is your choice, when you feel ready. We all need to hear your story, Mary, not just about Franz, but what happened to you as a child. It's your story to tell."

"I wish you had been here yesterday, Fergus."

"Go on."

"When they were taking me for my medical, I could smell sweetgrass, and then I heard some drumming. There are native healers here. If…when...Noel comes, can she work with them, too?"

"Of course."

Little Current, the same day

Not so gentle were the police and media, both of whom were now running with the growing speculation that the late Franz Dietrich had been tied into dark forces: side deals, cover-ups, and the stench of blood money. And if Franz was the dealmaker, then what about Max Adler, his uncle? All the conjectures strung together; it seemed reasonable to ask whether Max's hotel was nothing more than an elaborate front for the Ecstasy trade. Manitoulin was already a thriving boating centre that provided easy access to America's great inland cities like Chicago, Detroit, and Milwaukee.

In short, the smell wouldn't go away while Mary had her thirty-day time-out. Rich Sawicki knew all too well that press conferences were tricky for police, even in the simplest of cases, and were particularly precarious once the judicial process had begun.

"No, no, no," Rich explained to one of the out-of-town reporters gathered around him in the detachment's main squad room for the press conference. "The remand order does *not* mean we are backing away from the murder charge. Dr. Fraser remains in custody in a detention centre. Both we and the crown attorney continue to believe there is sufficient evidence to charge her."

The reporter was dissatisfied with Rich's explanation and tried another tack. "What if she's found unfit to stand trial? Does she just walk away?"

Rich would like to throw the book at this jerk who had done no homework, but kept asking stupid questions under the self-redeeming theory that there were no stupid questions.

"The Criminal Code and the Mental Health Act are quite specific," Rich answered, now speaking deliberately but not quite masking his impatience. "If an accused, any accused, is found unfit to stand trial, then they are sent back to the original bail judge where the Crown can seek an order remanding the accused to a long-term psychiatric facility for an indeterminate time."

Another reporter, from a Sudbury radio station, joined in the attack. "For life? I mean real life?"

"Could be," said Rich. "The overriding issue is public safety."

"Kill once, could kill again, that it?"

"Listen up," Rich shot back quickly, anxious to explain himself before the press conference spun out of control. "What you said is too simplistic, even for a cop. We're getting ahead of ourselves, but I don't want you leaving here with that theory for your leads."

"So," another reporter took up the charge, "what *is* your opinion about, what's the term, the mentally disordered who commit crimes."

Rich weighed this question thoughtfully before he went on. "Just to clarify that last question, without any reference to the Fraser case, let me read something I brought along in anticipation of your questions."

No one challenged him. Rich fully understood, though, that the reporters' reticence did not mean they accepted his ground rules.

"Okay, then, the Health Ministry's answer in part reads: 'A single offence, even where the crime is very serious, such as murder, is not a good predictor of future violence. For example, research suggests that a person who has murdered a family member while in an extreme psychotic state is very unlikely to ever re-offend violently.'"

"I get your point, Detective, but Dr. Fraser didn't…isn't charged with killing a relative, so…"

"And I get your point. Now I know some of you have questions about the victim and the drug investigations now under way."

"Any busts yet?"

"We'll let you know if and when."

"Can you tell us why a task force has been organized?"

Before Rich could answer, Louisa Ledingham of the *Sudbury Star* fired another question at him.

"Was Dietrich involved?" asked Louisa, seeking confirmation for a story the paper had printed that morning, based on unnamed police sources. "I know we're getting close to the Fraser charge, but what can you say at this time?"

Rich relaxed. He and most cops in the area respected Louisa because she did her homework and protected her sources.

He also noticed that an older man, dressed in an expensive-looking black leather jacket and black turtleneck sweater, had entered the room. Max Adler. A lawyer Rich knew from Sudbury was with him. He concentrated on Louisa's question, to which he assumed she already knew the answer.

"Let me try to wrap up both questions with one answer. The lead investigators from the Sudbury Drug Squad and the RCMP will be holding their own press conference sometime early tomorrow. The OPP will be attending as a member of the Joint Forces Unit. We are also working with officials of the Canadian Customs and Revenue Agency, which is the first line of defense, particularly at our airports. At this point, I can say the JFU was organized in response to an increase in drug trafficking in the Sudbury and Manitoulin districts, specifically foreign sourced Ecstasy."

A hand was raised.

"I would like to finish before I answer more questions."

Rich took the reporters' silence as consent.

"Thanks. While the amounts involved are small, relative to larger centres, we believe we have an opportunity to knock out the supply lines. Louisa, you asked whether the late Franz Dietrich was involved. We can say this much, thanks to help from Interpol and Franz's own uncle, Maximillian Adler. Mr. Adler is back from Germany and has already given us a statement. He also indicated he wants to make it available."

The man in the black leather jacket held up his hand.

"Thank you, Detective," said Max. "I don't wish to interrupt your press conference, but I do wish to meet with the reporters later if you can recommend a place. Perhaps the—"

"Why not here? And now?" Louisa probed quickly. "We've all got deadlines, Detective. But let's be practical, Okay?"

Rich knew when to concede a point. "Would you like to read your own statement, Mr. Adler?"

"As you wish, Detective Sawicki," Max replied from the back of the room, speaking slowly, sounding more tired than thoughtful. "I need to do this."

A new energy swept the room. TV camera crews turned their lights back on, and reporters checked their tape recorders. Max's lawyer sensed trouble ahead, and whispered to his client to stick to the prepared statement The assembled reporters and police could not hear the exchange until Max shook his head, stepped away from his lawyer, and said audibly and curtly, "Mistakes, tragic mistakes, have been made, and I must rectify them."

His lawyer's concerns were well founded. Now that the drug investigation was underway, several of the JFU officers were speculating among themselves that if Max was responsible for bringing Franz to Canada, was Max a silent partner of some sort?

Rich, too, wondered whether Max was about to confess some criminal involvement, perhaps even in Franz's murder. *This is bizarre,* he told himself. *Bad guys usually don't hold press conferences. Most guilty minds seek absolution, though. And he already has his lawyer here. Better be prepared if he spills.*

Slowly, Max walked to the front of the room to face the media. He tried to stand tall, but faltered and had to grab the back of a nearby chair for balance. His blood sugar levels, always a problem, were low, affecting both his coordination and concentration. Nevertheless, when his lawyer insisted that Max issue a statement rather than make an appearance, Max had become irritated, and demanded that he be allowed to make peace with himself, at least.

Sawicki offered the older man a glass of water, from which Max gulped.

"I know what some of you must think of me," Max began, his voice trembling. "If I had not come to Canada with my hotel project, none of this would have happened. Franz, my beloved sister's son, would still be alive. I have no children of my own, and Franz's destiny was crucial to me. And, of course, Dr. Fraser would not be in jail."

As Max paused to drink more water, Isaiah Steen from the *Expositor* jotted a note that, while Max did not accuse Mary Fraser of killing Franz, neither did he say anything to defend or absolve her. Interesting. 'Does Max blame her for all this?' he asked himself. 'Or is he simply trying to divert the police away from his own guilt?'

Max steeled himself to go on. "But of course, you know that already. I feel very old now, so please excuse me if I ramble. I must tell you about Franz. Your authorities say we can take his body home to Saxony next week. This will be sad for my sister. Violent death has been a constant reminder of life's fragility for her. Our parents died in the Dresden firebombing by the Allies in 1945, and her husband was taken away by the East German secret police, the Stasi, during a crackdown on non-Communist political dissidents during the 1960s. Like so many other good people, he never returned. All because he helped distribute an underground paper. My sister did not remarry.

"I regret that I did not provide my sister or Franz with more assistance then, but I was too busy trying to improve my own lot, first as a simple bureaucrat for the Communists, later as a developer. But always, most determinedly so, staying removed from politics. We all try to survive in our own way.

"Now Franz is gone – another violent death for my sister and myself to deal with. I assure you, it is very painful. Without a strong man close to him, Franz had become quite obsessed with his grandfather, his father's father, a Wehrmacht officer who was killed during the Normandy landings. In turn, and in many ways – too many to my eternal regret – that is who Franz had become. His grandfather was Franz's hero: a daring young adventurer given an Iron Cross for crushing French resistance fighters without remorse.

"My lawyer is shaking his head, and so I must get to the point of why we are here and why your police are investigating Franz's death and his involvement in drugs. I am also told that I must not attribute guilt to anyone except myself. I would… May I sit for a moment, sir?"

Rich nodded his approval, and Marston refilled Max's water glass. Max sat heavily on a desk.

"Was my nephew involved in drugs? We knew he was using drugs, and indeed, that is why we brought him to Canada – to begin a new life. Perhaps I was too naïve, and too caught up in my own dreams. I now know from the German and Canadian police that Franz was using an inheritance from his grandfather to finance drug trafficking from Germany. Such an irony. His grandfather's wealth, no doubt stolen and amassed during the war and safely deposited in Swiss banks, was eventually used to hurt so many German youngsters, and now some Canadians, too.

"His mother and I, unfortunately, were more concerned about his mental balance. Franz was extremely bright and could be gracious at one moment, then suddenly becoming brutal and self-serving, telling us we would never understand him, never be free ourselves until we, too, used his drugs that would wipe out memory. Franz's new world order: no memory, no history, no conscience. I consulted a psychiatrist friend who told me Franz was showing classic psychopathic symptoms. Put him in a business, I was told; many firms value someone like him who enjoys having blood on his hands.

"That is why I brought him with me, partly out of guilt, I confess, and partly because I needed a more pragmatic partner to balance my vision. I must reconsider whether I will continue to work here, or even if I am still welcome.

"My lawyer is pointing to his watch. When lawyers become worried about the time they are spending with a client, then it truly is time to be worried. For the record, I was not involved in Franz's drug operations, neither here nor in Germany. Before I returned from Germany, I voluntarily provided police there with complete access to all my business and financial records. I am offering the same to Canadian officials. If Franz ever used my name, it was without my knowledge or approval.

"I am tired now, too tired for any questions, which I know journalists always have. If you report any of this, say that Max Adler has apologized for bringing his nephew to Canada in search of a new, life-giving vision that turned most deadly."

Max turned to Detective Sawicki, and made an attempt to salvage what was left of his energy – and his life.

"May I go now, sir? It is time to talk to my employees about their future."

Rich shrugged his shoulders, not quite convinced by what he had heard. But he also knew he still did not have any hard evidence to detain the old man. Yes, Franz used family wealth to finance drug shipments to Canada. Nazi blood money here on Manitoulin. But if his own hands are clean, then what? Let's wait for the forensic audits. What Max did was stupid, probably self-serving and immoral, but not a crime.

"You may go, Mr. Adler. But please, do not leave Manitoulin without letting us know."

The reporters appeared stunned as Max and his lawyer left. Then they pulled out their cell phones and tried to explain to their news editors what had just happened.

Early that evening

"Heading home?"

Rich Sawicki did not want to be the first to leave, even though the day had been long and demanding. The early news reports from the press conference had sparked more phone calls. A clerk from the Crown Attorney's office called to say that Cal McTavish expected a full transcript of Max's statement for review. Sawicki knew McTavish had been upset that the OPP had not held Max for further questioning without the media present.

"Not yet, Chris. Got some call backs to make first."

"Want me to handle some of those?"

"Nothing going on in your life?"

"None of your business, sir. Just give me a couple of those, and we both can get out of here sooner."

"Touchy, are we? Take this one then: An old woman from Sheg wants to see me about something. Have her call me in the morning, around ten."

The younger detective went back to his own desk, put some files away, and then made the call. The conversation did not last long, and he immediately made notes before he walked back to Sawicki's desk.

"I told her to come in tonight. She'll be here in—"

"I thought you wanted to get out of here," Rich snapped back quickly. "Dammit, Chris, I told you tomorrow—"

"She broke off before I could stall her. Besides, I think we should hear her tonight, before this gets all over the island."

"You do, do you? I gave you instructions, Constable!"

"Sir, it's about the Fraser case."

"And?"

"She says she knows who killed the German."

"She did it herself?"

"I don't think so. I could hear someone, perhaps a kid, in the background telling her to get in the car. Someone's coming with her."

"This for real, Chris?"

"She sounded all right, old and tired, but determined."

"How long before she gets here?"

"Let's say fifteen minutes."

"Too late to order in food."

"Anything else you want me to do, sir?"

"Check the interview rooms. Any coffee around?"

Chapter 22

Little Current, OPP squad room, later that evening

"Where in hell are they?" snarled Rich Sawicki. "Dammit! Grandma and whoever's coming with her, they could've walked here by now."

Marston tried to ignore him, "So what if they don't show?" he countered, more crisply than usual. "We've already got a suspect locked up, and evidence that rocks."

"No second thoughts, Chris?"

"That's bullshit, sir. I did my job and...and I really don't give a damn who Mary Fraser is, or that Fergus friend of hers. It's her fingerprints in the victim's blood, and that locks it for me."

"Leave Fraser out of this, Chris."

"If *you* can, sir!"

Marston's challenge bit deeply. But rather than argue, Rich shook his head, then slammed his hand on his desk, turning away. He worried that he might have charged Mary so quickly because he hadn't wanted to show favoritism. He could have, and should have, waited for the full DNA results. Rich feared it had been his professional self-image that had mattered: Was he tough enough to charge a woman who had so much to offer?

'Or just do my damn job,' Rich told himself. 'If I can.'

He was not alone. He had heard the squad room chatter. Every experienced officer in the squad worried that the detachment itself would be on trial if the wrong person was charged. For starters, the judge in Sudbury would be ticked off big-time, and so would McTavish.

Nor would the fallout stop there. Within the OPP's own ranks, the know-it-alls at headquarters in Orillia would be dumping on Inspector Robitaille from North Bay, who had supervised the investigation as case manager. In turn, Robitaille would be on Rich's head, a probability that had become a blistering reality.

Robitaille was already on his way to resume case command. It would take another ninety minutes before the inspector arrived, but he had made it abundantly clear he wanted in on major decisions.

"Give them five more minutes, Chris, and then go find 'em!"

Rich made a mental note of the time, trying to project a professional calm. Don't pre-judge this, he told himself. Reason it through. Hearsay? Could be she feels sorry for Mary Fraser? Perhaps she heard noises, but didn't see anything. Or perhaps she had a dream – the unconscious reasoning of a mind that doesn't want to see a good woman punished for killing a drug-dealing scumbag. Perhaps Mary's lawyer put the old woman up to this.

A few minutes passed, and Chris could not watch the clock any longer.

"Bring them in?"

"No, no, no, Constable," said Rich unable to keep sarcasm out of his voice. "Be nice. Let them wander around. Talk to a bunch of people. Yes, dammit, find them, bring them in ASAP, and for God's sake, don't let them near anyone else until we check this out. Are the interview rooms ready?"

"Yes, sir," said another constable.

"Video set up, too? Audio?"

"Almost."

"Both rooms?"

"Will be in a couple of minutes. Checking tapes and timer stamps. You want coffee?"

"Yeah, lots of it. Better get some tea, though, for grandma. Let's play nice, folks. I'll be upstairs waiting."

The lower street door of the two-story building opened just as Marston reached it, and an elderly native woman came in, followed by a young male, tall and thin, perhaps still a teenager, with a black ball cap pulled down over his eyes and a garbage bag dangling from one hand. The woman went to the counter and spoke to the civilian clerk.

"I told the detective I wanted to see him. My grandson, he's here, too."

"Did you call earlier, ma'am?"

"Needed to get gas. Takes time. It costs a lot."

"I think you're expected. Let me check, ma'am."

It was dark outside, with little traffic. There were no other visitors in the squad room. Two officers were working the phones, and the others pretended to be busy, fully aware of what was going down and the possible consequences. Marston told the clerk to bring the old woman and young man through to the squad room before heading there himself.

Grandma was small, shorter by at least a foot than most of the officers. Hard to tell her age, Chris thought. She could be in her seventies or eighties, judging by her grey hair gathered loosely in a ponytail. Her face was deeply etched with wrinkles, and the once full cheeks now drooped into heavy jowls. There was no doubt, though, from her expression that she was determined, set on a mission. When her grandson pulled back, looking around nervously, and wiping his nose with his sleeve, she stopped, stared hard into his face, then reached up and yanked the cap off his head.

To Chris's eye, he was a typical kid in a tough spot: spare frame slouched into an over-sized, black nylon sports jacket and cargo pants. His head was clean-shaven, but the bravado was gone from his wide shoulders, and his eyes were sullen rather than defiant. If anything, he dressed like an Afro-American street kid. Even grandma wore a bright red Tommy Hilfiger jacket.

"This is Shane. He wants to tell everything to the detective."

Marston was the first to respond, standing in the middle of the squad room.

"May I have your names, please?"

The old woman paused, looking around before answering. "Charity Shigwadja. I can spell that, if you want."

"Just write it out please, ma'am," said Chris, handing her a pad and pencil. "And your grandson?"

Shane didn't answer until his grandmother glared at him through thick glasses.

"Kanasawae, Shane Kanasawae."

"How old are you, Shane?"

"Nineteen, yeah, last June."

"If you will sit here for a moment, ma'am, I'll get Detective Sawicki."

"Okay. We can wait. Shane brought some clothes with him. They're in the bag on that chair over there, so nobody will trip over it. Okay?"

Without giving an answer, Chris bounded up the stairs to the second-floor interview room where Sawicki waited.

"They're here, Chris?"

"Yeah. They look serious. The grandson, Shane, even brought a bag of clothes, so he's thinking he ain't going home soon. But one question first."

"Go on."

"If we spook the old lady and the kid, do you think they'll walk out?"

"No, they made a decision and they've got a story to tell. Make sure we offer her some tea."

"Tea?"

"Yes, tea. We honor her. Hell, I'd give her tobacco if I could, because she's the key."

"Not the kid? He's here, too, so he must have a conscience."

"Maybe. But more importantly, his grandmother is here. She's the one who called us, and that means a lot in Ojibwa culture. Peltier tells me that's where the tribal wisdom sits – with the elders, especially the women. Respect that. Let grandma stay with him until we find out what he knows. And watch your language."

"Huh?"

"The Ojibwa see the legal system differently than we do, not as adversarial. Even the English language seems way too harsh and judgmental to most natives – too many adjectives and adverbs."

"Man, you want us to play patty-cake with the old lady?"

"Just protecting ourselves. Don't dig us into an even bigger hole."

"You're telling me something?"

"Yeah. Round one: We check out a few things with grandma and the kid together. If the story holds, then you get to interview the kid first. Not me. Just you. Whole world knows Fraser's already been charged, so let's keep this clean."

"So you want me to watch what I say? Don't deal 'em a race card?"

"You're close. Listen up. If the kid talks, we don't need a false confession that falls apart at trial."

"Christ, Rich, I'm not going to smack him around. Give me some credit. I've done interrogations before."

"Cool it, Chris. This isn't Winnipeg or Saskatoon."

"Just Manitoulin. So?"

"Some natives will confess because they think that's what we want them to say, and they don't want to insult us. Trust me on this: Harmony and respect are big values in native culture. If the kid did it, let him tell us. If he goes quiet for a bit, don't panic and don't lead him. If he has something to say, he'll get to it in his own time."

"You've got a bad sense about this one, don'tcha?"

"Not good, Chris, not good. My gut tells me this is going to be one crapping big mess before it's over. By the book, young guy. Just find out where McTavish will be tonight if we need him."

"Tell him why?"

"Try not to. But hell, we can't afford to blindside him."

Twenty minutes later, Rich and Chris settled Charity and Shane into an interview room. Charity was given a chair at the end of the long table facing the video camera on the opposite wall. Her grandson sat beside her, legs sprawled as he looked at the wall and the camera mounts.

"Mrs. Shigwadja, Charity, help me here," said Rich quietly. "Do you know who Fergus Fitzgerald is?"

"Yes. He gave me a drive one day."

"So you know him. Did you ever call him or send him anything?"

"Yes. I wanted to thank him."

"What did you give him?"

"A letter."

"Just a letter? Did you give him anything else?"

"Some money."

"How much?"

"About $500, I think. It was a lot, but my sister's family helped."

Rich opened a file, pulled out a sheet of paper, and handed it across the table.

"Is this the letter you wrote?"

"Yes."

"I want to ask you a question about the letter."

Rich waited a moment, and then took the silence as agreement.

"Your letter said the money was for Dr. Fraser's lawyer. 'She didn't do it,' you wrote. Help me here so I can understand. You believe Dr. Fraser didn't kill Franz Dietrich?"

"She didn't kill the young German."

"If Dr. Fraser didn't kill him, then you believe somebody else did. Is that correct?"

"Yes."

Rich suggested they take a break for a minute, now that they had linked the old woman to the letter. Charity smiled at him as he and Chris stepped into the hallway.

"Is she playing us? Why doesn't she get right to it, dammit? Rich, I know what you said, but this goes too far."

Sawicki raised an eyebrow, but didn't reply.

Once back in the interview room, Rich apologized for the interruption, then offered Charity more tea and picked up the thread of her last statement.

"Take your time, Charity. I appreciate this is difficult for you. May we start again?"

"Yes, please. It is the right time now."

"Thank you. Before I went out, you said you believe that Mary Fraser did not kill Franz Dietrich, and that you believe somebody else did. Do I have this right? Take your time if you want to think about this."

"What you said is true, Detective Sawicki. I have told you what I know to be true. Now I want my grandson to tell his story."

"Shane, are you ready?"

No answer. The strong overhead lights reflected off a thin sheen of sweat on his bald head.

"Shane, your grandmother says this is the right time."

"Yeah, Grandmother's pretty cool. Been there for me a lot. Lets me stay with her sometimes, and she tells me stories."

"About Mary Fraser?"

"No, not this time. Yeah, I did it."

"Did what, Shane? Help us here. First, though, it is my duty to tell you that you have the right to retain and instruct counsel without delay. If you are charged with an offence, you may apply to the Ontario Legal Aid Plan for assistance. Do you want a lawyer?"

"No."

"Are you sure?"

"Yeah."

"You're a stand-up guy, Shane, and we want to help. So what did you tell your grandmother?"

There was a long pause – and both Rich and Chris held themselves dead still.

Finally Shane, in the low, respectful voice that Rich was sure his grandmother had ingrained in him since early childhood, cut into the silence. "I killed him. Franz. That's why she sent the money to that Irish guy. Thought it might help."

It was Rich's turn to hold back, knowing he should confirm what he had been told. "Shane, I want to be clear about this. You killed Franz Dietrich. Is that what you told your grandmother?"

"Yeah, that what's I told her. Then we talked a lot."

Rich sat back, weighing what he had heard. He motioned for Chris to jump in.

"Shane, like hey, guy, you're a good grandson. And you've got an awesome grandmother. We all respect her. First of all, thanks big time for coming forward. We respect that. Now we want to talk to you and your grandmother separately, because we need to know more details."

"More questions?" asked Charity. "It is late for me."

Rich answered.

"Let me explain. Dr. Fraser is a good woman, and it's obvious that you want to help her. We all know that, but the evidence against her is strong, really tight. That's why she was charged. If she is innocent, however, then you'll have to help us with some more details. Detective Marston here will talk with Shane in another room, and Charity, you and I will have more tea here. Okay?"

She nodded, saying nothing.

As they left, Rich told Chris to read Shane his caution again and offer him a lawyer, and to be sure he did so on camera.

"Thanks for taking the oath, Charity."

"Telling truth is easy."

"Not everyone wants to hear the truth," said Rich, "so we have to protect you."

"Okay. What do you want me to tell you?"

"Just a few things. Let's start with where you were on the night Franz was murdered."

"He was not a good person. He sold Shane drugs."

"We can ask Shane about that, Charity, but first, I need to know where you were that night. At home? Visiting your sister?"

"I was home alone. Lester, my man, he died a long time ago. Bad heart."

"Does Shane stay with you sometimes?"

"Yes, since he was a child, when his mother went away. She used to be gone a lot. Little Shane would come over and play, and I would tell him stories."

"Do you tell him what to do?"

"No. It is good not to interfere. We respect our children. Sometimes we tell stories to show them how to live."

Rich wanted to move her mind back to the murder, and to what she saw, if anything. Repeating what Shane had told her could quickly be rejected as hearsay. Moreover, Charity looked weary, and Rich was worried that she might not be able to go on much longer.

"Charity, let's concentrate on what happened the night Franz was killed. Okay?"

"Okay."

"Did Shane come to your house that night?"

"I…think so."

"You think so?" said Rich, trying to keep panic from seeping into his voice. "Why do you think so, Charity? This is important."

"Because he was there in the morning when I got up to go to the bathroom."

"What was he doing?"

"Sleeping on the couch."

"In his pyjamas?"

"No, just his underwear."

"Where were his clothes?"

"He told me he put them with things to get washed."

"Did you wash his clothes then?"

"Not right away. Decided not to. He pulled on some old clothes he keeps at my place, and then left. Said he'd be away a few days, hunting."

Rich got up, told Charity he was getting her more tea, and went into the monitoring room. The case managers from North Bay had arrived, and already Inspector Robitaille was watching the video. They developed tactics as the session progressed. Standard interrogation procedure.

"Stick with the kid's clothes, Rich," said Robitaille. "Can't tell whether she's holding back, but we need to know why what's-his-name, Shane, wanted his clothes washed in the middle of the night. The rest of you agree?"

Heads nodded, and Rich went back to the interrogation room with more tea for Charity.

He noticed her eyelids were heavy, almost covering her pupils.

"Charity, I know it's late and we want to get you home as soon as we can. Just a few more questions. Okay?"

"Okay."

"When did you wash Shane's clothes?"

"I didn't."

"Oh?"

"I didn't think I could get the blood out."

"Blood? Do you remember how much blood, and what it was on?"

"Too much to wash with the other stuff. Mostly on his jacket and jeans. That's what I remember. Messy, like after a hunting trip."

"Where are the clothes now? At your house, or did Shane take them?"

"No. Not there."

"Where then?"

"I brought them here, in the garbage bag."

"Here? Downstairs? Really?"

"Seemed like right thing to do. Nobody else wanted them."

"Okay then. So where did you leave them?"

"One of the officers told me to put them on a chair so nobody would trip over them. So I did."

"I'll be back in a couple of minutes," said Rich, rushing out the door and bumping into Robatille as he did.

"You've got them stowed away, Rich," said Robitaille, almost screaming. "Tell me you have! Tell me it's not another monumental fuck up! Of all the incompetence. Of all the sloppy… Find that bag or you're going to…"

Once downstairs, Rich yelled for attention.

"Stop everything you're doing! Everything, dammit! Now! Nobody comes in or out. The old woman brought in a green garbage bag full of bloody clothes. Anyone see it?"

Everyone shook their head. They all looked under their desks. No green garbage bag. Sawicki and Robitaille looked stunned.

"Take another look," he yelled, pointing to a constable who had just returned from the washroom. "You, too! Everybody!"

"Sorry, sir, I needed a break. Couldn't wait."

"Christ, you're taking a leak and we're missing evidence."

"What're you looking for?"

"A garbage bag of clothes."

"Green?"

"No, you dimwit. Pink. Flaming pink. It's a green garbage bag, just like all—"

"Like this bag, sir?"

"Give it to me. Where in hell was it?"

"Put it in one of the lockup cells while I took a break. Thought perhaps the young guy might need a change of clothes later if we hold him overnight. Is it important?"

"Big guy," said Rich, "we owe ya. Hell, I owe ya."

Barely controlling a war whoop, he turned to Robitaille.

"Well, how 'bout that, Inspector? Not too shabby for incompetents, eh? Do you want to examine the clothes yourself, careful of course not to get any blood on you, or shall I ask my fine detectives to take over, sir?"

No answer.

"Okay, by the book, then," Rich said, striding into the middle of the squad room. "Got a lot of work ahead, folks. First, I go back to get grandma to confirm this is the bag she brought in and these clothes are the ones Shane left behind."

An older constable who usually handled community relations caught the upbeat.

"Want me to call the forensic guys in the Sault to match the blood and prints?"

"Yeah, get them here ASAP. Looks like we're starting all over again. It's not conclusive that the kid killed the German. Nothing we got so far wipes out the Fraser charge. Anything from Chris and the kid yet?"

Inspector Robitaille, rubbing his throbbing temples, stepped up to Rich.

"No hard feelings, eh? Nothing personal, of course."

"Of course, sir."

Robitaille moved on. "Any progress with Shane?"

"Nothing, I'm afraid. Just to be safe on this, Marston had the young native speak to the duty counsel on the 800 line to Toronto. Kid hasn't said much since. Just sits there."

"Look, Shane, we can sit here all night," said Chris. "That's your right. But heck, man, help yourself; are these your clothes or not?"

"Don't have to. That's what the lawyer man said. Be cool like."

"Okay. We arranged for you to talk to a lawyer, so it's only natural to take his advice. Got it, man. I understand that. Probably do the same myself, if I was sitting in your place, lots of bad stuff waiting for me. Like you said, be cool."

"You ain't never been like this, never been the loser, never—"

"Could have been, Shane. Caught a few breaks, though, and now I get to ask the questions. Tell ya what. Forget about the murder for a while. Franz, he can wait. Tell me, how'd ya meet him?"

"Easy. One of the construction guys, he told me Franz was looking for native stuff, like the old scrolls that are worth a lot. Needed someone who knows where the burial grounds are to sneak in after dark and prowl around. Sounded cool. Not much else to do here, except construction, or join the army. Just more people tellin' me what to do."

"Get paid?"

"Yeah, more money than I ever saw. Even promised to take me to Germany with him. Gonna to be partners, him and me. Took me into Sudbury couple of times. Met some bikers in a bar. Real scary, too. But they liked Franz."

"And you liked Franz? He was good to you."

"Like, say?"

"You rolled with him?"

"Rolled with him?"

"Never messed with you then?"

"Could be chin doubter sometimes, if he was usin'."

"Huh? Chin doubter?"

"You're not Nish, are you?"

"No, Shane. So what's it mean?"

"Chin doubter? He could screw me around. Real tight most of the time, then he'd start playin' games with me."

"That's why you killed him?"

"Not supposed to talk 'bout that. That's what the lawyer man said. Say nothin'."

"But that's not what your grandma told you."

No answer.

"She's a good woman, always been there for you, no games. That right?"

No answer.

"She said you had something to tell us."

No answer.

Still in his first year on the crime unit, Chris struggled with the silence. He knew everything he said was being monitored, and that if he bullied Shane too much, whatever Shane told him might not ever make it to open court. So he sat still for another minute, watching Shane fiddle with his shirt, becoming almost arrogant as the seconds ticked by. Buddy boy, Chris finally told himself, you're not baby-sitting, so either crack this kid or move out.

"So, she's a liar then," he said leaning into Shane's face, almost nose-to-nose. "If you won't talk to us, then your grandmother is a liar, a foolish old woman who makes up stuff. Just a miserable, stupid, old, rotten liar who wants to jerk us around."

"Leave her out of this. She's not a liar. She's—"

"Then it's time to stand up for her, Shane. Be the man today. Make her proud."

Shane got up, fists clenched. For a long moment, he looked out the window, and then faced Rich.

"Okay, okay, I did it. That's all. I hit him and he's dead. So leave me alone."

"Shane, that was good. You're a stand-up guy. Help me understand what happened."

"It was dark, no lights up there, and he looked like a bear, all big and scary-like, when I saw him."

"Bear? Don't play me, man. No time for *Winnie the Pooh*. Forget the bear shit. Just tell me why you were there."

"Hey, man, I got real scared."

"Yeah, so we all get scared in the dark. Just tell me what you did, how you hit him."

"Okay. If that's the way you want it. I was dealing some E for him, not much, and I had some money coming."

"Just to be clear, you were selling Ecstasy? E?"

"Not much now. Could'a been big with the tourists. Easy money for a few pills."

"Where were you?"

"On the construction site."

"For the new hotel?"

"Yeah, the one Franz's uncle's building. We met there sometimes because it's dark, and we can come in through the back trails from the village."

"What time?"

"Didn't check, but I had some beers in Espanola. Came back after the hockey game, so it musta been after midnight."

"Then what?"

"Didn't see Franz at first. Too dark. Thought he was holding back my money, so I was a little pissed off."

"And?"

"Then he just sorta dropped out of the sky, yelling and screaming at me, part human, part bear like, and he kept stompin' around trying to scare me. I told him I wanted my money, and he called me some fuckin' Indian, and said I was only gonna piss it away anyway like my ol' man, so what good was money to me? He threw some coins at me for a cheap bottle of wine."

"That made you angry, Shane?"

"He shouldn't have said what he did, about fuckin' Indians. I wanted my money, so I grabbed a piece of scaffolding, one of the big metal rods lying around, to scare him. I just wanted the money I was owed, but he kept coming at me, still screaming, so I hit him."

"How many blows? Do you remember?"

"Can't say."

"Stay with me, Shane. We're almost through. Are you saying you won't tell me or that you don't remember?"

"Don't remember. Happened too fast. Not what I wanted anyways."

"And no one else saw this. That's right?"

"Just Dr. Fraser."

"Dr. Mary Fraser?"

"She was there. Ya, just her. Excited like."

"Did she come with you?"

"No, she musta come alone."

"Did she do anything, or just stand there?"

"Hard to remember, but I think she got in front and yanked the metal bar from me. Howled something awful and then threw it away. We looked at him, Franz, for a bit. But he was clear dead, head all smashed in. Some blood on me. Her, too, I guess. Then I ran into the woods and went to Grandmother's and changed."

The door opened behind them, and Rich Sawicki reached in and handed Chris the garbage bag.

"Don't let him touch it again. Just ask him to identify it."

"Got it. Better stay with me in case he balks."

Chris turned back to Shane, who was now slumped in his seat, all resistance long gone.

"One last thing, Shane. Are these your clothes?"

"Yeah."

"Were you wearing them when Franz was killed?"

"Yeah, that's what I had on. Jeans and a shirt. Franz bought them for me. In Sudbury. Nice jacket, eh?"

Chapter 23

Next morning

Fergus finally went to war.

At first, he was euphoric when his friend Matt Peltier told him a young native man had been arrested. He tidied the house, changed the linens on the bed, picked flowers, all the while humming more Streisand and Diamond themes.

Around noon, though, Michael Balfour called.

"You've got good news, I hope, from McTavish," said Fergus. "When can I pick Mary up?"

"That's not why I called, Fergus."

"Huh? She's not coming home? That's it? Noooo."

"I'm afraid so. There are complications that—"

"Complications? COMPLICATIONS? Fucking Jesus, Michael, what's going on?" said Fergus, banging his coffee cup down on the kitchen counter, hard enough to chip the handle.

"Easy, man. We knew this might go south. Calmly does it. Just tell me what's going on in your mind."

"Forget me. My hand is bleeding a little, that's all. Oh man, I wish I had that righteous little prick McTavish by the—"

"Bleeding? What was that noise? Did you break something?"

"Mike, you wanna hold my hand? Sweet Jesus, fuck it, man. You're some lawyer. Mary's still in jail, and you want to give me a Band-Aid."

"I heard something breaking, Fergus."

"Bloody coffee cup."

"You dropped it?"

"It broke on the counter, so what the hell, I threw it through the window. Screw you!"

"Threw it? Are you alone?"

"Of course I'm alone, Mike. That native kid says he killed Dietrich, but oh no, Mary doesn't get to come home. Know what?"

"We're all sorry–"

"No, dammit! I'm going to McTavish myself. I know where he lives and I'll—"

"FERGUS! Listen to me. Okay? Just say okay."

"Okay what?"

"Okay that you'll listen to me before you make a real mess of this. McTavish is a jerk. We know that. But you're of no use to Mary if you can't control yourself. We'll—"

"Don't lecture me, man. I'll do whatever I want."

"Let me repeat. You're of no use to Mary with your raw anger. Take the long view. Good man. We'll find a way to get her out. But not at this moment, so tell me you won't go near McTavish without me there."

"Whatever!"

"Just say it, Ferg, that you won't go off half-cocked."

"Okay, dammit, for now. Okay, okay. I'll go fix the bloody window. But you fix McTavish. Just squeeze, really squeeze the shit out of him, any way you can."

Meanwhile, news that a young native had confessed to Franz's murder swept through the island. Most folks were stunned. The OPP would confirm only that Shane had been arrested, preferring not to comment until the bail hearing was held in a day or two. Nor would Shane's grandmother talk, still hoping she could bring him home soon, although given the horrific circumstances, it was unlikely he would be released on bail.

In truth, Shane's confession raised more questions than it resolved: questions mostly about Mary. Everyone knew she had blood on her hands. What was she doing hanging around with a native in the middle of the night? Downright strange, that Fraser woman. Her and a young native, would you believe it? And a much younger native at that.

Late afternoon

From: **Fergus Fitzgerald <Brendan@bmts.com**
To: **Conall Fitzgerald <Famtrack@corknet.ie**
Subject: **me again**

God, fella, you're worse than Michael Balfour, all a'tizzy because I wanted to tear off McTavish's balls for ripping out my heart. Okay, rant's over. The apocalypse passes. But lordy, it felt good, letting go and unleashing all that anger. I've bottled it up for much too long. Thanks, mate, for offering to send Mary flowers. Gracious indeed. More legal hurdles to get past.

Let me get back to basics, if only to clear my head.

The police are convinced Shane, the native kid, is guilty. Peltier now tells me the confession has been accepted as authentic, because he mentioned some crime scene evidence that had not been publicly released, something about a bearskin found at the scene. Moreover, the blood on the clothes he left with his grandmother matched Franz's blood type. Our cops spent considerable time talking to Shane's family and friends, but they haven't released any details.

So if the cops and the Crown believe the kid did it, why haven't the charges against Mary been withdrawn? Michael Balfour keeps telling me to be patient, but I'm left with the feeling I'm standing on a beach where the tide is pulling sand from under my feet, and there is absolutely nothing I can do about it.

The catch is this: Whatever the native kid did, Mary's prints still link her to the victim and, moreover, she did utter some nasty threats against Franz. But why didn't she stay snuggled in bed with me that night, and let the cops worry about the drugs? All the police forces around here have teamed up to investigate the increase in trafficking since Franz's arrival. Nasty bit of irony here, but it seems logical to conclude that they could have – dammit, should have – cleared up the mess and sent Franz packing. That in turn would have left Mary and me to get on with our lives.

Not Mary's way. She's not a spectator. She's not content to let problems pile up around her like I am, most of the time, not with all her admirable and loveable qualities. But now, quite literally, she's stuck with blood on her hands. So where's the logic in this? Shit just happens – perhaps that's the ultimate human condition.

Ignore that pretentious posturing if you like. Yeah, I'm venting. Back to the central question: Since Mary was at the crime scene, what are the legal consequences? Manitoulin has a righteous crown attorney who seems honor-bound to squeeze sin and crime out of rocks. His take on this, according to Michael Balfour, is that Mary could have been in cahoots with Shane, and thus could be charged as an accessory before the fact. Quite serious indeed, but I can't see her motivation. If Mary wasn't involved with Shane before the killing, which the Crown concedes is hypothetically possible, then why did she flee the scene? Does that make her an accessory after the fact, a lesser charge but still quite serious in a murder case?

There is more, Mike warns me. If Mary is charged, what happens to Noel Callaghan and her husband who whisked Mary off to the mental hospital in Sudbury only a few minutes before the OPP came knocking on our door? I had no idea what was happening when Mary slipped away that morning, but I certainly was in contact with Noel at least twice after I knew that Franz was dead. The police already know this, anyway.

What's next? For starters, it's become a big, big media story. The Toronto papers, bless their hyperactive imaginations, are running Mary's, Shane's, and Franz's pictures in a row with question marks. Much is also being made of the fact that she is a professor at the University of Toronto. And, according to a couple of unidentified faculty sources, she was always "a bit different," kept to herself, and once did time on the West Coast. Mike quickly emailed an explanation that she once had been held in jail overnight with an anti-logging group on Vancouver Island.

The Callaghans have asked Mike Balfour and me to dinner on Saturday, which is much appreciated, as I am not in the mood to cook for myself, and not yet ready to eat out in public. Mike may be able to shed more light on the next legal steps. If Mary is to be re-charged, then I gather she must be returned to the Superior Court in Sudbury before Judge Stroud, who remanded her for an assessment at the Forensic Detention Centre. We can certainly expect more fire and brimstone from McTavish, who was not exactly enthusiastic about Mary's remand in the first place.

Presumably, there is still an issue as to whether Mary is fit to stand trial, regardless of what charges she may be facing. Another "if", – if Mary does appear before Judge Stroud again, I'm curious as to whether Mike can get the detention centre to provide us with an interim report. She seems more at peace these days, particularly after a smudging ceremony. The native healers, so I'm told, believe that rituals – dancing, too, sometimes – are the best paths to the soul's inner rhythms. It's still much too soon, however, for Mary to overcome the traumatic memories that still bedevil her. In time, Noel says. Perhaps never. Just think about the perversity of that possibility, painful though it may be. Mary could end up with an indeterminate sentence in a psych hospital because she's involved in a murder she didn't commit. Oh God, where are You now?

Stay well, friend. I need to know there is somebody out there who reads all this, and reminds me that the sun will rise in the morning...if it isn't snowing.

F.

Chapter 24

The next day

By noon on Friday, the best Fergus could say was that it wasn't snowing. Cold and damp, yes, with most of the summer's flowers now gone from their yard, save for a row of bright yellow marigolds along the western face.

He had even given up watching TV or reading the papers. Today – again – no one had called him to say that Mary had been released, which was the only piece of information he was interested in.

Except for her watercolor, the one Mary had painted for him at the detention centre. The woman has style, he thought, and a gentle color sense that's so different from her assertive persona.

The colors were muted in this work: long lines of blues and greens, with a hint of yellow coming through. In the corner, though, the lower right, there were two dark shapes, not fully formed, but one had a tendril of some sort, perhaps an arm, that reached out to the other. *What's Mary saying to me,* Fergus pondered. But another part of him decided it was too painful to work through. The meaning would come later.

In Little Current a few hours later, the weekend ritual was taking shape. Mike Balfour tried to pack his briefcase and close his office. Friday evenings were his "forgetting" time, a time to kick back, or just putter around. The paperwork on two real estate deals was complete, and everything else on his desk could wait until Monday.

Or so he thought, until a clerk from the crown attorney's office hand-delivered all the documents and transcripts of Shane's interrogation and confession, which, by law, the Crown was obliged to share.

Mike suspected the timing of the delivery was deliberate. It was well known among the island's lawyers that McTavish liked to leave a clean desk on Friday afternoons, taking delight that he had shifted work and headaches to his opponents.

As usual, this made Mike angry enough to jam the file into a briefcase. Then he calmed down, changed his mind, and opened the file on his desk. The disclosures, he noted, made it tragically obvious that Shane had no idea why Mary was at the killing site.

"She was just there suddenly behind me," Shane had told the OPP. "Like I don't expect her, don't even know who she was until she gets in my face, screaming and running around wild-like, and then she yanks the metal bar out of my hands and flings it away."

The implication was clear: If Shane didn't know why Mary was there, then Mary could not be an accomplice. Her presence must be explained by some other motive. Indeed, was there ever any intent to kill in the first place?

What to do: Go home or return the volley?

Just past quarter to five, Mike called the crown attorney's office in Gore Bay. McTavish was still at his desk. The conversation about the significance of Shane's statement was brief and blunt. Cal dug in, and quickly dismissed Mike's claim that Mary should be released, or failing that, at least re-charged with a lesser offence for which bail might be possible. When Mike argued that Shane's statement raised reasonable doubt about Mary's role, Cal countered that the differences in interpretation should be left to a trial to be decided, particularly as to whether Shane had told the full truth.

"Who to believe? That's the crux of this, Mr. Balfour. Shane could be protecting her. Too much evidence against her to ignore. If she was innocent, as you claim, why didn't she simply call the OPP when she returned home? No, Mr. Balfour, she remains in custody. That's that, and I'm due home."

Mike was left fuming. Rather than argue the point, he hung up. Let intransigence and blinkered logic simmer for a day. More importantly, this would allow him time to go home, relax, and see what popped, he told himself. Don't bother Fergus with this, not yet anyway.

Within a few hours, Mike had mapped out a counterattack, satisfyingly nasty in its potential, which he planned to discuss with Noel, Don, and Fergus over dinner the next evening.

Saturday evening

At first, Fergus had only a tepid interest in Mike's squeeze play. He sat quietly to the side as Mike broached the legal tactic in the Callaghans' living room.

Sipping on good scotch with a trickle of water, Noel and Don quickly warmed to the ploy, so much so that they urged Mike to call McTavish right off, before they moved to the dining room. Let him squirm, they told Mike. Put him on the speakerphone so they could all hear. Fergus just shrugged.

The conversation began graciously, Mike apologizing for interrupting Cal's evening with his family. Then, Mike abruptly became cold and formal, telling Cal that he had been instructed to file a civil suit for false arrest and detention after Mary was cleared. The proposed settlement, said Mike, could reach six figures, at least.

Cal, ever the consummate professional, fell back on the mantra of his Teflon persona, informing Mike calmly that he was just doing his job, nothing personal, merely protecting public security. There seemed to be a standoff, until Mike suggested they might at least explore some accommodation to avoid unnecessary litigation, which inevitably could drag on for some time. Cal paused before responding that he was too busy to meet Mike, and, moreover, he was due in Sudbury on Monday for a regional Crowns' conference.

Quickly picking up Cal's hesitation, Mike changed tactics. "Okay, Cal, Tuesday morning it is then. Great idea; gives us both more time to review the case. Always enjoy working with you. Garry's at eight for breakfast... Fine, fine. My best to your wife."

Game to Mr. Balfour, and after a congratulatory clinking of glasses, Noel served dinner.

Everyone but Fergus tucked into the plain comfort food, as Noel called it: shepherd's pie to some, *pate chinois* to others, but simple to make, serve, and eat. Tossed salad on the side. Don served the red wine.

"Fergus, you're not eating," said Noel. "That's not like you, my friend."

Usually Fergus devoured such food, but this Saturday evening at the Callaghan home, he was in a foul mood, grumpy and anxious, unable to sit in one place for long. Even his glass of wine sat almost untouched.

Get him to talk, said the psychologist in Noel. With Mary in jail, it was obvious Fergus had been overwhelmed with a terrible and paralysing guilt that he had failed her. Not only had his appetite waned, but Noel noticed he was listless and unkempt, with dark circles under his eyes.

Everything appeared bleaker than it had before. He couldn't even find it in him to bring Mary flowers, or to sit by her bed and pretend he was Neil Diamond whispering quiet love songs.

Across the table, Mike looked just as uneasy.

"Just three days, Mike?" said Fergus, sitting back in his chair, arms crossed. "That's all we have? Our last real shot to change his mind?"

Mike arched his bushy eyebrows, patted his moustache, and nodded.

"And he gets to play God, is that it? The bloody, sanctimonious bastard!"

"Getting mad, Ferg, won't resolve this mess," Mike pointed out. "Not at all, not at all. Cal deals with angry people every day. Just part of his job, but offenders being put away does tend to make them apoplectic."

"So get even, that's your plan?"

"Get new information, man, that's what we're telling you. Stop feeling so..."

Mike didn't bother to finish his sentence, when he saw Fergus turn away.

Noel continued to fret about Fergus, although she smiled when she realized she was also worrying about all that good food being left untouched. Part of her wanted to rap his knuckles with her knife, but instead she took a gulp of wine.

"May I get into this, Mike? Some thoughts from another perspective?"

"Be my guest, but we should finish eating first, Noel. I never have shepherd's pie at home."

Noel turned to Fergus. "Fergus, we're all… No, let me start again. Let's break this down. We have two issues here – one legal, one medical – that unfortunately are intertwined. "

"So?" said Fergus.

"Just this. What I understand at this point, judging from what the detention centre staff tell me, is that Mary is close to remembering what happened when Franz was killed. Fragments at best, though, no full recollection. The anti-anxiety meds seem to be taking hold. She's relatively stable now, but her short-term memory is still blocked."

"That's good news, eh, Fergus?" said Mike. "Recovery is under way. Marvellous!"

"Not quite that fast, Mike," Noel cautioned. "Most likely, she will need to connect with someone or something she saw when Franz was killed. The trouble is that I doubt whether this can happen in the detention centre."

Don topped up the wine glasses. No one waved him off as they weighed the implications of what Noel had said.

Fergus managed a small grin that was really more a poorly disguised sneer.

"Simple, eh? Bloody easy? Tell me: Do we bust Mary into jail to meet Shane again, or do we bust him out to visit her?"

"Cute, Fergus, cute," acknowledged Noel with a smile. "If you want help, we're here. If you don't…make a choice, my friend. It's time."

"Noel, you're pushing too hard."

"Perhaps not hard enough, Fergus. Play with my food and I'll understand. But play with my mind and I'll…I'll… We're running out of time, Fergus. Your call."

"Just like that?"

"Afraid so. Just like that."

"No place to hide anymore."

"Not if you want to find Mary."

Fergus knuckled his eyes. "Okay."

"Okay what, Fergus?"

"Okay, Noel, tell me what you want."

"Find the mystery person."

"Jaysus. Where do I...?"

Noel's face opened into a big grin. "Start with grandma."

Sheguiandah, Sunday

Finding grandma, however, took Fergus on a much different route than he had been instructed to follow.

First of all, he didn't feel heroic, and he knew he definitely didn't look the role. If he was to have an epiphany this Sunday morning, shake off his doubts, and slay Mary's dragon, he needed a new body. Alone with only his reflection in the full-length antique mirror in the corner of the upstairs bedroom, he admitted to himself that his image left no room for fantasy or flattery. Same old, just more so: a middle-aged man wearing an old sweatshirt over his mismatched pyjamas, badly sagging in most of the wrong places and in desperate need of a haircut and a shave.

Mary, he thought fondly, always looked better in the morning, and took delight in preening before the mirror, checking color combinations, and adjusting every stray wisp of hair.

Secondly, as he stood there in front of the unforgiving mirror, Fergus found himself increasingly reluctant to make a cold call to a stranger. That was not his thing, never had been. He hadn't even liked making cold calls when he was a reporter. So he took Brendan for a long walk, and caught up with neglected house chores before he finally broke down and telephoned Matt Peltier at the OPP detachment.

"Where can I find her, Matt – the old lady – or do I just drive around the reserve?"

"You could do that."

"Or?"

"Skip the old lady. You know what she said anyway, Ferg."

"Yeah, I read the transcripts. You sound cautious. You're telling me something?"

"Yes."

"Why?"

"Why? I'm a cop, Ferg, with a cop's priorities."

"I know where you work, Matt. So?"

"So, Cal McTavish likes to be first in line for new developments. But he's left for Sudbury already."

"So you want me to lead you, ask questions? Yes or no?"

"Yes."

"Okay, we take the long way home. Whatever. Did you interview others after Shane's confession?"

"Yes, of course."

"The old lady's family?"

"Yes."

"The kid's mother?"

"No."

"Oh? The kid's father?"

"Yes."

"Know where he is?"

"No, not at the moment."

"More games. Where would you start then, Matt?"

"At his work, tonight."

"Once more, with feeling. Where does he work?"

"He's a security guard at the hotel site."

"Max's hotel site?"

"Yes. Sorry, must go, Ferg. Another call's waiting, but always glad to help."

By the time Fergus drove east that evening through the village of Sheguiandah to the hotel construction site, only a thin sliver of light remained. Off to Fergus's left, the structural steel for the hotel's second floor stood frozen in time against the clear evening sky. Stacks of concrete-forming boards were piled next to large holes, now partially water-filled.

Fergus parked near the construction trailer at the bottom of the hill, and got out to look around, only to be startled by a voice behind him. A bright light blinded his vision for a moment until he shielded his eyes, and made out the shape of a man with a big flashlight.

Fergus quickly sensed who the other man was, and for a second, questioned the accident of history that had brought them both to this place: two middle-aged men standing face-to-face in the mud from the late autumn squalls of rain and snow. Would we ever have met in any other context, he asked himself? Probably not. And yet we're here, so that must mean something. Is he as fearful as I am right now? Perhaps. Do we share anything more than fear?

An eternity passed. Neither man spoke as they sized each other up. Shane's father, Wilbur Kanasawae, looked to be in his late fifties, about Fergus's own age. He was wearing a green, hip-length jacket with some sort of security badge on the shoulder. Spirals of white hair stuck out the side of a well-weathered leather hat with a broad brim pulled down front and back, and a yellowed ponytail curled frontward around his neck. Shorter than Fergus, he was hunched a bit – beaten down by age or arthritis, Fergus thought, or perhaps both – but his chin was thrust forward, strong jaw set squarely, and one eye cocked at Fergus.

"Site's closed," said the guard, stepping out of the shadows. "Come back in the morning if ya want the super."

"Easy, man. I didn't come looking for work or money. Hey, can you get your light out of my bloody eyes?"

"Okay, but don't move. Stay back there where I can see ya."

Fergus's feet felt cold as he squished a few steps in the mud, admonishing himself for wearing hiking shoes instead of practical rubber boots. Should have known better.

"Okay now?"

"Why ya here? Reporter or sumptin'?"

"No…not anymore."

"Not anymore?"

"Not really, but that's not the point. I'm Fergus Fitzgerald."

"Heard 'bout ya. Ya live with the Fraser woman, way out the Town Line Road. She's in jail. Must be lonely. Me, too."

"Your woman's in jail?"

"No, my wife; she's been gone a long time. Got a good job in Michigan."

"That's why you work nights?"

"It's a job. Sometimes I can forget things when I'm alone."

"You're lucky," said Fergus. "I wish I could."

"That's why you're here?"

"No. I'm too old to run any more. I'm looking for a man."

"A man? Hmm. You don't look that way but who knows with white people."

Fergus laughed a little, and then trusted his instinct. "Forget me, I'm not important. I'm looking for Shane Kanasawae's father. I'm told he works here."

"Yeah, Shane's a good kid. Don't understand some things yet."

"You know Shane?"

"My son. Not much anymore. Stays mostly with his grandmother. Wanted to be a big man. Used to worry 'bout him and that dead guy."

"Franz?" said Fergus. "Franz Dietrich?"

"Yeah, the German with the drugs. Not much like his uncle. Mr. Adler, he's a good man."

"You're right about Max Adler. I liked his dreams."

The two men fidgeted for a few moments, not saying anything, just looking for a sense of common ground. Another eternity passed, until Fergus accepted that he liked the feel of this man and this place, understanding in his own prescient way that he was finally taking root on Manitoulin.

"Got any coffee in there?" said Fergus, pointing to the trailer.

"Sure. No milk, though."

"That's okay, black as my soul. I want to talk a little about Mary and your son. Perhaps we can help each other."

Chapter 25

Little Current, Three days later

Fergus finally had his showdown with Cal McTavish. Not quite the private dueling ground both might have preferred; instead, it was breakfast time at Garry's, a local restaurant where the scrambled eggs were always served with a side order of curious onlookers.

Garry's did have a laid-back feel about it – dark carpets, veneer-topped tables and chairs, a newsstand near the cash register for the local weeklies – and was typical in towns the size of Little Current, most of which could boast a place like Garry's.

Fergus understood the breakfast meeting with the crown attorney was the best chance of getting the murder charge dropped against Mary. And he had promised, albeit reluctantly, to play nice, to squeeze McTavish a little, but to otherwise make the little/big man feel wise and compassionate. That was the game plan, but he was so on edge that he'd have preferred to lift up his side of the table and dump Cal's breakfast into his lap. Hot coffee to go – no warning, no second chance.

It was tempting. Fergus swallowed his frustration with his coffee, and resolved to remain stoic, at least for the moment. But he was worried they had chosen the wrong place – too public and too casual for a showdown.

At first, the breakfast crowd took no notice of Fergus, Mike, and Cal at their corner table. None of the three ordered heavily – juice, muffins, and coffee as they settled in. But a couple, friendly in the way of small towns, had nodded to Cal when they arrived, and the casual recognition had made him even more nervous about why he'd agreed to meet in such a public place. Especially with Fitzgerald, he thought. Just a drifter shacked up with that dreadful woman.

"For the record, Mr. Balfour, I don't bluff. If you believe you have a case for a civil action, then it's your right to file suit. On the other hand, your client, or Mr. Fitzgerald here acting on behalf of Dr. Fraser, should realize how expensive that route is, and that the Crown certainly knows how to protect the people's interest."

"Interesting opening gambit, Mr. McTavish," said Mike. "Just tell me this then: Why are you here at all?"

"So we move quickly to cross-examination, is that it, Mr. Balfour?"

"More coffee, guys?" asked a waitress, hovering with a coffeepot.

Fergus nodded yes; the other two covered their cups.

Mike worried the meeting might not last much longer, and seemed headed more toward confrontation than conciliation. "It's too early to be so formal. Can't we be Cal and Mike, at least over breakfast?"

McTavish shrugged. "As you wish."

"So let's cut to the chase. If you're trying to scare us off and cover your own…uh...position if a civil case does come to court, then we might as well halt the charade. But, as I have told you many times before, Cal, I've always seen you as a reasonable person open to new ideas. So what shall it be?"

"Reason has its limits, Mr. Balfour – or Michael, as you prefer – but I would like at least some new information. We all must be accountable to someone higher."

Mike quickly translated Cal's answer: The high media profile of the case and the possibility that an innocent person had been detained meant Cal was in a sensitive position with the senior Crowns in Sudbury and Toronto. The obvious message from the top: Clean up the mess,

"New information?" he asked.

"Yes. Not theories. Facts."

"Okay, let Fergus tell you what Shane's father told him Sunday night."

"The father – he's the guard at the hotel site, right, Mr. Fitzgerald?"

"Yes. Good guy."

"Well then, I've already been briefed by the OPP. Curious, though. You're talking to him, too?"

"I was a good reporter myself once, Mr. McTavish. Wilbur wasn't hard to find."

"At times, the Charter gets in the…the way," Cal answered shaking his head. "What did he tell you? Do we have the same story?"

"Okay, then. He, ah, Shane's father, explained why my Mary was at the construction site when Franz was killed."

"He confirms that she was there, then?"

"That's not in question any more, is it, McTavish?"

"Just tell me what he said."

"Your way then. Straight up. For some time now, Wilbur said he had been worried that Franz was drawing his son into the drug business. Shane suddenly had a lot more money to spend, and several elders had warned him that Shane was selling drugs on First Nations land. Shane even tried to recruit some high school kids to help."

"Did his father have firsthand knowledge about the drugs?"

"Did he use himself? Is that what you're asking?"

"Ah, you have a legal bent, Mr. Fitzgerald. Answering a question with a question."

"That's not the point, McTavish. Shane's dad's not on trial here."

"Then get to the point. What did the father know?"

"Wilbur didn't say much. That's as clearly as I remember, and with no editorializing. That's the gist of it. But he did say that Shane and Franz used to meet late at night behind the hotel foundation. A couple of times he caught them exchanging money."

"So why didn't the father go to the OPP, or tell Franz's uncle directly?"

"I asked him that, too, but it's hard for some natives to interfere like that. So he asked Mary to intervene."

"With the OPP, or with Mr. Adler?"

"Fair question. From what I can gather from Wilbur, Mary thought she could protect the hotel project and the jobs if she could confront Franz directly."

"And…? How did she want to confront the victim? With a metal bar?"

"Whoa, McTavish! I concede you've got a job to do, but that's too bloody much, even from you!"

"Sensitive, are you? Did I strike a nerve?"

"Yeah, you're beginning to piss me off. Mary didn't thump Franz, and you know it. That's not what Wilbur asked Mary to do.

"True believer, are you?"

"In some people, McTavish. Like Wilbur, who is just a father worried about his kid. All he wanted Mary to do was warn Franz to stop dealing with Shane."

"And if Franz refused, which must have seemed possible, what did he propose then, Mr. Fitzgerald? Blunt force?"

"That was not the intent. If Franz didn't pull back, then she'd ask Max to send him home."

"Tell me, Mr. Fitzgerald, how was Dr. Fraser supposed to make this work?"

"Figure it out yourself. No, I take that back. Wilbur knew that Mary had leverage with Max, more leverage than anyone else on this island. If Mary ever pulled out, Max's big dream might never recover. Even Franz, parasite that he was, knew that. Was he evil? Yes. Was he stupid? No."

Mike leaned forward across the table, hands steepled in front of him. His voice was soft and deliberate.

"Well, well, well, Cal. We certainly have a new slant on Dr. Fraser's motivation. Agreed, she could have called in the OPP sooner, but she chose to consider a greater good at this time."

"Still, her prints are on the murder weapon."

"Yes, Cal," said Mike. "The physical evidence is real, but you also have Shane's confession. What this comes down to is that Mary is the only real witness you have. And she's Shane's witness, too, if, as I suspect, he is going to plead some form of self-defense."

Mike moved quickly on with what he considered to be the real purpose of the meeting.

"Now about Dr. Fraser – Mary – how can we bring her home for real therapy? The detention centre is…well, a detention centre. Its staff does a good job with the resources available, but Mary's there for assessment, not a cure or long-term therapy. Yes, a man is dead, but the lives of two other people hang on this. Can you help us, Cal?"

Cal turned away from the table and gestured to the waitress. "Check, please."

Mike said nothing, but Fergus rose angrily, so forcibly that he knocked over his chair. Mike tried to intervene, but not in time to prevent Fergus from reaching across the table and grabbing Cal's arm. "That's it? You just walk away?"

Cal, red-faced, shook free, and backed away from the table. "Stop making a scene," he hissed to Fergus.

Garry stared out from the serving window of his kitchen, holding a plate of rapidly cooling scrambled eggs and home fries. Some customers dropped their food. In rapid order, the hydro workers in their safety vests and boots moved in between Fergus and an elderly woman who had become so badly shaken that she spilled her coffee. One worker helped her to another chair, at a safer distance from the fray.

Fergus ignored them all. "No, not this way, McTavish. Not this time. I'm not letting you get away with this."

Cal pulled out his cell phone. "Stop, or I'll get the OPP here. One more step, Fitzgerald, and I'll have you charged!" He turned to Mike, "Balfour, get control of your client!"

Mike pulled back. "Don't look at me, Cal. He's right. And you're too stubborn to admit it."

Fergus moved closer and backed Cal into the restaurant's foyer.

"Go ahead, make your damn call, McTavish. Put more people in jail. Feels good, eh? Don't deal with the real shit. Yeah, Mary got her hands dirty trying to help some kid and you can't deal with that, let alone understand why. You just sit on the sidelines waiting for someone to screw up. Justice? Shit, that's not what you're peddling. Man, all you're offering is vengeance – sheer righteous vengeance. What kind of merciless God do you think you are?"

Cal looked stunned. Nobody, ever, had challenged him like this – not his wife and most certainly not his staff. There were no laws here to protect him, and he quickly sensed that he, too, was on trial. The restaurant was now dead silent, but Cal knew that word of a retreat could spread quickly. He stared at Fergus and began to say something, then turned and faced Mike.

"It seems, ah, we need to talk again, Mike, lawyer-to-lawyer, perhaps my office. I'll pay for breakfast this time."

"Big deal," interjected Fergus loudly. "Big whopping deal! Throw money at it. I'll pay for my own bloody coffee. You got a price?"

Cal stood his ground. "Save your money, Fitzgerald!"

"Why? In the name of God, why?"

"Explain it to your client, Mike. Lawyers are expensive. Call me in a couple of days. Gentlemen."

As Cal left Garry's, his emotions were still smarting. He was embarrassed to his core and his righteous self-image teetered on its pedestal. He intended to honor his commitment to meet Mike Balfour later, but what then? For a man seldom given to doubts, he'd lost his instinctive feel for the tree of good and evil, and the certainty that he could face down its temptations.

What to do? *No, no, no,* he argued with himself, *the truly righteous do not sit and cower. Never, ever. I must rise up and find my way again.*

And try he did. By late afternoon, Calvin John McTavish bluntly demanded that the OPP take him along to find Shane's father, to confirm what he had told Fergus. At first, the police insisted they could do their own investigations, and would send along a report to the Crown's office in due time. But it was to no avail.

Rich Sawicki, with unusual forbearance, did not press Cal for an explanation, since he and everyone else in the OPP detachment at Little Current knew within minutes what had taken place. After Cal had left Garry's, the elderly woman whom the hydro workers tried to protect was rushed to hospital with heart palpitations. She recovered quickly, but a report was made to the OPP about the disturbance, and even Garry had called to ask whether he could or should ban Fergus and Cal from the restaurant. The complaints were duly noted, but no one really wanted to muddy up a murder case with a report of a temper tantrum.

Cal's worries, though, went much deeper: He could not shake off what Fergus had screamed at him – that he was more dedicated to vengeance than to justice. Much of his mind wanted to dismiss Fergus as a loudmouth American trying to protect his free ride with the Fraser woman. Shacked up, yes, that's all they're doing, shacking up, unchurched even by a priest, holding themselves up as an intellectual elite, freethinking beyond law and decency.

And yet there was another side of Cal that could not condemn Fergus. Cal did pray more frequently than most folk: Almost every night with his wife and children, he sought the strength to follow God's will and if his family should stumble, to ask forgiveness for them. Yet Fergus's accusation stung, and he could not explain why to himself.

He thought so much about this paradox that he could not concentrate on the normal flow of work that came across his desk. Nor did a walk along the waterfront at lunchtime help to clear his mind, as it sometimes did.

No, no, no, I will not...I must not give in, he cautioned himself. I must not, just because I'm challenged. Fitzgerald sees vengeance, but I say deterrence. I put bad people away so they can't break the law again. I protect people, and then they whine and accuse me like they're some kind of evil spirits sending forth their own vengeance. And they talk about decency. Hypocrites!

Sheguiandah

"I assume you know where you're going," Cal said to Sawicki as the OPP cruiser turned on to a reserve road. "You know where the father lives?"

"One more left, and we're there."

They eventually found the house after twice asking for directions. Wilbur was waiting outside for them, sprawled listlessly on the top step. He hadn't gotten much sleep since Shane had been arrested, and sent to the regional detention centre to await trial. He offered Rich and Cal tea, and sat them around an old Formica-topped table. The cups were chipped, and the small house was sparsely furnished. It was also immaculately clean, Cal noticed with some surprise.

Without much questioning or prompting from Rich, Wilbur repeated what he had told Fergus the previous night. Yes, he had asked Mary to intervene with Franz to protect his son. Yes, he believed Mary was the best person to do this, even if it could cost him his job. And yes, he would come to court and say this again, if that was needed.

"Now may I ask a question?" Wilbur said to Cal.

"If it is brief, of course," said Cal. "I must get back to Gore Bay. There are too many files awaiting me."

"I understand. You are an important man. More busy than a watchman. Let me ask this: Why is Dr. Fraser still in jail if she was only trying to help Shane? I don't understand."

"What don't you understand, sir?"

"If anyone should be in jail, perhaps it should be me. Shane has told you that he killed the young German. That was wrong of him, and all of us are affected. Perhaps if I had been a better father, and had been here for him more, this would not have happened. So how do we restore peace and balance in our family? By putting Dr. Fraser in jail as well as Shane? Better let them go and take me instead."

"Really? You want us to put you in jail, is that it?" asked Cal "And yet you have committed no crime."

"Not according to *your* laws, Mr. McTavish. But I want to forgive myself and cleanse my heart. And if you help me do this, then perhaps you can forgive Dr. Fraser, and maybe even Shane a little."

For the second time that day, Calvin John McTavish sat stunned, unable to respond to the older man. Of course, they would not take Wilbur with them when they returned to Little Current. Cal's law did not allow for surrogate prisoners, but he was both moved and challenged by the profundity of Wilbur's sacrificial sense of justice and beyond that, the forgiving face of his uncommon decency.

Without saying anything more, Cal went outside, opened his cell phone, and prayed for a connection.

"Mr. Balfour, Michael, may I come to see you? As soon as possible, if I may. Thank you. Right away then."

Chapter 26

Sudbury, Three days later

It was Mary's day in court again, and everyone seemed confident of a positive outcome – everyone, that is, except Fergus, who expected another black hole to open up and swallow Mary into some nether world.

"Ah, Mr. McTavish, Mr. Balfour, back again so soon?" said Madam Justice Rita Stroud.

"And Dr. Fraser as well, I see."

Mary Fraser was able to stand this time, holding onto the front of the prisoner's dock. Earlier in the day, OPP constables had brought her from the North Bay forensic detention centre in North Bay.

Technically, Mary had still been a prisoner during the ninety-minute drive to Sudbury where she was scheduled to appear again before Justice Stroud. But she was not in handcuffs, and the two young constables were unusually solicitous about her comfort, and even tried to joke a little. She didn't say much, though, content for the moment to watch the traffic flow along Highway 17 and to savor the ordinariness of the small villages and farms.

The day before, Fergus and Mike had brought her a heavier coat when they visited to explain the legal process that was about to unfold. Mary appeared able to accept that Franz was dead, and that she had been present when he was killed. Her remorse and grief had seemed quieter, more deeply internalized, as her own sense of survival strengthened.

Yet she admitted to only a fleeting recall of Shane's role, and why she had been with him at the hotel construction site. She couldn't remember meeting Wilbur, his dad, at all. "Don't push her," Noel had counselled. "Her memory fragments will link in time. What's really crucial here is to help put her tragedies back into the context of an otherwise loving life."

As the court hearing began, Fergus noticed Max sitting in one of the back rows next to Wilbur and a well-dressed young Ojibwa man, whom he assumed was Shane's lawyer. Fergus was too far away to hear what the men said during the formal hand-shaking, but he was intrigued when Max pulled an envelope from the inside pocket of his blazer and handed it to the lawyer. Wilbur nodded and held himself a little straighter, as did Max.

Across the aisle from the defense table sat several OPP officers, including both Rich Sawicki and Matt Peltier. While Rich was relieved that Mary would be freed, his stomach was churning in anticipation of that afternoon's press conference. Someone, sure as hell, was reviewing police procedures, since it was painfully obvious that Dr. Fraser had been charged too quickly, and that perhaps racial bias had been part of the decision to do so.

"Are you ready to proceed, Mr. McTavish?" asked Justice Stroud in a stern tone that made her query sound more like a command than a question.

Cal, too, knew he would be judged, and had been advised by his superiors to take the moral high ground: Be magnanimous and gracious in defense of justice. And above all else, don't complicate the case against the young native who had been charged with Franz's murder.

Much of what Cal explained in support of his motion to withdraw charges against Mary was a recitation of facts already well known to the court: when and how Franz was killed, the forensic evidence linking Mary's prints to the murder weapon, her threats to Franz both at the Toronto airport and in Little Current, and her flight to Sudbury just as the OPP began their investigation.

"There is no doubt in my mind, Madam Justice," said Cal, "that the charges against Dr. Fraser were the result of solid professional police work, given the evidence that existed at the time. In summary, the charge against Dr. Fraser reflected motive, opportunity, and strong physical evidence."

Justice Stroud stopped making notes, and leaned back in her chair, running a finger over her chin, her eyebrows raised more in cynicism than surprise. Shane's lawyer leaned forward, also weighing every word, as Cal now had to explain how Shane was involved.

Cal, however, did not follow the expected script. "As part of the Crown's decision to present this motion, we also considered whether subsidiary charges should be laid against Dr. Fraser and her psychologist, Dr. Noel Callaghan of Little Current. Police investigation did show that Dr. Fraser made no attempt to inform police about Mr. Dietrich's death and its circumstances. Without even telling her companion, Fergus Fitzgerald, she fled to Dr. Callaghan's office and was taken to the Northeast Mental Health Centre in Sudbury.

"Our perspective on these issues changed, of course, when a young associate of the victim came forward recently, and accepted sole responsibility for Mr. Dietrich's death. He now has been charged, and is in custody awaiting trial. Bail has been denied. Let me simply say I do not want to prejudice a fair trial at some later date, so, Madam Justice, I ask you to accept this limited description of the new and exculpatory evidence supporting Dr. Fraser's innocence.

"The law is quite clear on these matters. Dr. Fraser was under no legal obligation to inform the authorities, as…" Cal paused, meticulously choosing his words, "...as we cannot say whether she participated in the planning and execution of the murder or whether she helped the accused avoid arrest. Good citizens do make a 911 call when they witness a crime, but they do so voluntarily. As we understand, however, Dr. Fraser had been undergoing treatment for post-traumatic stress disorder prior to Mr. Dietrich's death. Indeed, you will recall, Madam Justice, that I supported the defense motion for an assessment at the North Bay Forensic Detention Centre of Dr. Fraser's criminal responsibility in these matters. If you accept our brief to withdraw the charges against Dr. Fraser, then the assessment order will be rendered moot, and Dr. Fraser will be free to seek whatever therapy she and presumably Dr. Callaghan deem necessary.

"Similarly, we will not be charging Dr. Callaghan or her husband. We believe they acted in the best interests of their patient."

Justice Stroud leaned forward, took a quick look at Mary, then pointed a finger at Mike. "I assume, Mr. Balfour, that you concur on behalf of your client. If you have anything to say, please be brief, sir, as Dr. Fraser must be anxious to resume her freedom as expeditiously as possible."

Mike stood. "Thank you, Madam Justice. I do differ from Mr. McTavish in one aspect. Surely, though, in the name of decency and justice, he has more to say to Dr. Fraser in this most public of forums."

Justice Stroud paused for a moment. "I agree, Mr. Balfour. Mr. McTavish, I urge you to respond in kind sir?"

Cal, was hesitant to rise. He spent a few seconds straightening his notepads and files, precisely aligning each to the other. It was his way of sorting out emotion and reason, putting his brain back in sync, especially right now when he wanted to pounce on Mary Fraser although he knew better. Not now, he told himself. Get her later. Don't do it this way. Put on the mask.

"What can one say in these matters, Madam Justice? Surely we can be grateful that an injustice has been nipped in the bud, that Dr. Fraser can return to her life, and that considerable expense to the state has been spared. Our police, however, must be free to investigate and lay charges as they see fit."

"That is all you have to say, Mr. McTavish?" asked Justice Stroud. "A good woman suffering from childhood trauma has spent considerable time in detention. My understanding is that many First Nations people welcome her leadership gifts. Really!"

Cal's face reddened, and he paused to straighten his tie.

"Get to it, sir, or must I do your job for you?"

"No, no, of course not, Madam Justice. It is just…just that we must tread carefully here today, as other charges have been laid in the tragic death of Mr. Dietrich. We must not compound the errors – the very human errors, I might add.

"Still, we must attempt to see this matter through Dr. Fraser's perspective. Yes, yes, that's it, from Dr. Fraser's perspective, of course. If I were she, I would expect someone to apologize, to say they're sorry Yes, I can do that. Dr. Fraser, we regret what has happened to you, and let this moment stand as a reminder to everyone how human and frail we are in the midst of so much evil."

Justice Stroud wrinkled her nose and cocked one eyebrow. "Mr. Balfour, are you satisfied now, sir?"

"Hmm. Let me say I am satisfied the appropriate words can be found somewhere in what Mr. McTavish has said. Thank you, Madam Justice. Now please, your ruling on behalf of my client. Justice delayed is justice denied."

"Yes, I, too, know that cliché, Mr. Balfour. Dr. Fraser, please stand. The Crown's motion to withdraw the charges against you is accepted. You are free to go with the most heartfelt apologies of this court. Court is adjourned. "

Judge Stroud banged her gavel with unusual vigor, and left the bench. Her work was done.

Fergus waited for Mary to sign a few papers. There had been exuberant hugs all around with Mike and Noel. Even Cal crossed the aisle to congratulate Mike, although the congratulations were brief.

And then, finally, it was time for Mary and Fergus to leave.

"Before you go out there…"

"Yes, Fergus…"

"Listen to this, Mary."

He pulled out a portable CD player with one disc already loaded.

"Streisand and Diamond?"

"No, just Barbra. This is what I've been playing over and over."

"You did bring me flowers. I remember that, Fergus."

"Close."

"Memories then, Fergus. 'I remember the time that happiness was...'"

"Memories are good, Mary."

"Oh Lord, man, I thought I had lost them all."

"Not all, Mary. We'll find your memories. Okay?"

"Oh yes, you loving man. Then play it, Fergus."

And so he did.

As Fergus and Mary slipped away to Noel's van, Wilbur, Max, and the young Ojibwa lawyer were also slow to leave. Max simply stood there, gently holding Wilbur by the shoulders, trying to reassure him that his son's life was not over. The lawyer – Simon Corbiere – stood a little to the side, looping the belt of his new black overcoat, long and fashionable like some well-established Bay Street lawyer's. Simon had cut off his ponytail when he entered Laurentian University as an undergraduate. Called to the bar after graduating high in his class at Queen's University law school, he had joined a prestigious Sudbury law firm, but still firmly believed that he would in time come back to the reserve, and perhaps oversee the introduction of native-run community sentencing circles as a form of restorative justice. But not until he was established.

Such had been his vision and goal...until his family had reached out last week and pulled him back to defend Shane Kanasawae, using the tenuous line of defense that evil spirits had made Shane kill Franz. To Simon, this was bogeyman stuff that he knew many natives here still believed in, but didn't talk much about. Evil spirits didn't leave fingerprints, let alone DNA. Ever see a mug shot of an evil spirit?

This was his first major case since his call to the bar, but if he was nervous, he didn't let it show.

The attention, he realized, came with a price: How he defended Shane would be carefully scrutinized by both the Ojibwa community and the legal profession, particularly if he based his defense on Shane's contention that paranormal forces were involved in what some natives accepted as a ritual killing. Simon knew his childhood friends back on the reserve at M'Chigeeng would tell him it was way out, man, so run with it, but his law school buddies would probably counter that this was spooky old stuff, myths better left to storytellers and anthropologists. Indeed, a bearwalker defense could be translated as radical and therefore risky, both for his client and himself. This case might not be the good career move he had first believed, but his mother was a cousin of Shane's grandmother, and the women were talking. Sometimes, Simon told himself, it was good to listen and respect the elders.

Meanwhile, he had already put in a request for a transcript of today's proceedings.

Only two reporters remained on the courthouse steps: Isaiah Steen from the *Manitoulin Expositor* and Louisa Ledingham from the *Sudbury Star*. All the electronic types had left with their sound bites of Mary's walk into freedom. Isaiah and Louisa were hanging back, because they sensed that Max had changed. For the first time since Franz's death, he seemed more comfortable with himself. Less rigid, with even a slight smile.

They were intrigued, because it was evident Max wanted to share Wilbur's guilt. Why?

"Mr. Adler, Louisa Ledingham from the *Sudbury Star*," Louisa called over to him. "May we have a word with you, sir?"

"Ah, Fraulein Ledingham, I thought I saw you in court. Yes, certainly you may have a word. But I am afraid we must leave quickly to visit Shane, and advise him of some issues. You will understand, of course."

"We understand, of course, sir."

Isaiah nodded, but decided to pose the one question that had been intriguing him all afternoon.

"Mr. Adler, Isaiah Steen from the *Manitoulin Expositor*. You're going to visit Shane, Max. May I call you Max? Thanks. I can understand Shane's dad rushing over with Shane's lawyer, but it does strike me as odd, Max, that you're going along, too."

"Oh? Why should I not go?"

"Free country, of course. You can go where you like, but Shane did confess that he killed your nephew."

"You are aware, are you not, Herr Steen, that I have apologized for bringing Franz to Manitoulin. So why can I not help Wilbur? There is much left to understand about why Franz is dead. Wilbur and I, though, are both family men with heavy hearts, so why should I not help him?"

Isaiah looked over at Louisa, and she closed her notebook, signaling to him that he was pushing too hard. Simon also noticed the gesture and began to guide Max and Wilbur to his car.

Isaiah remained curious about what Max had just said. His instincts demanded that he ask the follow-up question, where the jackpot answers lay.

"Okay, Max, you want to help Wilbur. I caught that. Man helping man. The Canadian way. But how are you helping him? Just being friendly and sympathetic, or what?"

"I am still German, practical, very much to the point," Max replied. "I prefer action. Hence, I have retained Simon Corbiere to represent Shane."

"You're paying Shane's legal bills?"

"That is what I said. Does it not seem right that I do so, or can only Canadians help Canadians? Such a curious country, so sensitive at times. We live in a big world, Herr Steen."

Louisa re-opened her notebook. "I realize you must leave quickly, but may I ask Mr. Corbiere one last question?"

Simon stepped forward, his shoulder and face muscles tensing.

"Can you tell us, then, how you plan to defend Shane? Some sort of self-defense plea?"

"Yes."

"Yes? Just yes? Not one that the Crown will roll over on."

Simon coughed as he tried not to rise to the bait.

"I will leave the Crown's case to Mr. McTavish."

"And your case?"

"There is time to say only this: Mr. Adler and Mr. Kanasawae have consulted with me, and I shall be formally informing the Crown in the morning of our position."

"You seem to have trouble with your position, sir."

"Not at all. There is a process in play."

"Ah, the process knows all," said Louisa, shaking her head. "Good try, guy. Just tell us what base you're on. If you *are* confident in your position, that is. Or I can report that you are still working out the defense."

Max looked at Simon, holding out one hand palm up, telling Simon the decision was his.

Simon nodded back before answering. Either say nothing, he said to himself, or take a chance and put the idea in play. Go for broke.

"Shane has told us he believed Franz was a bearwalker, intent on killing him," he finally said.

"For real? This is for real? Bearwalker – the old Indian myth, dark creature in the forest?"

"Not a myth for Shane, or for his family. That is his defense. Look up the case law yourself."

"Oh my God, Isaiah, he could be right," Louisa blurted out.

Then she turned on Max. "You believe in this, Mr. Adler?"

"I'm here, am I not, Fraulein?"

"Being here and believing are two different matters, sir. Do you believe that the bearwalker exists?"

"It is not that simple. Nothing is, when we look into the night at things we do not fully understand," said Max. "Wilbur and I share a great grief that goes beyond death itself. We must be careful here. Very, very careful about what the skeptics among your readers will say about this."

Louisa refused to give up. "If you're worried about public opinion, then now is the time to explain what you believe."

Max pulled himself erect, nodding slowly as he did. "Just this, then, from an old man who has seen too much tragedy in his life. I respect the beliefs of my Ojibwa friends about the bearwalker. I must even confess that these stories about the bearwalker resonate deeply within me. Perhaps that is why I am here; perhaps because these stories parallel my family's history in Germany. Perhaps because, in the end, we all end up in the same place – from different countries using different names for what has happened. Call evil what you may, give it whatever name you like, but yes, I believe in spirits that can steal your soul. Now we must go."

Chapter 27

The next day

From: **Fergus Fitzgerald <Brendan@bmts.com**
To: **Conall Fitzgerald <Famtrack@corknet.ie**
Subject: **poltergeists**

Life is better here – for the moment anyway – with Mary home. So good, broken only when the kid lawyer pesters me as to whether Mary can recall any hint of a bearwalker. Lord, he might as well be looking for leprechauns. If you have any to spare in Cork, send them over, will ya? Collect. I can just hear ya saying "that poor Ferg, a right eedjit and all, wants the wee folk to help him out." All I want is for her to be well again, snuggling against my backside, so we can get on with life and catch up with the dreams that have been on hold for so long. But oh, no, man, that's not the freedom we have. Freedom, of course, is bloody well not there for easy picking, as anyone Irish ought to know. The Germans, too, in an ironic way. Ever read Goethe? Years ago, I picked up an English translation of his *Faust* when I stopped over in Weimar on a German holiday. "Let's plunge ourselves into the roar of time," he wrote. "It's only action that can make a man." Sounds invigorating, but it's not the Fitzgerald way. Max's, though. Now there's a man.

Okay, rant's over. Mary is starting to recover, thanks to Noel and a native healer, an amazing team who might someday be the makings of a good book about a partnership that really does take healing beyond conventional boundaries. Her blood pressure is under control again, and she's sleeping better. And no, in case you're wondering, not everything is back to normal.

But what's normal these days?

"Just hug me," she says.

"Horizontal hugs?" I ask.

"Okay," she replies, "but without presumptions."

I wish I could help more, but her healers say my role is to affirm who she is. Trouble is, I can't look at her without setting off my own guilt that I could have prevented this if I had returned Franz to Germany as an undesirable.

Noel keeps telling me the root of Mary's troubles is much deeper than watching Franz's violent death. If I understand the healing process correctly, first she must deal with the abuse in her childhood before she moves on to the murder trauma. Mary's own explanation is that she feels like she's restoring an old masterpiece, removing one layer of paint at a time to find the original images and elegance. She should know, art historian that she is. Think about it. How ironic! Most of the troubles here started when the natives grew concerned that the Germans – Franz really – were trying to pirate ancient burial scrolls from the hotel site. Instead, Franz ends up dead, and we white folk are trying to save Mary's memories.

Yes, yes, I will try to explain the bearwalker phenomenon in a moment. Trust me, it ain't a voodoo show for the tourists. Nor is it a fanciful story about things that go bump in the night, like a Stephen King poltergeist.

Let me stay focused on Mary. As I said, Mary is getting the healing she needs. I've told you about Noel Callaghan, the ex-nun psychologist, and her GP husband, Don. They've teamed up with a native healer from the Wicki First Nation to provide cross-cultural healing. Truly, these people are pioneers who are finally being accepted by the Ontario medical establishment. Even some non-natives are turning to this team for holistic healing. Just imagine, centuries ago, the first Europeans who came here thought of the natives as savages. Now we are finally starting to understand their unique gifts that evolve more from the natural world than from technology.

The other day, I came across a slim book by a Yale-trained psychiatrist, Carl Hammerschlag, who left the U.S. East Coast to work among the Pueblo tribes in New Mexico. Interesting stuff. "Do you know how to dance?" a clan chief asked him when he first arrived. Not what Hammerschlag had expected, but eventually his answer came down to this: "It is the left brain that knows how to speak, but the right brain remembers the lyrics to songs. You need both to dance. You need both to remain healthy."

Yeah, I can hear ya muttering that loud Irish music and jigs can cure anything. No, friend, not that kind of dancing. Another time, perhaps, so let me be serious for a bit. Mary, in many ways, is learning to dance again. Not always beautifully though; in fact, the native healer cautions that her immediate reaction will be quite wretched. First, Mary has to go through a series of four sweat lodges to purge her system from the residual elements of the various drugs she was given at the Sudbury and North Bay hospitals. Read 'vomiting' and 'diarrhea' here. Ritual healing in other cultures is usually not as dramatic, but hey, Christians have baptisms and lots of folk sit in spas and steam rooms.

So natives build sweat lodges from materials at hand, and pour water over heated stones. Other people do this, too –refreshing, I'm told – but many natives here hold to the ancient belief that the rocks are invested with the spirits of their ancestors and the steam is the breath of their grandparents. "Sweating with your ancestors breathing on you," said Hammerschlag, "has a healing influence."

Not my way. This is a struggle for me, after battling the rituals of organized religion so much of my life. But it works for some people, so why not Mary? She came back to Manitoulin – perhaps was drawn back is a better explanation – to recover something missing in her life. Perhaps this is her first dance step.

My overriding concern, obviously, is whether Mary will be able to dance in time for Shane's trial. As I've said before, she's Shane's only real hope. The bearwalker defense has been used before – the first time in 1945 in a murder also on the Sheguiandah reserve. James Nahwaikezhik, a thirty-three-year-old native, told police he had killed his father, whom he believed helped cast the spell of a bearwalker on him. When James returned to Manitoulin after working at a northern lumber camp, his mother urged him to find a wife and gave him love potions. Old newspaper reports said he was obsessed with sexual fantasies and had fierce headaches. Neighbors told him they saw a fireball circling his house, traditionally believed to be a sign of a bearwalker. A blind witch doctor prescribed herbal brews, but the headaches persisted.

In the end, James testified that he believed the only way to overcome the curse was to kill both his parents. And so he went to their house in the middle of the night with a rifle and screaming, "Why have you been bearwalking me?" He shot his father when the old man answered the door, but fortunately, his mother escaped through a rear door. Although his lawyer pleaded insanity, a government psychiatrist said he was sane and had acted on a belief held since childhood. The jury agreed, and Nahwaikezhik was sentenced to death by hanging. The sentence was later commuted to life imprisonment, just twelve hours before his scheduled execution in the Sudbury jail.

Some precedent, only now with a slightly more humane face. Shane still faces a life sentence with no chance for parole for at least ten years, perhaps even twenty-five. That's mandatory for second-degree murder here. Since Shane didn't bring a weapon, the Crown can't prove intent. It looks as though the Crown will agree to a trial by judge alone, since nobody wants to roll the dice with a jury trial about a bearwalker.

If that jail term isn't bad enough, the suicide rate for native prisoners with long sentences is much higher than for non-native inmates. Too many come home in a coffin. There are moments when I wish Shane's lawyer would plead guilty to a lesser charge like manslaughter and forget the bearwalker. But then again, I seem to prefer the easier way.

Take care, friend, and at least say a prayer to St. Jude for us.

F.

Chapter 28

Gore Bay, April 2000

Most of the winter's ice had gone from the harbor, and one tourist hotel had opened early to cater to the anticipated influx of lawyers and media, for what was being is called "the bearwalker trial." Long strings of cars jammed the narrow side streets adjacent to the old courthouse, high on the hillside overlooking the North Channel.

"Bearwalker defense, indeed," Cal McTavish snorted at his Crown colleagues as they entered the courtroom. "Just evil personified. I know evil, and if there is evil in this case, it's not the bearwalker."

Shane Kanasawae and his lawyer, Simon Corbiere, had already elected trial by judge alone, as it had become abundantly clear that the outcome might depend on complex, philosophical arguments. Simon, waiting at the defense table, looked at the note he had written to himself late the previous night: Does evil have rights? He then passed the note to his associate, Harley Reif, the older attorney who had been retained to represent Mary Fraser's legal interests if the need arose. Reif frowned at Simon, but said nothing.

The trial was being held in the small, hundred-and-fifteen-year-old stone courthouse that looked more like a simple church with its high windows and ceiling under a gabled roof.

"Are you ready with your opening statement, Mr. McTavish?" asked Mr. Justice McWilliams of the Ontario

Supreme Court, his deep rumbling voice easily heard in the back rows. While William George McWilliams had not sought this assignment, Ontario's Chief Justice made it known that he wanted someone with both judicial experience in northern Ontario and a steady mind, sensitive to the cultural issues at play. Until several years ago, McWilliams, a tall angular man now in his mid-fifties, had been a partner in a small law firm in Kenora in northwestern Ontario, near the Manitoba border.

"Of course, sir," said Cal McTavish, putting aside his notes and moving quickly to stand in the centre. "I shall be brief, as we have a full confession by Mr. Kanasawae. Indeed, my colleague, Mr. Corbiere, has stipulated that his client's confession stands with one small exception, which he will no doubt deal with later in his own statement."

"Mr. McTavish," Justice McWilliams cut in quickly, "It is not your purpose to speak for the defense counsel. Move on, please."

Cal, taken aback, retreated to the Crown's table where he looked at his notes, straightened his tie, and marched back into the fray. Only a curt nod of his head acknowledged that the judge would not allow him to patronize Simon Corbiere.

"Of course, sir," replied Cal, partly turning to point at the defense table. "Indeed, we can be prompt because so little of what the Crown will present is in doubt. The first point I shall make is that Shane Kanasawae is not some unfortunate person who was in the wrong place at the wrong time and acted merely to defend himself. Not at all, sir, not at all."

Shane, for his part, sat almost motionless in his chair, looking straight forward as his lawyers had told him to do. They had also advised him not to wear the ritual dark suit, white shirt, and conservative tie normally chosen for male defendants to project an aura of responsibility and respect for the court. "Look native," they had said. "Look like you believe in native ways: jean jacket, cargo pants, and braided hair. No jewelry, just one band to hold your hair in place." His grandmother, father, and even Fergus and Mary were not allowed in court, because they might be called as witnesses later in the trial.

Cal continued. "Over the next few days – and I do hope it will be days and not weeks…."

McWilliams appeared to be annoyed, having been told in advance that McTavish was stubborn, and seldom took the easy way in anything. Better to draw a line in the sand now.

"Mr. McTavish, please get on with it. It is my usual practice to grant counsel considerable latitude in opening remarks, particularly with no jury present. You seem, however, to enjoy speaking not only for the Crown, but also for Mr. Corbiere, and now for me. Your point, sir?"

"Ah, yes, my point, sir. Shane Kanasawae, by his own admission, killed Franz Dietrich this past October during the commission of a criminal act. He intended to meet the victim late at night in an isolated place to conclude a drug deal. Money was to be exchanged. You will hear testimony from representatives of the Joint Forces Unit established to halt the accelerated influx of drugs into the Sudbury region and onto this island. Both Mr. Dietrich and Mr. Kanasawae were well known to the JFU. We will also introduce evidence that both Mr. Dietrich and Mr. Kanasawae have associated with biker gangs, such as the Hells Angels, that now dominate the drug trade in the north as well as in southern Ontario. Indeed, Mr. Kanasawae was remanded without bail, in part for his own safety.

"You will also hear, sir, that trafficking charges against Mr. Kanasawae have been deferred pending the resolution of the murder charges against him. No, Your Honor, Shane Kanasawae is not some innocent abroad. If Mr. Dietrich were still alive, it is highly probable that he, too, would be charged with drug trafficking. The evidence will show that Mr. Dietrich and Mr. Kanasawae were habitual criminals with access to international drug supply lines. I have been asked by the JFU not to comment further on the international aspects of this case. While Mr. Kanasawae may have been dealing at the outer edges of this web, he was nonetheless part of the web."

At the defense table, Harley Reif whispered, "Now! Do it."

"Your Honor, I object," Simon said, rising to his feet. "The Crown's allegations are way too much—"

"Mr. Corbiere, we have not met before. But let me advise you to frame your objections closer to the law. I'm afraid 'way too much' is not very much at all. Or shall we let Mr. McTavish continue?"

Simon looked back at Harley, breathed into his cupped hands covering his mouth to calm himself, and then went on. "Thank you, Your Honor. Your point is well taken."

"Thank you, Mr. Corbiere. And now, may I hear your point?"

"Of course, sir. Shane Kanasawae is on trial for murder, not drug trafficking, for which he has not even been charged, let alone convicted. Mr. McTavish, in his well-known zeal, is confusing the two cases. I ask you, sir, to rule out all mention of possible drug charges, that they cannot be properly heard here."

"Mr. McTavish, do you wish to reply?"

"Indeed, Your Honor. The accused's drug involvement speaks to his credibility and the state of his mind when Mr. Dietrich was murdered. I seek some leeway on this matter, sir."

"Hmm, Mr. Corbiere, no, not this time. Your objection is overruled, but I caution Mr. McTavish to restrict his comments on the alleged drug dealings until they are properly heard, if and when Mr. Kanasawae is charged. Continue, Mr. McTavish."

Over at the defense table, Harley Reif grinned triumphantly at Simon.

Having lost his momentum, which Simon knew had been Harley's real intention, Cal McTavish retreated to his notes again, flipped through a couple of pages, and then spun sharply to face the bench.

"Let me go on to the next point of my opening remarks, Your Honor. Much will be made about the mythical bearwalker. I most certainly will leave that portion of the defense to Mr. Corbiere, because the existence of a bearwalker is central to their claim of self-defense. I await with considerable interest whatever physical evidence exists other than some colorful paintings and drawings by the island's more imaginative artists.

"But this is not an art show. It is a criminal trial set in motion by the most serious of offences. Murder, sir, in the context I have sketched, is murder most evil. The only physical evidence produced about a bear is an old, tattered bearskin located near the victim's body and bearing the victim's blood. Police investigators believe it was purchased by the victim for the hotel shortly after he arrived in Canada last year, and was eventually destined to hang in the hotel his uncle is building. Quite similar indeed to the bearskins that hang in many hunting lodges, sir. It is an inanimate object, incapable of action, reason, intent, or simply put, killing anyone.

"The central question the Crown poses about the accused is whether an accused involved in a serious criminal matter should be allowed to claim self-defense when he murders a co-conspirator in another matter. Arguably not, Mr. Justice. Was he angry? Possibly. Even scared? Perhaps. But Shane Kanasawae could have chosen a different life. He could have chosen not to be involved in the drug trade, and most certainly, he could have chosen not to meet the victim that fateful night. He made choices, all wrong, and now he is on trial. To grant that he acted in self-defense would be an affront to Canadian justice. This would send the wrong message to all criminals that arguing 'the bogeyman made me do it' can remove any trace of personal responsibility. This is modern Canada, long removed from primitive times and ancient superstitions. We are a rational society. Irrational beliefs do not justify irrational acts. This is what really is at stake, sir: the rule of law.

"Now, let me turn to the only witness who actually saw the murder, Dr. Mary Fraser, or more specifically to her credibility as a witness. I ask the Court's indulgence in doing so, as I recognize that witnesses should be challenged only while testifying when they are able to respond promptly. However, I do believe that what I seek to say at this time is in Dr. Fraser's best interests. May I speak to my reasons, Your Honor?"

Mr. Justice McWilliams pondered the request for a moment, and then addressed the defense. "Mr. Corbiere, I am disposed to allow Mr. McTavish to proceed, to speak to his reasons, but Dr. Fraser is your witness and you may comment if you wish."

Simon and Harley huddled, and quickly concluded to trust McWilliams's instinct for fair play. They also realized that Mary's credibility would be challenged at some point, so why not test the water now?

"We have no objection, Your Honor."

McWilliams looked pleasantly surprised at the answer, as he had expected a contentious sidebar discussion or a conference in chambers. "Very well, then, Mr. McTavish, you may present your reasons."

"Thank you, sir. There is no doubt that Dr. Fraser is an accomplished woman and recognized as a world-class scholar, whose integrity has never been challenged. An Ojibwa herself, she was adopted by a white family in Peterborough, and is now on leave from her position as a tenured professor at the University of Toronto. We also acknowledge that she is considered Canada's ranking expert on native symbols. That is why she was recruited by the victim's uncle, Max Adler of Dresden, Germany, to assist in the development of his hotel on this island, which was to cater primarily to Germans interested in Ojibwa culture and art.

"Having said this, however, we must also raise questions about Dr. Fraser's mental stability. I understand that she is still under a psychologist's care as the result of serious and abusive traumatic events in her childhood. My reason for raising this issue is to minimize the time I will need to examine this witness. I seek your indulgence in this matter, sir."

"Mr. Corbiere?"

"No objections, Your Honor, so long as the Crown does not discuss the credibility of specific evidence that Dr. Fraser may present. In any event, her recent medical and judicial history is well known. We, and Dr. Fraser presumably, have nothing to hide."

"Continue then, Mr. McTavish."

"Let me be clear, Your Honor, lest my colleague find reason to object, that Dr. Fraser is not on trial here. Moreover, let me concede that the murder charge against her was dropped following Shane Kanasawae's confession. Both the accused and his father, Wilbur Kanasawae, told OPP investigators that Wilbur had asked Dr. Fraser to intervene. You will be able to assess the credibility of Mr. Kanasawae and his son on this particular matter if and when they are called as defense witnesses. At this time, I am not challenging the veracity of their statements, only that Your Honor will have his own opportunity to explore their reasoning.

"During the brief period when the OPP had charged Dr. Fraser with murder, her legal counsel at the time, Michael Balfour, proposed, and I agreed, that she should be remanded to the North Bay Forensic Detention Centre for an assessment as to whether she was criminally responsible for the victim's death. We were advised both by hospital staff and by Dr. Fraser's own psychologist, Dr. Noel Callaghan of Little Current, that traumatic events in Dr. Fraser's life were causing horrifying flashbacks and memory repression. Indeed, Dr. Fraser was barely able to communicate with Madam Justice Rita Stroud during the assessment hearing. We do acknowledge that Dr. Fraser became less agitated during the time she was in the detention centre, and that the more serious manifestations of her mental problems were easing.

"In many ways, however, all this is moot because Dr. Fraser was released following Shane's confession. However, I understand she is still being treated for PTSD. The Crown will present expert witnesses to testify whether full recovery is ever possible. Indeed, many military veterans with PTSD as the result of combat experience remain in treatment all their lives.

"Now we are at the nub of the matter. The Crown will be seeking to determine whether Dr. Fraser's memory has been restored to the point where she can credibly testify as to what she saw when the accused murdered Mr. Dietrich. Will she be testifying as one of Canada's most accomplished scholars, attentive to detail with excellent recall, or have her sympathy and imagination woven a story that reflects only what she would have preferred to have happened?"

Simon jumped up. "Your Honor, I object. The Crown is going well beyond Dr. Fraser's history, casting doubts about her integrity and memory."

"I agree, Mr. Corbiere. Your objection is sustained. Mr. McTavish, you're well beyond compassion now. Wrap it up quickly. You are in danger of damaging your own credibility."

"Very well, then, sir. In recent months, I have learned to appreciate the elasticity of memory when it is stretched by trauma and misshapen beyond reality. In the days ahead, the Crown will be asking what Mary Fraser really did see, and what she can remember."

"Mr. Corbiere, are you ready to proceed or shall we adjourn until this afternoon?"

"Yes, Your Honor."

"Yes what?"

"I would like to proceed, sir, as my opening remarks will be brief."

"Very well, then. While brevity is much admired in this court, I do ask that you be thorough."

"Thank you, Your Honor. The Crown is absolutely right...up to a point. My client, Shane Kanasawae, is on trial for murder, to which he has already confessed. Most of the facts of the case are quite simple. Shane and Franz Dietrich met at the hotel site by prior arrangement. This was not a chance meeting, nor did Shane lie in wait for Mr. Dietrich. They had a business arrangement to conclude, albeit about drugs. The deal went bad, Shane hit the victim several times with a piece of construction scaffolding, and Mr. Dietrich died quickly. Dr. Fraser tried to intervene, but arrived too late and unfortunately picked up the murder weapon, leaving her prints on it.

"The central issue, as argued by the Crown, is why Shane hit Franz. Yes, Shane did flee the scene, and avoided the police investigation for some time. Yet he did surrender himself to the OPP, and voluntarily gave the OPP his confession. Subsequent investigation did show traces of the victim's blood on my client's clothes, and also on the laundry hamper in his grandmother's home in Sheguiandah.

"What does this say? That they are good people caught up in an unfortunate situation? Yes, I believe so. But more than that, Your Honor. Begin with the fact that the victim brought a bearskin to the hotel site on the night he died. The bearskin belonged to his uncle, but traces of Mr. Dietrich's blood were discovered on the bear's head, which was found almost severed from the body. The head also showed several marks that suggested it had received blows from a piece of scaffolding. The question we shall address is not so much why Shane struck the bearskin, as why Mr. Dietrich brought it with him that night, and why, as we shall show, he wore it. Why?

"Let me move on to Shane's signed statement, corroborated by both audio- and videotaping. When Shane tried to mention that he had seen what looked like a bear, Detective Constable Chris Marston said, according to the transcript to be entered into evidence: 'Bear? Don't play me, man. No time for Winnie the Pooh. Forget the bear shit.'

"A few moments later, according to the statement, Shane tried to explain again. I again read what Shane said, for the record: 'Then he just sorta dropped out of the sky, yelling and screaming at me, part human, part bear like, and he kept stomping around trying to scare me. I told him I just wanted my money, and he called me some fucking Indian, and said I was only gonna piss it away like my old man, so what good was money to me. He threw some coins at me for a cheap bottle of wine.'

"My point here, Your Honor, is that neither the police nor the crown attorney made any attempt to explore why the victim brought a bearskin to the site, let alone the significance of the bear in native culture, particularly the bearwalker legends, which are well known among the Ojibwa here. In recent years, the bearwalker has been the subject of well-received books and films. Again, Your Honor, as we present our case, please ask yourself: Why did the victim come dressed in a bearskin? Was it just a trophy, as the Crown suggests, or was Franz Dietrich trying to intimidate Shane?

"The evidence will also show that the bearskin itself was struck several times, and was eventually found several meters from the victim's body. Again, we will ask why the bearskin was struck. If it were an inanimate object, as the Crown suggests, then why would anyone bother with it? We will show, through witnesses, that not only did my client believe in the powers of the bearwalker, but also that the victim himself had shown considerable interest in the power of this story. Did Mr. Dietrich believe in the bearwalker? He was well aware that many natives did. We will show that, despite protests from Dr. Fraser, the victim wanted to call the main bar in his uncle's lodge 'The Bearwalker Room' to give their German guests an authentic feel of native life, albeit its dark side."

Simon paused for a moment, turned, and looked to his colleague. Harley shrugged and shook his head.

Simon's eyes opened wide as he stared at the ceiling before facing the judge.

"Is there a problem, Mr. Corbiere?" said Justice McWilliams. "It's unusual to break at this point."

"Well, ah, yes," responded Simon nervously. "It seems that, well, ah, we must advise the court that, ah, it is still uncertain as to whether Dr. Fraser will be able to testify. My colleague and I, ah, remain confident that you will see her as a credible witness.

"Ultimately, her credibility depends on *your* perception of her fitness, not the Crown's questions. If I were less confident about Dr. Fraser, I might have objected strenuously about the crown attorney's characterization of her. And more to the point, we would not have asked her to testify.

"Whether she does appear, however, is up to her. So far, as the Crown knows, she has not given the police any statement, and indeed has not indicated to us whether she will appear as a defense witness."

"Is that all, Mr. Corbiere?"

"Yes, Your Honor."

Even though McWilliams would have liked to ask more questions about Mary Fraser's condition, he decided not to intervene, at least not at this point.

"Very well then, gentlemen, we can proceed with the Crown's next witness after lunch. You will be ready then, Mr. McTavish? Good. Court is adjourned until one-thirty this afternoon."

Chapter 29

After the lunch break, Cal McTavish methodically questioned his first witness to nail down the brutality of the killing.

"So, Dr. Charlebois, you were called by the OPP as acting coroner. Is that correct?"

"Yes, it was my turn on the rotation."

"Without going into detail at this time, how did Mr. Dietrich die?"

"From a massive blow to the skull."

"That is the official cause?"

"More formally then, if you wish, the cause of death was blunt cranial cerebral trauma. My initial observation was confirmed by the post-mortem in Sudbury."

"Tell me, Doctor, what happens inside the skull as a result of this type of blow?"

"There is a rapid acceleration of the brain inside the skull and, ah, the axons between the nerves begin to tear."

"But my understanding, Doctor, is that axons are nerve fibres that carry nerve impulses around the body."

"Yes. Think of them as electrical wiring."

"When its axons are torn, what happens to the life of the brain?"

"Brain activity begins to shut down, often quite suddenly. Intensive haemorrhaging follows the initial trauma."

"Can you tell the court where the victim was hit – in what part of the skull, that is?"

"The blow was to the rear of his skull. He was found face down, confirming that he had been hit from behind."

"Did your examination reveal any other injuries?"

"Just bruises and lacerations on his arms."

"What do they suggest, Doctor?"

"Defensive wounds. There was no damage to his face or legs."

Cal looked at his notes again, cleared his throat.

"Now, Dr. Charlebois, let us move on to the accused, Mr. Kanawasae. Did you examine the accused after he was arrested?"

"Yes, sir, as requested by Detective Sawicki."

Cal then handed her a police file. "And you wrote this report?"

"Yes, that is my report."

"Would you please read the highlighted portions?"

"Of course. It reads: 'Aside from some shortness of breath, unusual for his age and probably due to smoking, Shane is physically fit with no evidence of serious health problems or recent injuries.'"

"Let me ask you this question then: Was Mr. Kanawasae's body bruised in any way? Was there any sign that he had been struck, or involved in a fight?"

"No, there were no bruises on his body."

"Were there any scratch marks from nails or claws?"

"Nothing."

"No physical sign that he had been attacked?"

"Nothing."

"Thank you, Doctor."

"Mr. Corbiere, do you wish to cross-examine this witness?"

"No, Your Honor."

"Hmm. As you wish Mr. Corbiere. Dr. Charlebois, you are excused. Let us take a five-minute break, and then, Mr. McTavish, you may call your next witness."

Simon Corbiere and Harley Reif led their client to the defense conference room off the main courtroom. They were grateful to be out of the court for even a few moments. They didn't speak – that is, until Shane lit up a cigarette and blew smoke at Simon.

"Geez, when you going to fight back, lawyer-man?"

"Put the cigarette out, Shane. There's no smoking in—"

"Fuck you! That bitch Charlebois says like I'm a coward or something, and all you can do is worry about my smoking."

"No, Shane, it's not going well, not at all. But this is what we expected," said Harley. "This is what we told you and your dad. Remember. All the bad news first and then—"

"Cut the crap," Shane interjected, banging the table in front of him. "Screw the judge and the fucking lawyers. Yes, Your Honor, No, Your Honor. May it please Your Honor. Shit! That judge... Man, he just sits up there, says fuck all, stares at me sometimes. And even then I think he don't really see *me* here: just another stupid Indian he's gonna put away. Lots of us in prison anyway. Always room for one more."

Simon took his client by the shoulders. "Listen to me. You're on trial, and so am I, and so is every Aboriginal on the island. Yes, I got a break and moved on. But you're the man here, and you've got to hold it together when you go in. Sit tall, be strong, brother, and when the time comes, tomorrow perhaps, tell your story."

"Oh geez, just tell my story that I whacked him. Busted open his head like a pumpkin."

"No, remind them you're the stand-up guy who turned himself in. That's your strength, man."

"So ya want me to forget what I seen: the bearwalker coming at me, arms up and yelling something fierce."

"Shane, you believe in the bearwalker, and so does your grandmother. I…well, I know the stories. But convincing a white judge… Face it, guy, I don't know. There's only been one other case like this, and it went badly."

"Old man Adler paying you to say this?"

"Yes, but I chose to be here. So what it's going to be, Shane: cool red man or a fucking Indian out there, running scared?"

The bailiff interrupted with a knock on the door. "Time, folks."

Shane said nothing as they returned to the courtroom.

Cal McTavish moved his next witness quickly into the heart of her testimony. "Dr. Kellman, you're a well-educated person and the principal curator for native artefacts at the Royal Ontario Museum in Toronto. For the record, is that correct?"

"Yes."

"And the ROM is not only Ontario's largest museum, but it is generally regarded as one of the finest in the world. I'm sure you agree."

Julia Kellman smiled, enjoying the fulsome flattery and prestige by association. She would be retiring within the year, and having lived alone for most of her life, was already wondering what she would do with her time. Best not to burn bridges with the native community, she frequently told herself.

"I most definitely would agree to that description. We have—"

"Please, let me move on, Doctor. Your collections of native artefacts, particularly Ojibwa, are considered comprehensive."

"Yes, we work with many collectors and, of course, our native-born ethnologists. Yes, we have extensive collections."

"All appropriately catalogued?"

"Of course. We take great care that nothing is lost. We see ourselves as stewards, not owners."

"Well, then," said McTavish, moving closer to the witness, barely holding back a smug grin, and obviously confident of the answer he was pursuing, "tell us, does the ROM have a bearwalker in its collections, or even a piece of a bearwalker?"

"Not that I am aware of."

"That was carefully stated, Dr. Kellman, but let me reframe the question. If the ROM did have a bearwalker in its collection, surely you would know about it?"

"Oh, obviously yes. It is my responsibility to know such things. I have read the legends, appreciated the fine artistic renderings, and even attended a viewing of *The Bearwalker* film. Most intriguing."

"But I repeat, and please indulge me on this line of questioning, have you ever seen a bearwalker?"

"No. Never."

"So then, Dr. Kellman, you have no objective proof that the legends are true."

"For many natives, Mr. McTavish, the issue is not one of objective truth, as you say, but belief."

"Confine your answer to my question, please, Doctor. Have you any scientific and objective proof that a bearwalker exists?"

"No, not as your question is framed – none."

"Thank you, Doctor."

"Mr. Corbiere, do you wish to cross?"

"Yes, Your Honor, just one question."

Simon rose from the defense table.

"Dr. Kellman, I heard you answer Mr. McTavish that the issue is not about objective truth, but about belief.

Before I ask my question, is that substantially what you said?"

Judge McWilliams raised a hand to halt Simon, and asked the court reporter to read the curator's full answer on that point.

"Thank you, Your Honor. Now, Dr. Kellman, please feel free to complete your remarks about belief."

"Well then, let me pick up the thread of that idea. Yes, many natives, particularly on Manitoulin, believe in the old legends. They hold that the spirit world is part of their everyday life, both good spirits and bad spirits. In turn, this is what inspires their creative people. That is all I was going to say."

"Thank you, Doctor," said Simon, returning to his chair.

"Do you wish to re-cross at this time, Mr. McTavish?" asked Justice McWilliams.

"Yes, Your Honor. Dr. Kellman, you have an appreciation for native art. But, Doctor, who really knows what inspires the wonderfully creative mind? Have you personally questioned the Ojibwa artists as to the links between their beliefs and their art? Where does their imagination come from? Which comes first: the art or the legends?"

"Interestingly put, Mr. McTavish, but I'm afraid I can't answer you. I suppose it depends on the legend and the artist."

"Ever the academic, eh, Dr. Kellman? So then, to sum up, if I may: You have no objective proof that a bearwalker exists, nor do you have any specific, objective knowledge about the links and causality between art, legends, and beliefs. In a general sense then, Doctor, do you agree with my summary?"

"In a general sense, do I agree? You must appreciate, Mr. McTavish, this is not how I might phrase my considered position. But in a rough sense, I do concede the direction of your logic. Yes, I have no objective proof of a bearwalker. That is as far as I want to go, if only out of respect for native beliefs. I really do regard—"

"Thank you, Doctor, you have been most helpful."

Simon looked at Harley Reif, and the two exchanged slight smiles.

Chapter 30

The next morning

Even with every seat taken, the courtroom was quiet as Simon Corbiere introduced his first witnesses. Noel Callaghan confirmed she had been treating Mary for PTSD flashbacks before Franz was killed. Cal McTavish jabbed lightly at Noel during his cross-examination, questioning her objectivity, but it was obvious he didn't want to challenge her professional diagnosis, or get into Mary's childhood abuse issues, at least at that time.

Simon was keen to get to his next witness, Father Murray J. Courtney, a lanky, forty-something Jesuit anthropologist who had spent several summers helping out at the Holy Cross Mission at the big Wikwemikong Reserve on the eastern end of the island.

As Father Courtney was sworn in, the defense strategy became obvious to Justice McWilliams. Interesting, he mused to himself. If the testimony of the theologian bombed, then so would the defense's case. Simon had to discredit the Crown's contention that irrational beliefs – at least so considered by mainstream standards of wisdom and science – could never justify an irrational act like murder. On the other hand, if Simon could prove that belief sometimes could justify the end, then the defense would have created a much more credible foundation by which to assess the testimony of other witnesses.

Cal McTavish, for his part, saw Father Courtney as a renegade scholar, one whom the Vatican had reprimanded several times for advocating that native spirituality and foundational ethics had much to offer Catholicism and other Christian churches. This is animism, if not outright paganism, declared the Congregation for the Doctrine of the Faith when it examined Courtney's acceptance of the aboriginal belief that animals have souls. As a result, in the early nineties the Vatican had banned him from teaching at Catholic universities for a year. He doesn't even dress like a priest, thought Cal, taking stock of Courtney, who sat in the witness chair in a rumpled blazer, grey turtleneck sweater, cotton pants, and hiking boots. Priests should wear their collars in court, he thought. Absolutely! The man has no respect for anybody. Outrageous! And that scruffy hair – demonic almost.

Simon Corbiere saw a much different person: the awesomely intelligent man who had taught him as a high school student, many years earlier, to see the possibility of beauty in all things, enjoy ritual, but always dig beneath the symbolism for meaning. It had been ten or twelve years since they had seen each other, and Simon was struck by Father Courtney's full mane of silver-grey hair. A lush beard and bushy eyebrows framed his open, confident face, making him look like a scholar of old, or even an explorer of sorts, prepared to climb a mountain to see the other side.

Simon moved to establish Father Courtney's credentials.

"Your doctorate is from Fordham University in New York, is that right, Father?"

"That's right, in 1991. Finally."

"What was your doctoral dissertation about?"

"A comparative analysis of aboriginal spiritualities around the world and Christian belief systems."

"Was it well received, Father?"

"Oh, some academic journals and theologians nit-picked, but yes, it was generally well received. Very gratifying and humbling in its own way. After all those years, travelling and writing in many countries."

"That's not unusual, though, is it, Jesuits who move around combining scholarship and pastoral work?"

"Those whose health holds, anyway. Yes. We are called to long journeys, in my case with indigenous peoples in Mexico, Haiti, Brazil, and, ah, the Philippines."

"As well as the Ojibwa here."

"Of course, Mr. Corbiere. I didn't mean to forget Manitoulin. It's just that, well, my journey as a Jesuit really started here. I'm talking about my fascination with the overlap of Christian and native cultures. The symbols differ from culture to culture and country to country, but the meanings are the same in most cases."

"You are considered an expert in this field, then?"

Father Courtney winced and then scratched behind one ear and cleared his throat. "People tell me that."

"Can you speak louder, Father? I'm not sure the court can hear you."

"Oh, yes, of course. How's my voice now? Better? About being an expert then. Such a presumptive word. I'm not comfortable with that label. Look, I just enjoy what I do, and trust to God's providence that my work will help others."

Simon nodded, and reminded himself to speak slowly. Be calm, guy, he thought. Like an elder. Not as soft-spoken, though.

"Let me get to the heart of this, Father. Your scholarship is well known and I am sure is accepted by the Court, and perhaps even by the Crown. No objection to that, Mr. McTavish? Good. Father, you obviously believe in God?"

"There are many words that mean the same, sir: Great Father, Manitou, Allah, many more that—"

"Your point is taken, Father, but I asked a simple question: Do you believe in God? Yes or no?"

"Well now, do lawyers always want simple answers to complex questions? A most curious habit, Mr. Corbiere. Are truth and justice always that simple? When I was in Haiti with—"

"Another time, Father. Please bear with me. Your answer is important, as I have framed the question. Do you believe in God? Yes or no?"

"A simple answer then. Yes. Of course."

"No doubts ever, Father?"

"Doubts are part of life, sir. I'm a scholar, not a mystic, but with the belief that ultimately my questions will be answered. Yes, that is what I do, who I am... Forgive me, I tend to ramble at times."

"Now, Father, do you also believe in evil?"

"The answer you seek is more complex. God, Supreme Being – the list is long – is everywhere to the believer. I see God in the earth and the skies around us, in the very nature of humanity. Even science can trace creation back to a nanosecond before the Big Bang. There are miracles and revelations, some of which I obviously concede were created only by hysteria and charlatans. But most of us accept, even as our Charter of Rights implies, that God is everywhere."

"But do you believe in evil, Father?"

Before Father Courtney could respond, Cal jumped up to object.

"Objection, Your Honor. Where is this going? This is a murder trial, and my young colleague is taking us far away from the evidential trail into theological speculation. I'm as God-fearing as the next person – more so, my wife tells me – but clearly and simply, Your Honor, murder is evil, most evil."

Justice McWilliams was caught off-guard by the objection, as he was more taken with Father Courtney's testimony than he was with the usual run of criminal evidence. Still, he privately wondered why the priest referred to the Charter of Rights at this point. What would Corbiere do with this testimony from his own witness? Eventual grounds for an appeal?

"Before I rule on your objection, Mr. McTavish, I, too, would like to know where Mr. Corbiere is going with this. Be brief, though."

"Very well, Your Honor," said Simon. "As I tried to convey during my opening remarks, we are not here to debate whether my client killed Mr. Dietrich. The more important question I raised was why he did so and what was his state of mind at the time. Is his belief in the bearwalker credible? To answer this, we must convince you, sir, that evil exists, or at the very least that the belief in evil, in all its forms, is both credible and reasonable. May I continue, or does my colleague wish to argue that evil does not exist?"

"Mr. McTavish, I'm inclined to let Mr. Corbiere continue with his line of questions on this. Unless you would like to reframe your objection?"

Cal looked back to his own staff, who could only shrug. No one wanted to test the constitutional right to freedom of religion. If one was free to believe in God, was he not also free to believe in evil?

"Not at this time, Your Honor."

"Proceed, Mr. Corbiere, but I do caution you to get to your point."

"Thank you," said Simon, looking at his notes to pick up on his line of questioning. "So, Father, once more unto the breach. Let me repeat the question: Do you believe in evil?"

"Very well. Interesting process, this, almost worse than my inquisition at the Vatican. My answer must be yes; I have seen too much of evil to say no."

"Are we all responsible, then, for our own evil choices?"

"Most of us, certainly."

"Most of us? Please elaborate."

"Cultural influences exist, obviously, but more importantly, so do neurological diseases, the really nasty ones that diminish the capacity to choose between good and bad, or even to be aware of consequences."

"Like schizophrenia?"

"Yes, of course. Also, and much more common on Manitoulin, with victims of fetal alcohol syndrome. And even with some types of psychopaths, often charming, highly intelligent people who have little or no sense of remorse."

Justice McWilliams gave way to impatience. "Please move on, Mr. Corbiere. With all due respect to your witness, you are not plowing new ground."

"My next question will get us there, Your Honor. Now, Father, since evil exists, do you believe in evil spirits, as my client says he does?"

"That's not a question that allows for an easy answer."

"Oh? Really?" said Simon with some frustration. "You either believe, or you don't believe. You're a scholar, you're well-traveled, and most certainly you understand what I am asking you."

"Indeed. What I was trying to say is that within my own Church, opinions vary. Some theologians distinguish between the spirit of evil and evil spirits. More recently, even the Vatican, in its revised rituals for exorcism distinguishes between obsession and possession. The concept of evil spirits is too primitive for some, shall we say, modern minds."

"But, Father? Is there a 'but'?"

"As you say, Mr. Corbiere, I'm a scholar. People like me are addicted to 'buts.' There are at least two formal rituals in the Catholic Church – and in most Christian faiths – that specifically recognize the existence of the ultimate evil spirit. The language of both baptism and exorcism demands the rejection of Satan."

"Have you ever seen Satan, Father?"

"No, I haven't. I haven't seen God either, but I believe in God."

"So, do you believe in Satan? A simple yes or no please."

"The Church's updated catechism says the devil, or Satan, and other demons were fallen angels."

"And, as you say, Father, that's what the Church catechism teaches. But you belong to the Church's intellectual elite. Just tell us what you believe. Again I ask: Do you, Doctor Murray J. Courtney, believe in Satan?"

"Yes, I do. Angels are real. So, therefore, are fallen angels. Perhaps some are here in this courtroom."

"Finally, Father, and Your Honor, we circle back to the bearwalker. Since you respect the Supreme Beings in other faiths, do you accept those faiths' concepts of evil spirits as well?"

"Logically one must follow the other, however culturally alien some forms of evil may appear. It's arrogant, even hypocritical, to dismiss them as old stories, little more than worn-out metaphors to entertain children."

"Hypocritical? Explain please."

"Most belief systems have evolved from oral histories and faith witnesses. Some become quite triumphant as time goes on and forget their humble origins. I am much taken with the work of William Asikinack at Saskatchewan's Indian Federated College. His point is that stories, such as the bearwalker, are as real to Aboriginals as the Bible is to Christians."

"Your Honor," Cal interjected, "expert testimony is one thing. But these are obscure references. If the defense wants to cite William Asikinack, let Mr. Asikinack testify here himself."

Justice McWilliams made a note in his court book that, while Father Courtney's remark was definitely hearsay, it went to the heart of the case.

"Sustained. Hmm. Mr. Corbiere, let's end this line of questioning quickly, but I do want you to provide the appropriate academic citations supporting Father Courtney's remarks. By five o'clock tomorrow afternoon, shall we say?"

Simon Corbiere agreed and then ran a finger under his shirt collar, smoothed his hair, and found his way again.

"I repeat, Father: Do you accept the various concepts of evil spirits held by, shall we say, the Judeo-Christian faiths? Just yes or no, please, this time, Father."

"Yes, I accept that other forms of evil exist. There's another point I want to make, if I may."

Simon, wary of treading into unknown fields, stepped back and looked first at Harley Reif who shrugged, and then to the bench for guidance. Justice McWilliams was intrigued, but didn't want to signal any comment at this time. "He's your witness, Mr. Corbiere. You opened the door on this."

In turn, Simon feared that if he closed off Father Courtney, his reluctance to pose more questions might undermine the logic of his case. Take a chance, he told himself. No other option, pal. Go for it.

"I usually prefer to ask the questions, Father, but you're the expert in this field."

"I realize that what I said may seem bizarre coming from a person with my education and who represents a church of princes and palaces, with minutely defined dogma and canon law all wrapped in the presumption of one holy and apostolic church, triumphant in history, at least in its own eyes."

Father Courtney paused to pull a handkerchief from an inside pocket of his jacket and mopped his brow before continuing. He knew his superiors might find his views difficult to defend if the local bishop took exception.

"How then does all this play out on Manitoulin Island, the spiritual centre of Ojibwa culture? Not easily, I'm afraid. For too many years, the Church aggressively tried to repress native spirituality. Many Ojibwa rituals were banned outright.

"Mercifully, we have moved away from that self-serving dominance. No physical church means more to me today than the church at West Bay, or M'Cheeng in Ojibwa. There the Catholic mass is celebrated amid native spiritual symbols. Smudging ceremonies often precede mass. Even the baptismal font, where believers are asked to reject Satan, is built on the back of a turtle, central to the Ojibwa creation story. Yes, I do believe in the spirit I call God, and in Satan, and yes, I respect that the bearwalker is a powerful symbol of evil for many Ojibwa believers."

Simon was tempted to probe deeper, but decided to let Father Courtney's last statement stand on its own.

As Simon returned to his seat, Cal McTavish didn't even pretend to look at his notes when he approached Father Courtney for the cross-examination.

"Ah, Father, you're not wearing the traditional Roman collar, the usual symbol of your priesthood. Does this mean that you reject some or all of your church's teachings?"

Simon wanted to object, but Harley pulled him back as Father Courtney grinned at the question.

"Not at all, Mr. McTavish. Many Jesuits wear suits and ties, now, or more casual clothes, like the people we serve. Nobody seems to mind. Do you?"

"Just checking, Father, about the framework for your beliefs. Now you took an oath to tell the truth when you took the stand."

"Yes. I—"

"A simple 'yes' will suffice. As a priest, oaths and vows are important to you. Yes?"

"Yes."

"Tell me then, have you ever broken your priestly vows?"

Simon went ballistic, almost jumping across the defense table.

"Objection, Your Honor. This is...this is outrageous. Father Courtney is not on trial here, nor are his vows. This is the rankest form of harassment."

Cal McTavish did not give ground. "Your Honor, Mr. Corbiere's own questions centered largely on the witness's beliefs, both as a scholar and a priest. We all know his own Church silenced him for a year. Father Courtney also cited specific Church rituals. Since Mr. Corbiere opened that door, I intend to examine the relationship between Father Courtney and his church. May I continue?"

Mr. Justice McWilliams pursed his lips. The dividing line between church and state was always a tricky issue, but since he was trying the case without a jury, he decided to hear more.

"Objection overruled. Yes, you may continue, Mr. McTavish, but I also remind you that the witness is not on trial here. So be brief, sir."

"Thank you, Your Honor," said Cal, turning to face the witness.

"I repeat the question, Father. Have you ever broken your priestly vows?"

"Hmm. Have I ever broken my vows of obedience and celibacy? Is that what you're asking?"

"Those will do. Yes. Have you ever broken them?"

"I discuss my moral life with my spiritual advisor and confessor on a regular basis."

"And?"

"My sins are forgiven, and I start anew."

"What sins? Have you broken your vows? Can you be trusted?"

"I suppose that is a matter for God, and here, I presume, for the judge of this case."

"You're evading the intent of my question, Father, and you know—"

Simon objected again. "Objection, Your Honor. The Crown is badgering the witness with presumptions that are way out of line."

"Objection sustained. I agree, Mr. Corbiere. Do you have any other questions, Mr. McTavish?"

"Ah…yes. I did mean to ask it sooner, as I do for all so-called expert witnesses."

"Go ahead then."

"What were you paid to testify here today?"

"Come again?"

"You've invested considerable time in the development of your scholarly insights, and you don't live here anymore. Surely you have a fee?"

"Are you implying that I'm for sale?"

Simon began to object but Harley pulled him down.

"Those are your words, Father," said McTavish. "Do they fit?"

"No more than you're paid to question me. Are lawyers for hire?"

"You're evading my question, Father. Surely you can distinguish between sins of commission and sins of omission."

"Neat point, Mr. McTavish. For the record then, the defense is paying my travel expenses and I'm bunking at the Jesuit mission here."

"That's all? No gratuities?"

"Yes. One."

"Oh? Can you explain?"

"I prefer a relatively simple life, sir. I did suggest that the defense team and Herr Adler make a contribution to the library at the Ojibwa high school at Wicki. Whether they do so is up to them."

Cal withdrew, knowing he had pushed too far.

"Mr. Corbiere. Re-cross?"

"Just one question. Father, do you still say mass as a priest in good standing?"

"I was in good standing when I arrived here this morning. And yes, I said mass."

"Thank you. That is all, Your Honor."

Chapter 31

At home, that evening

Fergus tried to avoid discussing the trial with Mary.

So far, she had given no hint that she would be able to testify about what she had seen the night of the murder. Only once had she asked about Shane, but she didn't seem to comprehend or even care about the answer. Her therapy was progressing well, although the purging, as expected, was both physically and mentally draining, and she had only a fitful interest in life beyond her own quest for sanity.

In the dark night of his own soul, Fergus accepted the Crown's argument that Mary's memory might be so twisted that her testimony could be a tortuous waste of time – an incoherent babble at worst, or just a blank stare. He knew that Cal would pounce on any sign of weakness, and the experience of being questioned could put Mary's long-term recovery at risk. Be cool, man, had been the advice from both Simon and Noel. Let tomorrow dawn, like any other day.

Not that simple, thought Fergus. Put my faith in small steps instead – many, many small steps, and not big romantic bounds. Ease into this, put dinner on the table for her, and light a candle.

For the moment, Mary seemed to be keeping her cool better than Fergus was. She was not irritated when Simon Corbiere called to advise her he was considering taking more time with the Jesuit anthropologist before possibly calling her as a witness. Fergus, of course, understood the ploy could give Mary more time.

A few hours later, however, Mary grew unusually quiet as they locked up their house for the night. She didn't linger over the computer. When Fergus inquired what she would wear in the morning, she shrugged, and when he asked if she would like to talk about the trial, she suddenly turned, almost stumbling as she ran up the stairs.

Frozen, Fergus could only watch. Ah shit, he told himself, shit, bloody shit, she's shutting down again. He knew he should have told Noel that Mary wasn't sleeping well and sometimes got up in the middle of the night to stare out the window. But she usually came back to bed, explaining that her various medications had given her a fragile bladder.

He believed her – well, he almost did – because there was a deeper, darker part of his subconscious that told him there was another layer to Mary's story that her therapy hadn't yet reached, a layer repressed in some nether world of shame or guilt. What really rankled was that no one could tell him when the fog would ever lift.

By the time Fergus had followed Mary into their bedroom, the lights were out. He slipped in quietly and fumbled for his nightclothes, until he realized that she was not yet in bed. He waited a few seconds for sounds from the bathroom, and, hearing nothing, turned his head to look for her.

She's gone again. Oh Lord, will it ever end? Now what is she up to?

Then he saw her form by the window overlooking the valley, which was now only a murky blend of dark greens, blues, and blacks.

Her sobbing crept slowly into his awareness, a gentle heaving and a catching of breath. She had a blanket wrapped around her because the room was cold, as they preferred to sleep with the windows open. Her feet, though, were bare and she was shivering.

Fergus tried not to startle her, coughing as he approached. "Mary, are you okay?"

"I can't see it all, just..."

"Come back to bed with me. You'll freeze standing here."

Fergus put his arm around her, and tried to lead her away from the window. She pulled away, and faced the window. Noel had told him to expect this. Night sweats and terrors might strike, as Mary moved beyond her repressed memories, and began to face the prospect of telling the judge what she had seen. "It's still a risk," Noel had told him. "There's something she has to face – we both know that – but we might lose her again, perhaps for a long time, if it's too much."

Noel had even suggested that Simon and Harley ask Mr. Justice McWilliams to delay Mary's testimony for a few days, but in the end, they all agreed such a delay might only serve to weaken her credibility as a witness. "Just help her through the night, Fergus," said Noel. "Let her find strength and peace in the ordinary things around her. We'll drop by for coffee about eight and drive you to Gore Bay."

Now, standing in the grey gloom of the night, Mary seemed fully awake.

"We have to go there, Fergus, now. Will you take me?"

"Where, Mary? Gore Bay? It's too early for to travel."

"Not the courthouse. Not now. Not yet."

Fergus, unsure of what Mary meant, decided to listen for a bit.

Several moments passed, and then Mary turned to face him.

"I can't see it all, Fergus. It comes in and out, just wisps and…" Her words petered out.

Fergus paused a moment. "You can't see Shane, is that it?"

"Not just Shane. Not even… Just take me there, Fergus. I... I need to feel it again."

Another pause. "But where, Mary? The construction site, where Franz died?"

"Yes. There. I want to see where I stood."

"Now? It's almost midnight. See what?"

"Why can't you do what I… No, no, that's not fair. Help me through this, my loving, sweet man who shares my hell. I need to know what's real and what's—"

Fergus was too intrigued to remain silent. "So there's something else? Oh Lord, you saw something else? That's it?"

Mary turned away again, arms wrapped tightly around herself as she leaned forward, her forehead on the window glass.

"Maybe."

"Maybe? Somebody else was there?"

That possibility hung in the air so ominously that Fergus could barely breathe. Mary was slow to respond. Suddenly, her body stiffened, and her head snapped around as she tried to fight off the implications of what she had said. "No. None of your damn questions, Fergus. Just be with me. I can see it, and then I can't. There's a voice I almost hear – like it's from another world – and it's squeezing my memory dry. I'm lost again, Fergus, and I don't know what's real anymore."

For a few moments, Fergus felt just as lost. He remembered a Mi'kmaq print his wife had given him the Christmas before she died. It was a simple sketch of two persons sitting on separate rocks, probably at low tide in the Bay of Fundy off the Atlantic between Nova Scotia and New Brunswick. Yet they were elementally linked by the sky and sun overhead and the water and earth beneath them.

"I'm still here, Mary, and I'm very, very real. It's good, so, so good, yeah, woman of my life."

"It was good, wasn't it? Before all this, I mean. Do you ever wish you hadn't come here with me?"

"Shhh. We'll have none of that. Best get dressed warmly, and I'll make some coffee, and get us a flashlight."

Chapter 32

The next morning

Harley Reif was stunned when Fergus told him about Mary's new doubts. The two men were in the rear booth of a Gore Bay restaurant, heads huddled over coffee. Harley was due in court shortly, but Mary had opted instead for an unusually long visit to the restaurant's washroom.

"No games, Harley. Bloody hell, I'm not sure I can hold Mary together much longer."

"I know that, Fergus, and so does Simon. But she needs to make her statement to the cops before she ever testifies in court."

"Dammit, Harley, you weren't there last night, so where in hell do you get off? Just listen, please. We went back to the hotel site because there's a terrible guilt burning inside her that comes from God knows where. All I could do was kneel with her in the mud, just be there for her."

"She didn't tell you? After all this, you just let her go back to bed?"

"What I know, Harley, is not important. She had to face this moment by herself, feel it her way, and when it was over, she put a finger to my lips and asked me to take her home and let her sleep."

"And?"

"And I'll be there again if she needs me. But I'm still frightened to death, Harley, terribly, sweet-Jesus-frightened that I... we...well, all of us could lose her again."

Harley tried again to shape his strategy. "Still no idea of what she saw?"

"No, dammit! All I really know is that one way or another, today or tomorrow, Mary first has to make a formal statement to the cops. It might take several hours. Routine drill, Peltier tells me. Bullshit! Nothing with cops is ever routine, but if she makes a credible statement, if…"

"That's a load of 'ifs,' Fergus. We could ask for more time."

"More time? Shit, no. That's what I'm trying to tell you. We're running out of time. Mary either pulls it together now – or perhaps never."

"Easy, Ferg. Take a breath. I'm scared, too, but if you don't know what Mary's going to say, then Simon and I don't know either. Which brings us to the worst-case scenario. Hypothetical, of course, but nonetheless possible: She blows up again, or breaks down, becomes rambling and incoherent on the stand, lashing out, so badly that she's no longer a credible witness. McWilliams gets turned off, the media howl, and Mary becomes useless to Simon's case. And to Shane's freedom."

"So what is it, Harley? First Shane's dad goes on the stand, and then Mary?"

"Whenever, Fergus, whenever she can."

Assailed by the voices and images haunting her, Mary was slow to rejoin them from her refuge in the washroom. Fergus reached out, but she turned away, and walked to the restaurant door on the hillside street. Stepping outside, she stared blankly over the dull grey rooftops of the small shops and homes, below to the rippling blue water of Gore Bay. She closed her eyes tightly and squeezed the palms of her hands into her ears, completely oblivious to the fact that Fergus and Harley had joined her. All Fergus could do was shake his head, then guide her gently back to the car. Harley watched, barely breathing, scared that she might never be able to testify

When court began later that morning, Simon called Wilbur Kanasawae as the next witness for the defense. Wilbur was clearly not comfortable in the witness chair: fidgety, running a hand through his scraggy hair, which he had washed that morning, along with his green work shirt. More seconds passed while he dried his sweaty palms on his thighs. When Simon asked why he didn't intervene himself, instead of asking Mary Fraser to rescue his son from Franz's influence, Wilbur looked down for a long moment before answering.

"I…I…never was much of a father. Away too much. Let his grandmother look after him, my wife's mother. She doesn't think much of me, either. Don't see her much. Just pass her on the road sometimes."

Simon nodded. "Grandmothers raise a lot of Aboriginal children, isn't that right, Mr. Kanasawae?"

Cal McTavish sat up straight. "Objection, Your Honor. Counsel is leading his witness."

"Sustained. Rephrase your question, Mr. Corbiere."

"Well, I meant… Yes, of course. Mr. Kanasawae, please tell the court, do many grandmothers raise their grandchildren?"

"Happens a lot. We try to respect our elders."

"As do I, sir," said Simon quickly, anxious to get to the core of Wilbur's testimony without spooking his witness. "Dr. Fraser then, she's not Shane's grandmother. So why did you turn to her for help?"

"Easy. She's a good woman and looks out for all the natives working on the hotel. Talks to everybody. Teaches at the big schools down in Toronto. Guess that's why Mr. Adler hired her."

"I see. Did you ever talk to her about Shane, your son?"

"Sometimes."

"In her office?"

"At the grocery store in town."

"Why?"

"To get food. Didn't need much, just coffee, tea, milk – the usual."

"Sorry, Mr. Kanasawae. Of course, you were shopping. But can you tell me why you spoke to Dr. Fraser about your son? That's what we need to know."

"Shane don't talk to me anymore. But my cousin who works in the reserve office has been telling me Shane must be getting lot of money from the young German. Bought himself a pickup and goes into Sudbury a lot. New clothes, too. Someone saw him selling drugs near the high school. The police've been asking questions, too."

Cal didn't even bother to stand this time: "Objection. Hearsay, Your Honor."

"Sustained. Unless you have a point with this, Mr. Corbiere."

"Agreed, Your Honor. I realize this is hearsay, but I seek some leeway here. The issue here is not whether my client was dealing drugs. But we do need to understand Wilbur Kanasawae's state of mind when he asked Dr. Fraser to intervene."

"The difference is noted, but it's tenuous. Be careful, or you and I will be having a little chat."

Wilber looked puzzled, and Simon apologized to the older man for the lawyer-talk before going on.

"Did you tell this to Dr. Fraser?"

"Yes."

"And did you call her at some later date?"

"Yes. She gave me her number, and told me to call if I needed help."

"Oh. Can you tell us when you called her, Mr. Kanasawae?"

"I was doing my rounds, probably about eleven-thirty, up on the hill, checking the construction site."

As Wilbur reached for the water glass, Simon handed two sheets of paper to the judge. "Your Honor, we are submitting telephone records for Dr. Fraser's cell phone. We have highlighted the call she received from Mr. Kanasawae at 11:38 p.m. on the evening before Mr. Dietrich's body was found."

Simon turned back to address his witness.

"And what did you say to Dr. Fraser?"

"Didn't have to say much. Told her I had just left Shane and I had a bad feeling he was heading for trouble, more than he could handle. Could she help? She said she'd try. Didn't talk much more."

"I understand. Now, can you tell us what happened when you saw Shane at the construction site the night Mr. Dietrich was killed?"

"First, I saw Shane standing alone by a pile of scaffolding and wood. Scared me at first 'cause I didn't recognize him. Thought he was a thief or something."

"Did you tell him to leave?"

"Tried to, but he wouldn't listen. Probably drinking a lot. At first, he was mumbling so bad that I asked him to tell it again, so I could understand him. He pulled himself together a bit. Said he was waiting for Mr. Dietrich. Franz. So I asked him again to leave and he...he told me to bugger off. Called me a stupid old man who never did anything for him, so why should he listen to me now? And then...then...I...ah…he said…I can't…"

Justice McWilliams asked Wilbur if he wanted a few minutes to compose himself. Wilbur took a sip of water, offered by Simon, cleared his throat, and tried to wipe away the dampness welling up in his eyes.

"No, I can go on. Thank you, though, but I must live with Shane's words. He told me then that in the darkness, any fool with a stiff prick could screw a woman and get her pregnant, but that didn't make me his father, just some fucking stupid Indian who drank too much. I hadn't been there for him before, so why get in his face now? That's what he told me."

"Did you leave him then?"

"No, I felt I had to try again. He was angry, yeah, but he was still my son and it was time to be his father."

"To be his father. I see. What did you do?"

"I tried to get closer to him but he moved away and began yelling at me. I thought he was scared. He told me he had to wait, because Franz owed him a lot of money. He said he owed some bikers money and if he couldn't pay, they would… He didn't finish the sentence, just pushed me away, and told me to go hide in my guardhouse. Forget I ever knew him."

"Mr. Kanasawae, I know this is hard for you to come here and explain to the court what happened. But I would like to ask you one more question about Shane. Did he physically threaten you? Did he pick up any of the construction materials, or point a knife or gun at you?"

"No, I thought he was too scared himself. All he wanted was his money."

"What about the late Mr. Dietrich? Did you speak to him that night?"

"No, not then, but I knew that Franz liked to wander around up there in the dark most nights. Anybody else, I would have run him off, but he's Mr. Adler's nephew."

"I see," said Simon. "You left the hotel site then, is that right?"

"Finished my route, and went back to the security shack down the hill. That's my job."

"Now let's move on. Why did you call Dr. Fraser and not the police?"

"Like I said, she's a good woman. Strong, too. If Shane wouldn't listen, then I thought perhaps she could convince Franz to leave. If he didn't, then she could go to Mr. Adler, or perhaps the police herself. If anyone could protect Shane, I thought she could."

Simon consulted some papers on his desk, spoke with Harley, then returned to face the witness stand. Wilbur had covered his face and eyes with his hands, as he recalled the humiliation and helplessness he had felt that night. "Just a few more questions," Simon said softly, showing a measure of respect for the older man. "In an earlier statement, you told the police that you found Mr. Dietrich's body about 12:45 a.m. Is that right, sir?"

"Yes, on my hourly rounds."

"Did he, the victim, appear to be dead?"

"Not my job to say so. He wasn't moving, no sign of breathing, so I left like the security manual says. Didn't touch nothing. I called the police. That's my job."

"And Dr. Fraser?"

"No. I'd called her already, but didn't know if she had come. She wasn't there when I found the body. And nobody asked me about her. So I didn't say anything."

"You just did your job." Simon scratched his forehead before going on. "What about your son, Shane, why didn't you tell the police that you had seen him on the site an hour or so earlier?"

"Shane, he's my son, whatever he says about me. Probably wrong what I did, but I guess I owed him that much. When we talked, that was just family, him and me, no one else mattered."

"I see, sir. Now what about Dr. Fraser? Did you talk to her the next morning?"

"No. I heard later she had gone to Sudbury. Sick-like."

"Before that, Mr. Kanasawae, did you see her come to the hotel site?"

"No."

"She didn't check in with you at your trailer?"

"No."

"Are there any other routes to the hotel site, other than past your security post?"

"Lots of paths from the roads in the village."

"One last question. And please take as much time as you need. Don't rush."

"Okay."

"Just tell the judge again what you wanted Mary, Dr. Fraser, to do."

"I guess to do what I couldn't do. I don't know how to speak to Shane anymore, but she can... She can lead us away from these evil spirits. I wanted her to bring Shane back to me, not to hurt Franz or anything, just help Shane remember who he is."

"That's all, Your Honor."

"Mr. McTavish, do you wish to cross at this time?"

"Just a few questions, sir. Mr. Kanasawae, first, let me thank you for sharing what must have been a painful moment. Every parent in this room feels the profound depth of your son's rejection, a soul-rending of biblical proportions. Tell me then, did you really expect that Dr. Fraser would wave a fairy wand, and make everything better? Did it never cross your mind that the accused, your son, would resort to killing Franz out of a misguided desire for revenge? If he was angry enough to push you, his father, away, were you not also worried that he could kill

Mr. Dietrich? Did it ever occur to you that Dr. Fraser might simply stand by and watch Shane execute Mr. Dietrich?"

Both Harley and Simon were on their feet shouting "Objection" even before Cal had finished his line of questioning. Reporters were scribbling madly as Harley gave way to Simon.

"Did it ever occur to the crown attorney that he is speculating wildly?" Simon yelled, barely holding himself back from crossing the aisle. "Who's the executioner here? Dr. Fraser is not on trial, and yet, without the smallest shred of evidence or reason, the Crown accuses her of complicity. Your Honor, that venom has no place in—"

"That is enough, Mr. Corbiere."

"My apologies to this court, Your Honor," Simon said as he returned to his seat.

"Mr. McTavish?"

"Just exploring Mr. Kanasawae's state of mind, Your Honor. Mr. Corbiere did open that door."

"Save your speculation for your closing, Mr. McTavish. You are free, of course, to challenge Dr. Fraser when she takes the stand, but your speculations are clearly prejudicial until that time. Objection, objections, whatever, from whomever – they're upheld. Let's break for fifteen minutes. You have one more witness, Mr. Corbiere?"

"Yes, Your Honor. Dr. Fraser. I hope so, anyway."

With the court back in session, Simon reluctantly confessed to Justice McWilliams that his next witness would not be available. "My understanding is that she may be able to make her statement to the police this morning, but she stills tires easily. That's all I can say at this moment. Perhaps she will be more able tomorrow morning."

Equally perplexed and more than a little frustrated, Justice McWilliams called the two lawyers to his bench.

Simon proposed adjourning for the rest of the day, given, he said, that Mary was the only witness to the killing and the fragility of her mind was well known to everybody. After some eye-rolling and hand-wringing, even Cal agreed with the defense, more anxious to get Mary on the stand than to move on to the formal summations. Curious, thought McWilliams, but he accepted Simon's motion.

Fergus was simply grateful to spend the day with Mary. After leaving the restaurant, he drove her first to the OPP office, and waited while she gave a formal statement. Then he took her home to their farmhouse without asking a single question. She, in turn, said nothing to him, sitting still with eyes shut most of the way, stirring only when he made the sharp turn down the lane to their house. Be steady, he told himself, and trust the simple pace of their lives to restore her courage and calm. Let her find her own rhythms.

Trust he did, even though he had no idea of what she was going to say in court. Whatever she had seen on her return visit to the hotel site was still private, he sensed: bits and pieces of memory coming together, but not quite organized with the analytical vigour she had once applied to everything in her life. Her therapists had already told Fergus to expect that Mary might never be able to concentrate as intensely as before. She might become more intuitive perhaps, but she would process information more slowly.

On balance, Fergus conceded that life was becoming more satisfying for both of them. She was not quite the feisty Mary again, but she had become more settled in the past few days, well rooted in who she was and why she was now at this turning point – with its attendant risks – in her life.

Like the ebbing of a storm surge, Mary's confusion was beginning to recede. There were still occasional lapses, when she snapped at him. But, on balance, life went on, its old rhythms renewed. She even hugged Fergus a couple of times – a sense of hope, he thought, as he felt her arms around him and the warmth of her body. No tears, not even any bad dreams.

The next morning

When he got up, Fergus noticed with growing relief that when Mary took her shower, he heard no intensely painful scrubbing of her scars. Instead, he heard only the gentle flow of the warm water. Mary even reached out to him, flicking water as he shaved at the nearby sink.

"I'm ready," she told Fergus, "if you are."

He was, and he joined her in the shower – a long soapy shower, so long and sensuously soapy that they were almost late for court.

Chapter 33

The rush left Fergus and Mary almost giddy, at least until Fergus opened the door, and encountered the packed crowd staring at them and the chatter that followed. Mary's appearance startled those who hadn't seen her for several months – she was thinner, with deep bags under her eyes. She had let her hair grow longer, falling well below her shoulders, and held in place by a narrow band of beaded braid.

As Simon Corbiere sorted his notes, a few curiosity seekers chattered, undoubtedly drawn by the chance that the "uppity woman" from Toronto would break down again. A few native elders, however, did sense a change in her, and quietly wondered whether evil spirits were finally allowing her some peace.

Justice McWilliams, too, was worried that Mary might be too fragile to make it through her testimony. He would be left to make a decision without testimony from the only real witness to the murder. Do I adjourn until she's ready? he asked himself. Or do I call a mistrial?

From the press table, Isaiah Steen saw that Mary was breathing more easily, and wondered if she was willing herself to become more fully native. He made a note that Mary showed higher energy, better posture even, and that she answered Simon's preliminary questions with a strong voice. Full sentences, almost professorial again. As if she were free of something. "What?" he scribbled hurriedly, circling the word several times, and then added another: "Deal?"

Simon Corbiere led Mary gently through his first questions.

"Was Wilbur Kanasawae a friend? How well did you know him?"

"Not a friend in the social sense," answered Mary easily. "We were never in each other's homes. It was not that sort of relationship. But I did meet him in the construction office from time to time. Max Adler introduced us, and explained that we were both security guards. Wilbur protected the property, while my role was to protect Ojibwa culture."

"So you were not surprised when he called to ask for help?"

"I was surprised by the hour, which was almost midnight."

"How long did it take you to arrive at the hotel site?"

"Probably no more than fifteen minutes."

"Very promptly then."

Simon led Mary, step by step, to explain how she had arrived at the construction site, and what she first saw as she climbed the gentle grade leading up to the hotel foundation.

"How well could you see?"

"Not well. The night was dark with no moon, but there was a single light at the top of the main access road that was maintained through the night for security purposes. The lamp had an effective radius, though, of no more than seven or eight meters, ten at best."

"So then, could you make out anything or anybody?"

"Just Shane, standing alone with his back to me. Wilbur had remained in the gatehouse after calling me."

With the basics of the setting out of the way, Simon knew he was approaching the crucial moment when Mary had to confirm the basis for Shane's self-defense plea...and move Justice McWilliams's mindset beyond anthropological theories. Make-or-break time. Shane could yet take a ride to

Kingston Penitentiary. Mary seemed okay, he told himself, but don't hurry this.

"Now, Dr. Fraser," he said, moving closer, "I want you to explain in your own words – take your time – what you were thinking after Wilbur called. Why didn't you call the police?"

"It's hard to recall exactly what went through my mind, so much has happened since then. But..." She paused.

"But what?"

"I do recall that Wilbur wanted to save his son before the police intervened. Rumors were flying about drugs on Manitoulin, and Shane's future had come down to one last chance before he was charged with a serious crime. No, I can't recreate the phone call word for word, but...well, there is no doubt that's what Wilbur was asking me to do."

"If not the police, Dr. Fraser, then why didn't you call Franz or drive to the Adler home first?"

"Simply call Franz? Oh no, that was never an option for me. My relationship with Franz had been stormy almost from the first time we met in Germany. When I rejected his offers of sex and drugs, he became quite...agitated, and I regrettably responded in kind. If nothing else, he reminded me of painful things that had happened to me as a child. Life has its ironies, though, and in the end, it was Franz who laid the complaint, and it was me the OPP warned not to threaten him again. After that, I avoided him and went on with my work."

"And could you get on with your work?"

"It's time for me to say what must be said."

"What must be said?" McTavish interjected. "Your Honor, it's clearly evident that the witness is speaking from a script. Given Dr. Fraser's medical history, we need to know whether this is her story or something that defense counsel has prepared for her. How do we know what she really remembers?"

Simon slammed his papers down. "And it's clearly evident to me, Your Honor, that the Crown is harassing the witness with…yes, with those wild speculations."

Justice McWilliams, however, had lost patience with the constant crossfire between the lawyers, and pounded his gavel.

"Both of you, sit down," he thundered. "Since this is a trial by judge alone, let me speak to Dr. Fraser directly. No, Mr. McTavish, I will ask the questions here. Sit!"

You righteous son of a bitch, he added to himself.

Both lawyers obediently sat.

"Dr. Fraser, this court appreciates your appearance here today after all you've been through, but we are at a point that we all know has to be addressed, however painful it may be for you. Just one question then, which I acknowledge rises from the Crown's objection. You said, I believe, that it is time for you to say what must be said. Have I quoted you correctly?"

"Yes, Your Honor," Mary answered without hesitation.

"Well then, are those your own words, or were you told to say them?"

Mary smiled, struck by the irony.

"Told to say them? Sir, my words are always, well, *my* words. Indeed, the words were not clear to me until a few hours ago when, if you must know, I was showering. If that sounds strange, well, that's how my mind works. Can we go on?"

"Thank you, Dr. Fraser," said Justice McWilliams. "Mr. Corbiere, your witness, if you have more questions."

"Ah then, Dr. Fraser," Simon said, rising again, "please tell the court, in your own words, what you saw as you approached the construction site."

Pausing for a moment, Mary twisted several strands of hair around her right index finger. "My own words. Thank you. It is time to say this; yes, it is definitely time. Let me start with my acknowledgment – confession, really – that I was unable to intervene in time to prevent Mr. Dietrich's's death. There is no other way to make sense of this: I failed, and the sight of his mutilated body will stay with me for a long time. Perhaps if I had called the police, or even Franz himself, things might have worked out differently.

"What did I see that night as I approached? As I came up the hill, I could make out Shane with his back to me, waving a long object in front of him, not hitting anyone. Just waving something in front of him. Beyond Shane, I made out a dark figure, arms raised and yelling something I could not understand. Then the figure came closer, and jumped over some construction boards. As I recall, Shane didn't move, but kept waving what I recognized later as a piece of metal scaffolding. As the figure got nearer, it became easier to see that it was wearing a bearskin of some sort tied loosely around the neck and arms, and it was screaming at Shane. The voice, it sounded like Franz.

"All this was happening too quickly for me to get between them. The bearskin creature rushed at Shane, ignoring the blows to its arms and upper body. Then Shane lifted the metal bar, and slammed it down one last time. That's when I realized Franz was the mysterious figure. As he spun around, the bearskin flew off, and there was no mistaking who had been wearing it."

"Could you see Franz clearly? What was he wearing under the bearskin?"

"Wearing? Just pants and a turtleneck. Both black. But that hair of his, so blond… It was still white at first, until the blood—"

"Thank you, Dr. Fraser. We do have the forensic report in evidence. What happened next?"

"By the time I got to Franz, Shane had moved away from him, and was smashing the head of the bearskin on the ground, again and again. I grabbed the bar from him and flung it as far away as I could. I had to stop this madness, that's all I could think at that point. And then I saw Franz's body again, lying face down with a very bloody wound to the back of his head. It's hard to remember much after that, just an enormous sense that I must flee. Somehow I knew Franz was dead. He wasn't moving."

"If you believed he was dead, why did you not call the police?"

"Was I a coward? I ask myself that frequently. There's a fine line between cowardice and PTSD, I'm told, but the distinction is for rational minds, and best drawn in the calm of clinical assessments."

"Your memories, Dr. Fraser. Are you comfortable now that you are reliving for this court what happened?"

"Comfortable? No, not at all. I do recall my days at the North Bay hospital, trying to relive that night, and the journey has often been terrifying as my memories have returned. For most of my life, my mind was my protection. Oh Lord, I was so vain, about my doctorate. I knew who I was. No identity loss. No life-long obsession with childhood abuse. My father died in prison, I'm told, at Stony Plains, and my mother is…my mother is…well, nobody seems to know. Lost or dead, I don't know. But they can't hurt me anymore.

"Or so I thought. Repression has its price, and what I do know now is that reason had deserted me as I stood looking at Franz's body. My body began shaking, and now Franz is dead."

Simon came forward, and almost touched Mary on the arm.

"Dr. Fraser, let me quickly pose my final question, before I ask for a recess. From what you saw that dreadful night, was Shane attacking Franz, or was he defending himself?"

"I can see it. Yes, yes, I still see it. Franz was running at Shane, trying to scare him for whatever reason. Why, I don't know. But Franz was jumping around in a bearskin, yelling at Shane. And yes, Franz knew the intimidating significance of the bearwalker in Ojibwa culture. Oh, he could be self-obsessed, evil. He was so taken with the dark side of tribal mythology that he had wanted to call the hotel's main bar 'The Bearwalker Room', complete with flashing yellow lights and a tape of growling sounds."

"Dr. Fraser, I repeat: Was Shane attacking Franz, or defending himself?"

"Mr. Corbiere, I will answer you," said Mary, for the first time sounding impatient, "in my own way, sir. In context. Most people are able to dismiss horror stories, just as they dismiss horror movies. They can put the bogeymen back in the plastic case and return it to Blockbuster. Most people, that is; but not all, particularly those who live in tribal societies with their own symbols of good and evil. Given who he is, Shane had every reason to defend himself. Just think of this. Even when Shane had knocked Franz down, he continued striking the head of the bearskin – not Franz, but the bearskin – again and again. It was the bearwalker he wanted to kill, not Franz."

"Thank you, Dr. Fraser," said Simon. "No more questions, Your Honor, but I do suggest that we break for a few minutes."

After a fifteen-minute recess, the court reconvened.

"Mr. McTavish."

"Thank you, Your Honor. There are a few details I think should be clarified. Let's see, you went home after discovering that the accused had already killed Mr. Dietriich. Is that correct, for the record?"

"Yes. I drove back to our house."

"What time was that?"

"I don't recall checking my watch, but I think it was before one."

"Did you discuss what had happened with your, ah, partner, as you described Mr. Fitzgerald in your statement?"

"No."

"So you came home and went right to sleep. Is that correct?"

"I, ah, we…"

"Dr. Fraser, may I remind you that you are under oath. Simple question: Did you go to sleep when you came home or…?"

"If you must, sir," said Mary, her shoulders beginning to hunch, "we made love."

"You simply went home, you say, and made love. How nice. Except for Mr. Dietrich, of course, or did his death not bother you at all?"

Simon thought about objecting, but decided not to derail Mary's train of thought.

"I needed Fergus to hold me. Then we went to sleep."

Cal moved closer to the witness box. "So you did not tell Mr. Fitzgerald what had happened. Then, or later perhaps?"

"No. I left the house again while he was still asleep."

"I see. I must apologize for intruding on your personal life, Dr. Fraser. But I am curious about your sense of recollection of these events. Your answers have been detailed and logical. Yet you told Mr. Corbiere several times that you were unable to arrive at the construction site in time to prevent Franz Dietrich's death. You watched a brutal killing, and then went home, and had sexual relations with your partner without telling him what you had witnessed. Then you left him a few hours later, again without telling him about the murder. Is this correct?"

"Yes."

"And then you left to see your psychologist, as Dr. Callaghan has testified. Is that correct?"

"I knew I needed help."

"How is it then that you were able to see so much detail as you ran up the hill toward the hotel construction site? We have been told there was no moon that night and only one lamp provided light. My sense, Dr. Fraser, is that your memory may still be selective and perhaps even creative."

"Objection, Your Honor," Simon finally interjected. "Speculation."

"Sustained. Rephrase, Mr. McTavish."

"Just this then. How did you see so much detail?"

"I could not get there on time."

"Could not get there. I see," said Cal, drawing out each word. "Your words. While they do not answer my question, they do suggest to me that something prevented you from arriving. So, Dr. Fraser, did your car break down?

Did you get lost? Or did you simply fall, running up the hill?"

"No, no, not like that."

"Something else then?"

"Yes."

"Somebody stopped you?"

"Nooooo," said Mary, her face flushed. Her voice rose in pitch as frustration turned into anxiety. "No one. I was alone."

Fergus barely breathed at this point. If nobody else was there, then Mary must be alone with her guilt. But for what? He could only shake his head when Harley Reif turned around and looked at him for some hint as to where Mary was going with her answers.

"You were alone," Cal continued, barking out his words. "You were too late. Nothing held you up. I am left with the conclusion, Dr. Fraser, that you stood there and watched Shane Kanasawae kill Franz Dietrich. Just stood there and watched. Did that excite you? Perhaps sexually? Your own blood rising… How could any decent person stand by, and watch Franz die? Tell us why you just stood there. Did you *want* Shane to kill Franz for you?"

Simon jumped to his feet to object, but Justice McWilliams waved him down. "I need to hear Dr. Fraser's answer. Continue."

"That is preposterous!" Mary responded sharply. "Why would I—"

"Because you threatened him once before. According to OPP files, you said, and let me read here from Mr. Dietrich's complaint: 'Natives have their own special ways of getting rid of bad people.' You didn't deny then saying this. Do you deny it now?"

"No. I was angry with Franz when I said that. Yes, my words were intemperate, but he was unrepentantly evil.

I was using whatever words I knew to protect myself from a vicious predator. But what I said has nothing to do with Shane. Many of our people believe in evil spirits like the bear—"

"Yes, yes, like a bearwalker," McTavish cut in. "You're a highly educated woman, Doctor, and surely you must agree with Dr. Kellman – from the ROM, no less, and a former colleague of yours – that there is no objective proof that bearwalkers exist. You had nothing to fear from the victim's silly masquerade, and yet you stood there and watched Mr. Dietrich die. Face down in the mud. You didn't even call an ambulance, let alone the police."

"Objection," Simon shouted. "This is pure conjecture, Your Honor. If the Crown has a question, let him ask it."

"Sustained. Get to your point, Mr. McTavish."

Cal appeared to be chastened for a moment. He retreated to his notes on the Crown table, then suddenly wheeled around, the hem of his gown flying widely as he did.

"Who are you really, Dr. Mary Fraser? Ojibwa-born, internationally successful, and now back here to find yourself? A fine but troubled mind. Oh yes. That's what we're told. You're in the care of healers and psychologists. How convenient. No, no, Dr. Mary Fraser. It's an exorcist you need. Do you agree?"

"EXORCIST!" exploded Simon. "Your Honor, this egregious abuse is pure slander."

"Agreed. Control yourself, Mr. McTavish. You've gone much too far. Let the witness speak for herself. Please, Dr. Fraser, tell us why you were unable to intervene on time. It *is* an important point."

Harley Reif tried to control his own apprehension. Good God, he told himself, McTavish is after her again.

We embarrassed him once, and now it's payback time. Would he recharge her as an accessory after the fact? If Shane is found guilty, he just might – Cal McTavish, Avenging Angel. An exorcist? Maybe for himself!

Mary was too stunned to speak. Instinct took hold, and for a moment, she wanted to escape from this horrible person bearing down on her. Her hands tightened around each other, knuckles almost white, until she summoned the strength to raise her head to find Fergus. He was still there, face still quiet and composed, still comfortable with whatever she planned to say. She remembered what he had said to her earlier in the morning: "Today is your moment and your story. Find peace in what you want to say."

She took a deep breath to centre herself. "You may not understand this, Mr. McTavish, but I froze. My feet would not move, and my voice could not even scream. I felt as if I was locked into a nightmare. For terrifying moments, I did not see Shane or even Franz. I just saw yet another figure watching, unable or unwilling to help. Not a man. No, no, not a man. This I know. I still feel the helplessness I felt as a child, when my mother was unable to protect me. In that horrible moment when Shane was hitting Franz, I became that young girl again. My father was with me, and he was hurting me down there, and perhaps others were, too. And if I cried, then someone pushed a cigarette into my buttock. I can't see the faces; it's the image of my mother that's clearest, standing off to the side near the door, just watching what was happening to me, unwilling or unable to protect me."

McTavish, for the first time, was lost, not sure whether to back away and let Justice McWilliams take what he could from the tortured images. But what's credible here? Perhaps nothing? That's the issue. Best, then, to underscore the main point.

"So you did nothing. You froze, you said. You watched the killing. Is that what you're saying, Dr. Fraser?"

"No, it wasn't like that. Yes, what was happening in front of me was horrible, but so were the images in my head. Everything was all jumbled together. Shane and Franz and my mother and… Oh God, more than anything, I remember holding myself still and silently screaming that I did not want to be like her. Sometimes, even now as fear overwhelms me, I can finally hear my own words: 'Oh God, if You really exist, don't make me like her. Not like her. Let it end.'"

Justice McWilliams tried to remain impassive but failed. He was blocked by a painful sadness of his own and was barely able to speak.

"Anything more, Mr. McTavish?" he asked.

Cal's adrenaline was spent. She's still quite mad, he thought, that's obvious. Leave it. "No, I think not, Your Honor. No more questions."

"Mr. Corbiere, can we adjourn?"

Simon looked at Mary, who was suddenly and quite unexpectedly calm.

"I want to explain something," Mary told him. "May I please, sir?"

"Re-cross, Your Honor."

It was now Simon who was in a difficult position. There's more to Mary's story, that's obvious, he thought. But Shane is my client, and I don't dare bring alternative theories into play at this late point. Crown's already screwing around with that. Still, McTavish may have shaken her credibility. The only thing is to bring Mary back to her rational world.

"Dr. Fraser, we need to know what happened then. How did you overcome the paralysis you just described? How did you process what happened?"

"How did I process...?" she repeated. "That sounds so mechanical. No, no, it wasn't automatic. Emotional strength doesn't flow like that. I had to will myself to move beyond the colliding images, and not to fail Shane the way my mother had failed me. I had to move beyond my fear."

Simon said nothing for a few seconds, wondering whether anyone was ever beyond fear. One trial, but two interlocking fears from the Ojibwa past. He had come to realize that Mary's fear, however still painful, was rooted in childhood abuse, the memories of which she might never be fully free. Shane's bearwalker fear, he also knew, was ancient and part of the mythical core of Ojibwa beliefs.

As Shane's lawyer, he knew he had to link the two fears. But would a white judge understand? This was crucial to his radical and risky case, as his lawyer friends advised him.

Then the mantra of his generation kicked in. Never back away, he told himself. Go for it!

"Do you feel beyond fear now?"

Mary coughed to clear her throat, and then lifted her head and looked him steadily in the eye. "Fear is part of life, Mr. Corbiere. It's always there. Not that we all have the same fears. Me? I have been away too long to see evil spirits in the dark woods. But they are part of Ojibwa history and mythology. If I accept my people again and accept Manitoulin as my home, then there is part of me that accepts their fears. Yes, I believe the bearwalker exists in the hearts and minds of my people. And yes, I saw fear on Shane's face, eyes wild with terror, hands thrown up in front of him. But not panic. No, no, he's not a coward. That's not who the Ojibwa are. He stood his ground, and in the end, he knew the only way to survive was to kill the curse before it killed him. Think of him and think of me what you will, but these are the fears my people must deal with."

"The defense rests, Your Honor."

Chapter 34

Later that evening

From: **Fergus Fitzgerald <Brendan@bmts.com**
To: **Conall Fitzgerald <Famtrack@corknet.ie**
Subject: **on hold**

Still no word, and we wait yet again. Everything's on the back burner until McWilliams makes his ruling. I think the decision will come down to credibility. Either he believes Mary and the young native...or he doesn't. If he sees Mary as some kind of evil spirit, then we're in deep trouble.

McWilliams's simplest decision is to take Shane Kanasawae's confession at face value, find him guilty, and pack him off to prison. Or does McWilliams seek justice elsewhere where it can restore community balance and begin the healing? Methinks that's what Shane's grandmother was expecting.

Mary is tired tonight, but I don't think she realizes she may still be in jeopardy if Shane is found guilty. Cal McTavish, the crown attorney here, as much as said he believes she needs an exorcist. Not quite Satan's child, but close enough to the Puritan times in

Massachusetts when the 17th century leaders hung 27 young women one year.

Do you remember what Miller (Arthur, that is, not Henry) said in *The Crucible* about that? "This is a sharp time now, a precise time – we live no longer in that dusky afternoon when evil mixed with good and befuddled the world." Lovely phrase, that: "a precise time." Lives could change tomorrow, and if so, my guilt might back up like an overflowing sewer.

There are still moments when I am not quite sure whether I have made any difference. Franz is dead, but I can't change that. Shane may go to prison, but I can't change that. But Mary is recovering, and I *can* rejoice in that small miracle.

Perhaps that's all we can hope for – small miracles that come one at a time, never well ordered and sometimes hard to see or hear. I now believe in your Celtic thin place, that tipping point between reality and possibility, some even say between the human and the divine. That place, it's there. I can feel it.

If all goes well, we plan to buy the house we're now renting. Mary wants to stay here awhile, and let her healing run its full course.

Fortunately, Max Adler has come full circle, the good son in search of a resting place for his parents' souls. I like him, even if he did bring Franz into our lives. The hotel concept is dead, he says. Manitoulin doesn't need pretend-natives, searching for an identity that wasn't theirs in the first place. Instead, Max wants Mary to help him create a hospice for the other Marys coming back with all their scars. Yeah, they're coming full circle here, Mary and Max, and who knows how many more Marys and Maxes, all moving back into the light and away from the bogeymen that haunt all our lives.

Perhaps Dresden's sense of perpetual resurrection will take hold here. That is if – why is there always one more damnable, conditional 'if'? – Mary has a life beyond whatever the judge rules.

So, cousin, it's late and I must end this for now. You said your invitation to visit Cork is still open. Thank you kindly. If we do come we might take the long route east via Boston. It's time Mary met my family. Perhaps you might want to join us, with your Ma as well.

F.

PS. Just as I was about to send you the above, I was distracted by a knock on the door. It was Wilbur, father of the accused, standing there.

"I brought you something," he said and handed me a battered thermos.

"It's tea. For you and Dr. Fraser."

Flabbergasted, I stood there for a few seconds before I asked him in. He declined, saying something about his work boots being muddy and all.

"Long night ahead of us," he said. "I'm used to it, but I thought you might need help."

Words failed me, and I could only take the thermos, not knowing whether to hug him or shake his hand or whatever. I knew the tea wasn't for sale. So I simply listened:

"Whatever happens to my son will happen," said Wilbur, "but he will still be my son, and you will still be my friend. Now I must go to work." And he was gone.

F.

Chapter 35

The next morning

Shortly before dawn, Justice William George McWilliams gave up on sleep. His mind would not stop probing what the law meant by "reasonable." For him, that was at the core of this case. Everything else would come down to whether it was reasonable to believe in a bearwalker.

So what did "reasonable" mean? Even half-awake, his methodical mind took over, and began breaking down the question. Several definitions came back to him from previous cases before he settled on one: Reasonable is not extreme or excessive; reasonable is no more or no less than what may be expected.

His choice made, his mind was at the point where he used his usual method of reviewing his trial notes, and organizing some preliminary answers to the questions raised.

He opened his laptop.

> Does the confession stand? Yes, there is no need to doubt what the accused said. The confession was voluntary, the accused had access to a lawyer, and the forensic evidence was consistent with both the confession and the testimony of the one witness to the homicide.
>
> Were the witnesses credible? No doubts about the testimony from the police, coroner,

museum curator, the accused's father, and the psychologist. The anthropologist-priest's theories are intriguing. While his comments cannot establish guilt or innocence on their own, they do add perspective about the central issue of reasonableness, which in turn must be tested against the accused's plea of self-defense.

Testimony from the only witness who saw the homicide, Dr. Fraser, is more difficult to evaluate. The Crown aggressively challenged her memory and mental stability, but in the end did not undermine her testimony. Allegations that she chose not to intervene, and therefore willingly contributed to the victim's death, were unsubstantiated conjecture. I'm satisfied that Dr. Fraser was unable to intervene as she had intended. Also, her version ties into and gives weight to what both the accused and his father said. Was she credible? Given her demeanour and obvious sincerity, yes, her testimony is credible. Still, it, too, must be tested against the reasonableness of the defense claim.

What black-letter law in the Criminal Code and case precedents are relevant to the plea of self-defense against unprovoked assault? Both Crown and defense summations point to Section 34(2b) that says that defendant must "believe, on reasonable grounds, that he cannot otherwise preserve himself from death or grievous bodily harm." However, the attached commentary says the use of the word "reasonable" imports an objective element.

There are no contradictions in case law, either. R vs. Westhaver (1992) says failure to retreat does not necessarily preclude use of Section 34. Also, the defendant need not be reduced to a state of frenzy. Nor, says Antley (1963), must the defendant have waited to be struck first.

What, then, is reasonable? The Crown argues that death occurred during a felonious transaction, thus reducing or eliminating any claim to reasonableness. But neither Mr. Dietrich nor Mr. Kanasawae had been charged, let alone convicted, as the result of the on-going drug investigations. The defense relied on Patel (1994): "An honest but reasonable mistake is permitted…. The question to be asked is whether Defendant reasonably believed in the circumstances that he/she was being unlawfully assaulted, not whether D was unlawfully assaulted. There is no formal requirement that danger to D be imminent."

Is there any specific precedent to the bearwalker defense? The defendant in Nahwaikezhik (1945) was convicted of murder when the jury rejected his insanity defense. Defendant claimed his father had cast a bearwalker spell on him. But the insanity claim undermined belief in the bearwalker curse. Insanity is not claimed by the Kanasawae defense team.

Conclusion? Objectively, there's no proof that a bearwalker exists. The defendant's claim of self-defense does meet all pertinent criteria except whether the circumstances and fears were reasonable. I'm not comfortable, however, that it is the court's role to determine whether belief in the bearwalker curse is both rational and reasonable. And yet this is the core of this case. What separates beliefs held by mainstream religions from Aboriginal beliefs? More importantly, is there a line to be drawn? We heard expert testimony that the differences may be largely matters of symbolism and ritual. Old stories are held to be as important to natives as the Bible is to Christians. I'm grateful for Dr. Fraser's moving testimony that such fears are real in the hearts and minds of her people, and the accused exhibited these fears. Can I find that belief in the bearwalker is unreasonable beyond reasonable doubt? Perhaps yes in Ottawa or Toronto, but not necessarily on Manitoulin Island.

On balance, I therefore find Shane Kanasawae's claim of self-defense is reasonable, and that he is not guilty of 2nd degree murder.

Save

Later that morning

At 10:24 a.m., as recorded by the court clerk, Shane Kanasawae was a free man again, and Cal McTavish could only stare at the ceiling of the courtroom. He didn't even see Fergus and Mary walk down the aisle and out the door.

Epilogue

Boston, June 2000

With 33,931 other people standing and screaming around them, and banks of lights glaring down from above, Fergus didn't know what to make of Mary.

They were in Fenway Park, home of the Boston Red Sox, who were trailing the New York Yankees 4-to-3 in the eighth inning. He thought she looked a little silly in the Red Sox ball cap, now perched backwards on her head. A bright red Red Sox T-shirt, about two sizes too big, hung down well below her hips.

"So, why are you doing this for me?" said Fergus, sipping his paper cup of Narragansett beer. "It's a wedding present, and I'm grateful beyond words, but tell me, how did you get these seats looking down at the Green Monster?"

They were sitting in the bleacher seats atop the twenty-three-foot wall that guarded the short left field fence from line-drive hitters looking for an easy home run. Fenway was sacred to its fans, and nothing was more sacred than "the Monster."

Mary was feisty and taking charge again. There had been no hold up when they had crossed the border, in spite of Fergus's fey sense that something would go wrong. Their wedding at the Boston College chapel in Weston had gone well. Even Fergus's older brother had given him a back-thumping hug. Their aunt, the nun, cried a little, and said her late brother, their father, would have been pleased. His family settled, she said, God's will. She even had a whisky.

"How does a Toronto egghead get tickets like these?" asked Mary. "Is that what you're asking?"

"Yeah, some folks wait for years for these tickets."

"So?"

"So, how did you do it?"

"My secret."

"Come on, indulge me. We're married. We're supposed to share stuff, so bloody hell, woman, where did the tickets come from?"

"I'll tell you this much, and that's all. What's the use of being a world-class expert if you can't reach out to world-class friends? I know people here. That's all I'm saying...for now."

The sell-out crowd turned quiet as the Sox left two base runners stranded and still trailed the Yanks. Again.

"For now?" asked Fergus, picking up the loose thread in her reply.

"First, the curse," said Mary, reaching into her bag. "I know about that, too."

"You never cease to amaze me, woman," said Fergus, scratching his thin hair. "The curse of the Bambino, our bogeyman that has kept the Red Sox from winning the World Series since we sold Babe Ruth to the Yankees in 1920. Williams couldn't get us there. Not Yaz, not—"

"Yes, my sweet man, I know. But every tribe has its bogeyman: the Ojibwa, the Germans, and man, so do the Boston Irish. Hold this bowl."

"For?"

"For this tobacco," Mary answered, as she shredded a cigarette, and then dropped a match into it.

"You're smudging! God, can you do this here?"

"If you believe in the curse, Fergus, then believe in the good spirits as well. And find your balance. This I believe."

St. Louis, Mo., October 28, 2004

The Red Sox defeated the St. Louis Cardinals 3 to 0, thus sweeping the World Series and ending the curse. The *Boston Globe* sold out the next morning with a one-word headline on its front page: "YES!"

Acknowledgments

Oh, for the memories. About Monique, of course, my late wife, who was with me on Manitoulin when we first came across the Bearwalker myth. Over a hurried lunch, we eventually arrived at the Little Current Library and the back files of the Bearwalker murder trial in 1994.

Yes, that trial inspired this book, and so did a courageous grandmother with an indelible sense of justice. In the writing of this story, of course, the final characters and narrative are composites from my own imagination, along with the settings in both Canada and Germany. Monique was an enthusiastic partner in this quest from the beginning, usually asking tough questions that I couldn't immediately answer, and pushing me deeper into the complexities of the old Ojibwa Bearwalker myth and German fascination with Aboriginal art and North America.

Our first visit to the Library introduced us to the *Manitoulin Expositor*, truly one of Canada's finest weekly newspapers. One of its writers, Mike Erskine, and later his wife Linda, became very good friends and probing readers of the first BW draft.

Also generous with his time and experience was Detective Constable Mike Corrigan, crime scene specialist with the Ontario Provincial Police. Like the Erskines, Mike cared for my ego and demanded legal clarity on behalf of all readers.

From Toronto, Chris Marston and Francine Robitaillie provided incisive readings of the first draft and great advice. More immediate responses came from neighbors down the Georgian Bay shorelines near Leith, Marg and her late husband John.

Professionals in many fields guided me with great patience: Dr. Barbara Erskine of the Native Health Center in Little Current; Stacy Hammer, then assistant Crown Attorney at Gore Bay; David Hay, Crown Attorney in Grey-Bruce; Dr. Rayuda Kuka, director of the North Eastern Mental Health Center in Sudbury; John Dempster of the North Bay Forensic Detention Center; Dr. Brian Rudrick, pathologist at Bruce-Grey Regional Hospital; Bonita Johnson, Sexual Assault Councilor in Owen Sound; the late Dr. Jack Bailey and Ron Wakegiijig, pioneers in cross-culture medicine in Northern Ontario; Gerard Fischer, chief of the Buffalo Tribe in Germany who welcomed me into his home.

I am particularly indebted to Cheryl Freedman, a professional editor Toronto and witty friend. My only instruction to her was that I wanted the "best possible" final manuscript. And that she did, my first exposure to on-line editing and unflinching devotion to serial commas. Her return pages looked like a bad case of measles with many, many red commas. But she was a joy with whom to work, such was my confidence in and my appreciation of her skills.

When the writing and editing were complete, I sought the opinion of a two-time winner of the Arthur Ellis award for crime writing, Dr. Barbara Fradkin, a retired clinical Psychologist. Her review: "Powerful and intelligent."

As she does with so many writers, Donna Carrick of Carrick Publishing carried *Bearwalker Alibi* into the light of both the print and ebook editions - a caring and dedicated professional in every sense.

About Jake Doherty:

Bearwalker Alibi is Jake's second novel, written after meticulous research in both the Dresden area of Germany and Northern Ontario, particularly Manitoulin Island, Sudbury and North Bay.

His attention to detail and psychological roots of his main characters reflect 40 years in journalism as a reporter, editor and finally publisher of the *The Hamilton Spectator*. He received a Master Degree (Journalism) from Columbia University in New York in 1960. He also has a business degree from St. Francis Xavier University in Nova Scotia.

More recently, he was co-founder, editor and contributor of the *Sun Media's Summer Mystery Series*, followed by an anthology acclaimed by the *Globe and Mail's* mystery critic as "…perfect".

The Crime Writers of Canada, of which he is a member and former board member, described him his way:

"Jake came to crime writing not as a planned venture but more like a great plot that unfolds with its own inner force. Though born in New Brunswick, he now lives in Meaford, Ontario near Owen Sound, and spends considerable time on his deck, drinking white wine, or simply watching the sun go down on Georgian Bay. Most mornings though are spent writing in his basement office, and taking direction from P.D. James' "perennial fascination with the mystery of morality…rights vindicated, order restored."

He can be reached at jmdoherty@rogers.com.

Visit us at
http://www.carrickpublishing.com/

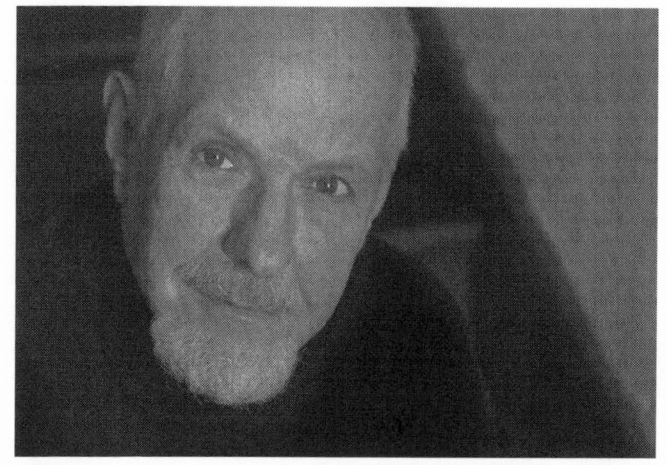